SIMPLE MAN

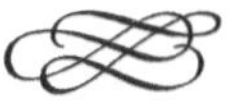

LYDIA MICHAELS

WWW.LYDIAMICHAELSBOOKS.COM

www.LydiaMichaelsBooks.com

Simple Man

Lydia Michaels

Published by Lydia Michaels

Print Copyright © 2023 Lydia Michaels

First Edition: Copyright 2013; Lydia Michaels

Listen to the Simple Man Playlist!
Click Here to Listen!

DEDICATION

To Michelle, you cardigan wearing book store,
I love you, admire you, and want to be you when I
grow up.
Cheers!
~Lydia

PROLOGUE

eptember

"WHO LEFT their pizza on the back of the toilet?"

Shane glanced up from his guitar only to catch Duce taking a huge bite out of said pizza. "You're disgusting, man. I haven't cleaned the john in weeks."

Duce plopped down beside him on the vintage couch—and by vintage, he meant seventies porn pea green with tarnished duct tape accents.

"It's all one big cycle, my friend. My immunities are superior. I can take it," Duce said as he shoveled the last bite of crust in his mouth. "Hand me a beer."

"Did we even order pizza tonight?" Sims asked from the floor, hands fused to a game controller, gaze plastered to the TV.

Shane stilled as he reached into the cooler parked beside the couch and thought about the last time they ordered pizza. He laughed. "Nope."

Duce shrugged. "Doesn't taste old."

"You're an idiot," Sims muttered as he decked Duce with a piece of trash he found on the floor.

Shane went back to strumming his guitar, not that anyone could hear him over the pounding stereo and the incessant loop of music coming from the video game on the television. His friends had showed up sometime that evening, waking him up and demanding beer. His trailer was the place they flocked to each weekend, which was fine with him. Since his truck wasn't working and he didn't have the money to fix it at the moment, having them come to his place was beyond convenient.

The stench of weed flowed from the backroom. "Who's in my room?" Shane yelled.

"Tucker. He's on the phone with Lisa."

"He's whipped," Russ said over the music and the popping crack of can tabs.

Lisa was one hot piece. Shane didn't hold it against Tucker for doing what the rest of them couldn't seem to do. Lisa was a good girl. Shane sort of hoped she'd hit it off with Tucker and bring some other good girls around for the rest of them. He'd never admit out loud how lonely he sometimes was, but deep down he thought it would be awesome to have a girl look at him the way Lisa sometimes looked at Tucker.

Shaking off his thoughts on the comforts of dating, he got back to the topic at hand. "That better not be my stash he's smoking."

"You said you were out," Duce pouted, eating another slice of mystery pizza.

"No," Shane corrected. "I said I didn't have any for you. Dude, where the fuck are you getting the pizza?"

"This is from that box over there," Duce mumbled over a mouthful of cold cheese and sauce, shrugging toward the box on the floor.

Shane's lip curled. "You're disgusting. That's from last week."

There was a sudden pounding coming from the aluminum door. Everyone quieted and stared. Shane did a quick head count. Everyone they hung with was already there.

The pounding rattled the door again. "Shane? Shane, it's Noel. Let me in."

He frowned. What the hell was his sister doing there? Standing from the couch, he walked to the back room. Tucker was lounging on Shane's unmade bed, joint between his lips, phone to his ear.

"That better not be my shit," Shane warned before slamming the bedroom door.

He stumbled to the front door. Fuck, he was wasted. Thumb pressed into the latch, he threw the meager aluminum panel wide. "What are you doing here, Noel?"

His sister stood on the sand lot outside his trailer looking a little dried up and sour. Climbing up the crooked, metal step, she shoved past him and scowled at his company.

"Hey, Noel," Duce greeted.

She glared. "Don't you guys ever go home?"

They all shrugged. Shane waited as she took in the dirty space with clear revulsion. Hey, no one invited her. He loved his sister, she was the only family he had, but lately she'd been hanging with a crowd that was bad news. It royally pissed him off that—when she did stop by—she made a clear show of disdain for his home and often spoke to his friends in that stuck up, scornful manner she did so well.

By no means was he living the highlife, but that was a result of sacrificing so much to raise her when their parents died. He had no idea where this sudden sense of entitlement she presumed came from. She never used to be like that and he wanted his sweet little sister back.

So what if he and his friends killed a few cases of beer a night? And yeah, maybe he toked up from time to time. They weren't hurting anyone. To his way of thinking, what they did with their weekends was a lot better than what the people Noel hung around with did. He hated the fact that she thought those coked up assholes she hung with were actually friends. Yes, they had nicer cars and more money than Shane's friends, but that was because they were dealing.

He'd tried to talk to Noel, but every time he said one bad word about her 'friends' she flew off the handle and got all high and mighty on his ass, putting down his life from her pedestal. Where did she get off? The past few months their relationship had definitely been strained compared to what it once was.

Turning on him, Noel's sharp blue eyes zeroing in on his appearance and the one pack of warm beer dangling from the rings looped over his fingers, she snapped, "Shane, I need to talk to you."

He shot her an expectant look.

She huffed and glared at his friends. "Alone."

He didn't feel like dealing with her drama at the moment, already picking up on her self-righteous tone. "Sorry, sis, I'm sort of entertaining at the moment." He pulled the last beer from the rings and cracked it open, allowing the plastic to drift to the floor.

"Yeah, I can see I'm interrupting a great meeting of the minds here." She turned to his friends. "Go home."

"Hey!" Duce cried. He was still eating pizza.

"Don't talk to my friends like that. This is my place, not yours," Shane snapped.

Her jaw clenched. "Shane."

"Hey, Noel, how come you never come around anymore?" Sims called from his spot on the floor where his gaze was still drilled into the TV. His arms swung with animation as he played war on the game screen.

"To do what? Watch you losers knock out last year's record holders for most brain cells lost in one sitting?"

"More like record holders of awesomeness," Sims quipped.

"Yeah, that's what Tracy said," his sister commented dryly. Tracy was an acquaintance of Noel's—one Shane approved of. She and Sims had something going for a while, but Tracy bailed on account of Sims needing to *grow the fuck up*, in her words.

Noel rolled her eyes. "Did you cross those enemy lines in your game yet, big winner?"

Sims actually put down the controller and gave her a wounded look. "You're mean."

"Whatever. Tracy's my friend and, unfortunately, after she wasted two years on your ass, I've had to do insurmountable damage control. You and I aren't friends."

Sims stared at her as if trying to process what she'd said. Shrugging, he went back to his game.

"Shane, can we please talk?"

He plopped back onto the couch. "Talk."

She shifted from foot to foot. "Not here," she begged, growling through ground teeth.

He shrugged, hefting a bowl of stale chips into his lap and sifting through for the best ones. "This is where I am."

All of his life he'd done his best to be there for Noel. This new attitude wasn't doing it for him. When had they gone from friends to enemies? He wasn't any sort of expert on raising little sisters—never claimed to be—but he supposed he was trying for what might be called tough love. It sucked, because it went against his nature not to jump to her aide. That's all he'd done since she was little.

Noel was going through a stage—an ugly one—and he wasn't sure how to handle it. She was an adult now. He assumed she'd figure it out and go back to being cool sooner or later. Sometimes he really missed chilling with her, but this person, this bratty girl he didn't know, he wanted nothing to do with her.

There was a ruckus coming from the small kitchen across from the couch. Beer exploded from a can and Duce and Russ started hollering and cracking up as they mopped up the foamy spill with a rag.

"Jesus Christ, Shane, how do you live like this?"

She had a lot of nerve, especially when she hung out in the ghetto with bunch of drug dealing pricks who only managed to have the nicest phones and shoes as a result of criminal acts. At least he and his friends made honest livings. "You don't like it, there's the door."

The stereo was suddenly jacked up, bass trembling through the house. "This song's badass!" someone yelled.

Noel gave Shane an exasperated look as he drained his beer. Duce passed him a bottle of Jagermeister and he took a long swig. Tucker came out of the bedroom along with a huge cloud of skunked air.

Shane returned his sister's glare. "You gonna just stand there all night with a stick up your ass?" His vision blurred as he shifted, making room for Tucker.

Why couldn't she just go back to being the sweet girl she was six months ago? He was tired of worrying about her. She never stopped by anymore unless she wanted something from him. His days of bending over backward for her were over. She talked to him like he was a pile of shit. He didn't expect admiration, but he'd been a pretty good brother and didn't understand how she could judge him so harshly. What made her so perfect?

Duce bumped into Noel and splashed his drink down her jeans. "Sorry, Noel."

She growled. "Shane."

Shane listened in as Tucker told Sims what

Lisa had said. She was coming over. Sweet. "She bringing friends?"

"Shane."

Russ turned from whatever he was doing in the kitchen. "Is she bringing Holly Big Tits?"

"Shane!"

Goddamn it. *"What?"*

His sister looked beyond pissed. Her cheeks were flushed and she appeared about ready to cry. "I need four hundred dollars."

He snorted. He'd like four hundred dollars too. "What do I look like, Western Union?"

Four hundred was pretty steep for his pockets. He could probably hit up a friend for a loan, but he didn't trust her. She'd asked for money a few months ago—money he needed to pay bills—but Shane gave it to her. He figured she really needed it. A week later he saw her new tattoo. There was no way he was going to enable more dumb choices.

Her cold eyes narrowed. "I don't have anywhere else to go. I need the money."

For someone asking for that much money she was sure going about it in a bitchy way. "Uh, sorry, I'm broke." He turned to the television. "Let me try, Sims."

His sister's glare burned through him as he took the controller from Sims.

"Shane, I'm pregnant."

Everything stopped. The room grew suddenly silent. Someone even shut off the radio.

He turned to her in slow motion. His twenty-one-year-old sister glared at him like a petulant twelve-year-old.

He swallowed multiple times, giving his brain a moment to connect to his mouth. "What?" he whispered.

Her jaw worked as she raised her chin. She gave him the same conceited look she'd had since she was five, clearly thinking she was better than him. "I'm pregnant and I need four hundred dollars to take care of it."

"You're pregnant," he rasped. "Who the fuck is the father?"

His skin weighed like granite on his face as he scowled, a million thoughts racing through his head at once. This was his baby sister. After their twisted upbringing he couldn't help the paternal reaction he suffered at the idea of someone knocking her up.

She dropped her gaze to the filthy floor. "He's not important."

Oh, he'd kill the bastard. "Maybe to you. Who the fuck is it, Noel?"

She met his gaze head on. "I don't intend on telling him, so I don't intend on telling you."

A low whistle came from one of the guys. "That's messed up," Tucker commented. "A guy deserves to know."

"I'm gonna kill him," Shane hissed. "You're gonna tell me who he is and then I'm gonna get my bat and go kill the fucker."

"No, Shane—"

"No?" He laughed derisively. "With the company you've been keeping, I can only imagine the piece of shit that did this to you." Pregnant? *Fuck!* What about her future?

She drew back as though he'd slapped her. "Like you're Captain Responsible. You live in a fucking dumpster."

"*My* dumpster. You don't see me knocking on doors asking other people for hundreds of dollars to clean up my messes. Jesus, Noel…" He wanted to hug her and talk it out, but neither of them was in the right state of mind.

And she wanted to get an abortion… that wasn't a decision to rush into. He'd never felt more unprepared to handle a situation in his life. Well, that wasn't completely true. He never expected his parents to both die so suddenly. Would he ever catch a break?

Her lips tightened and she blinked. Her blue irises shimmered in the dim, smoky lighting. He needed to know who the father was. Someone was going to have to man up here. "Who's the father?"

"It's none of your business! Can you just give me the damn money? I won't ask again."

"Oh." He made an expression of feigned panic. "Won't you? Won't you ask me again for four hundred dollars?"

"You're an asshole," she whispered.

He was pissed. She had some nerve coming

in here acting superior and what not, begging for money, knocked up with some loser's kid. Fuck, she was his baby sister. He didn't want to think of her having sex, but what the hell…she was pregnant! She'd been his responsibility for too long. Someone needed to answer for this. She had her whole life ahead of her.

"Rather be an asshole than some douche that knocks up a young girl and can't be held responsible for his own actions. You better produce a name if you expect anything in return from me."

He was totally unprepared when she lunged at him. Open palmed slaps rained down on him over her shrill screams and cries. *"You fucking asshole!"*

"Yo!" One of the guys finally ripped her off of him. Sims. His gangly arms restrained her wild blows as he held her back and dragged her to the door.

"I hate you!" she screamed.

Shane dabbed his thumb to the corner of his mouth. When he drew it away blood showed on the pad of his finger. Her words hurt more than anything else. "What the fuck is wrong with you?"

"Me? What's wrong with you? I'm your sister!"

And he was supposed to protect her! He was furious with her, furious with himself, furious with the bastard that knocked her up, furious with the entire fucking world. But this shit was unacceptable. She was acting insane. His head was pounding and the words left his mouth before he could reel them back.

"Get the fuck out of my home. Go ask your loser baby daddy for money. You're his problem, not mine."

"Fuck you, Shane! Fuck you! Mommy and Daddy are probably rolling in their graves looking at what you've become. You're the fucking loser!"

Sims dragged her outside and the door slammed. Chest heaving, harsh breath panted past his bloody lip.

"What the fuck?" Duce stared, pie-eyed, beside him on the couch.

Shane yanked the bottle from his friend's hand and took a swig. Wiping his mouth on his sleeve, he growled at the burn working its way to his belly and swallowed another mouthful. He'd deal with this in the morning.

Somehow he'd find the money she needed. But first he had to make sure she was one hundred percent certain of her decision. It was a life altering one she needed to really think about. Right now he needed to fucking escape. "Someone put the music back on and hand me my guitar."

That quick, the music returned, his guitar filled his arms, and the evening continued as if nothing happened. But something had definitely happened. His worry for Noel seemed to sober him, but he couldn't deal. He doubled his efforts to wash the nightmare of his life away with sour booze and forced laughter.

He drank until he forgot about his sister, forgot about her problems, and forgot about how accurate her words likely were. He *was* a loser. She needed him and no matter how pissed he was, he needed to help her. Problem was, he didn't know where to get the money she needed or the first thing about babies if she decided to keep it.

~

SHANE'S BODY screamed in protest as he twisted in his sleep. Was something wet? He squinted into the dim filter of light streaming through the fallen venetian blinds. Duce slept, sprawled on the chair beside the flickering TV, a plate of something runny balanced precariously on his broad chest.

Shane's back protested as he sat up. A waterfall of empty cans clattered to the floor causing his friend to grumble in his sleep. Shane gripped his head as he tried to find his equilibrium as he fought the urge to puke. What time was it?

After digging the heels of his palms into his eye sockets he reached into his pocket for his phone. It was dead.

"What time is it?" he asked Duce in a hoarse voice.

Duce startled, sucking a snore deep into his lungs and coughing out of his sleep. "What? Is it my hit?"

Shane frowned and stood, not waiting for Duce to come around. His place was trashed, which was nothing unusual for, well, any day of the week. Jesus, who was gonna clean up this mess?

Shuffling on bare feet to the kitchenette he squinted at the oven clock. 1:32. Shit. It was already afternoon. "Duce, get up. It's late."

"I'm up. I'm up. I'm up." He rolled onto his side, which was quite ridiculous being that Duce was around two hundred and fifty pounds and the chair he sat on was swallowed by one thigh.

Shane opened the fridge and pushed the straggler beers to the side. His fingers folded around an open Gatorade and brought it to his lips, drinking greedily. Man, he was wasted last night.

His brain played over the evening and his gut twisted when he recalled Noel's little visit. God damn it, he didn't have the energy to deal with that shit today. But since their parents died, it had just been the two of them. He needed to figure out how to get her money, but first he needed to find out whose ass he needed to kick for putting her in this predicament.

He sighed. Noel wasn't like him. She was smart. She was working on an associate's degree from the community college and had some scholarships lined up for the next semester. These new friends of hers were fucking up her future and he needed to really sit down with her and make her understand they were no good. The tough love wasn't working. He wished he was better at talking about shit like this.

They'd end up fighting—bad fighting—but rather than get frustrated and walk away angry again, he'd tough it out until she wised up. He loved her. She was all he had. He'd given up so much to make sure one of them had a shot at a decent life. It was a no brainer making sure she was the one. If she didn't get away from those losers she'd end up just like them and all his sacrifices would have been for nothing.

"Come on, Duce, get up. I need you to give me a lift to Lakota."

Duce opened his eyes, stretched, farted, and sniffed the plate on his chest. "What do we gotta go there for?"

"I need to find Noel. I gotta find out who's responsible and then I need to kick someone's ass. After that I gotta figure out a way to get four hundred dollars so she can fix this or figure out how to get way more money than that and convince her to keep it."

"You think she's gonna tell you? Dude, were

you not here last night when she freaked? I think if any ass kickery is happening it's gonna be your little sister kicking yours. She was fucking fuming when she left."

Shane tried to recall what was said, but his memory was a fun house mirror. He remembered her attacking him and screaming, but couldn't recall exactly what she'd said. His gut knotted uncomfortably as he considered the way he spoke to her. Fuck. They needed to figure out how to be a family again, but first he needed to find her.

Hiding his concern, he shrugged. "She can be pissed all she wants. I'm not giving her a cent until I have a name."

And he needed to be certain she was sure about her choices. There were other options. Even if she didn't keep the baby, maybe someone else would want it. He didn't want his little sister haunted by hasty decisions.

Duce tossed the plate on the coffee table. A few cans fell to the floor. "Where're you going to get money like that? You've been saving up to fix the truck for weeks."

"I'll figure something out. Come on."

They cleaned themselves up and quickly filled a trash bag with garbage, tossing it outside the door of the trailer. That was a slight improvement. If he could get the beer and weed stink out of his home he'd be good.

"Crack that window to let some air in while we're gone."

Duce did as he asked and paused when Shane returned from the bedroom. "Seriously, man…what are you doing with the bat?"

"I told you. I'm kicking someone's ass."

Duce shook his head, stepped closer, and pried the Louisville out of his friend's hand. "No, man. You know better than that."

Duce was an odd guy. Of all his friends he was the dumbest, but at the same time he was also the most level headed and sometimes smartest. He was the diplomat. So long as they kept him fed, he'd do anything for any one of them.

They climbed into Duce's Ford Focus, which, due to his friend's generous size, was more like driving around in a roller skate. Sunny Acres, the mobile community where Shane lived, was about ten miles from Lakota. Neither would be considered nice neighborhoods. One was a ghetto and one was ready to order aluminum homes for good ol' lower class like himself.

He supposed he was what some might call white trash, but that wasn't the way it would always be. He'd once had a beautiful home and a decent future promised to him. When life got hard, he'd tried his best, but he was just a kid. He'd fucked up a lot, thinking he was doing right.

This place, Sunny Acres, this was just a pit stop. Eventually his hard work would pay off and he'd get the hell out of there. He needed to believe that or else he wouldn't have the strength to keep on going.

For a guy who'd been on his own since he was seventeen with an eleven-year-old sister to raise, he figured he was doing all right. Although Noel had always been sort of a self-sufficient kid, she still needed food and clothes, the likes of which he was supposed to provide.

Noel begged him not to let her go into the system. It was no easy task to get custody of his sister when he turned eighteen. The months leading up to his eighteenth birthday were hell. They'd just lost their parents, their home was temporarily held up with estate paperwork neither he nor Noel understood, and they'd gone to two separate foster families. He never thought after going through so much to be together, they'd end up treating each other the way they had over the past few months. Something definitely had to change.

He didn't think about how hard it would be to raise Noel. All he focused on was holding on to the family he had left. There were some services that helped them along the way, but he was an adult and she was a kid. So much fell on his shoulders once he took on the role of guardian.

After the will was cleared up, they'd held

onto their parent's house for a few years before the bank foreclosed on it. Then they'd moved to an apartment in Lakota. Shane hated it there, but it was all he could afford at the time. He felt responsible for unintentionally introducing her to the people she met in Lakota and now called friends.

He worked his ass off, flipping burgers and finally caught a break getting hooked up with a construction company. Pouring concrete paid good, but the work only held out as long as the weather did. Winters were always tough.

Once he'd saved up enough money he'd bought a trailer in Sunny Acres. All he had to worry about was lot rent, which was about a third of what he paid in rent for their apartment. However, by that time Noel was already graduating high school and free to do as she pleased.

He didn't approve of her friends in Lakota. She chose to stay there and if not for her cell phone, he wouldn't have been able to find her half the time.

It was difficult for Shane to watch her date, knowing she could do so much better than some guy working a double o 'seven job she couldn't answer for. This was supposed to be a phase, not the path her life followed. He'd tried so hard to give her as many opportunities as he could. He wanted his parents to look down on them and be proud. This was not where he expected her life to go.

When they reached Lakota, Duce drove them to Tracy's house, Noel's best friend, but Tracy claimed she hadn't seen Noel in over a week. They drove to two other friends' houses. Neither had heard from Noel in days, but one suggested they visit a guy named Davis Charles who lived over by the post office.

Duce drove them to the guy's house and Shane got out to knock on the door. His body pulsed with tension. In situations like this things could escalate quickly and he was prepared for anything. Who knew if she'd lied and actually gone to the father, but the father tossed her out on her ass?

His jaw clenched as he tried to distract the rage percolating inside of him. This may not be the father at all. He needed to play it cool in order to get some answers.

His knuckles rapped on the door again as he distracted himself with his surroundings. The house was a duplex, brick on one side, yellow siding on the other. Why did people do that? If someone shared a house wouldn't they want it to match?

A thin, disheveled woman opened the door with a runny nosed toddler hanging on her hip. "Can I help you?" There was no welcome in her tone.

"Uh, yeah. I'm looking for Davis Charles."

"What you want with Davis? He ain't got no money if that's what this is about."

"I need to ask him something."

She pursed her full lips and eyed him skeptically. "Fine, but I gots kids in here. You start fighting and I'm gonna call the cops, ya hear?"

He nodded.

She turned. "Davis! You got some people here to see you."

The door slammed in their faces. "Wholesome neighborhood," Duce commented under his breath.

The door opened and a tall, shirtless man stared down at them. He was tall, but skinny. "Who are you?"

"I'm Shane Martin. I'm trying to find my sister, Noel."

"Well, Noel ain't here. You probably find her over at Dan Nucci's place."

"Where's Dan live?"

Davis gave them directions and they hopped back in the roller skate and continued their search. But Dan Nucci didn't know where Noel was. Neither did his friend Mark Shields, or his friend Lauren Coats. It seemed everyone had an idea, but none of them panned out.

As it started getting dark, Shane dialed his sister's number for the hundredth time, only to have it go to voicemail.

"I gotta eat, Shane. I'm wilting away to nothing over here. And I'm almost out of gas."

Duce had done nothing but complain for the last hour.

They fueled up at a local station closer to Sunny Acres. While Duce wolfed down three hot dogs, Shane scrolled through his contacts and texted anyone who might know where Noel was hiding. No one had seen her since last night.

"She'll turn up, dude. She's probably out with her girls somewhere, licking her wounds."

Duce's words were poor comfort. Regardless of her age, Noel was his responsibility. He'd let her go her own way for the most part, because no one told him how to live when he was her age and she deserved the same. But he always looked out for her.

Over the last three years, as she'd become an adult, guilt seeped in for his lack of guidance. Not that his opinions were always welcomed, but he hadn't been there for her the way he could have been.

Truth be told, he'd sort of let his own life go adrift. Work had been sparse, money tight, and at the end of the week all he wanted to do was drink his worries away.

Shane untied his ponytail and ran his fingers through his dark, shoulder length hair, tying it back off his neck again. He had a gig tomorrow night and needed to find her before then or he'd have to cancel. Without his truck running and his friends holding nine to five jobs, he'd be limited to searching for her at night. His worry took a back seat to the surge of irritation. Her little disappearing act was going to cost him more money if she didn't turn up soon.

"Should we head back?" Duce asked as he crumpled up his wrapper and tossed it in the back of the roller skate.

Shane dialed again and cursed when it went straight to voicemail. He was out of ideas. Where the fuck could she be? Sighing, he said, "Yeah, I guess."

Duce started the car and backed out of the gas station. The thing buzzed down the highway as if powered by Duracell.

When Duce dropped him off, he entered his trailer and winced. It smelled like pot, piss, and beer. Rather than zone out on the couch like he usually would, Shane grabbed another trash bag and began cleaning up. He was anxious and it would only get worse if he sat around. He filled five big trash bags before the place looked decent again. The smell had dissipated, but wasn't completely gone.

He'd opened the small windows to let in some air and worked himself into a sweat. Filling a bucket with soapy water, he began scrubbing down the cabinets and walls. The water was black before he reached the living room.

Shane ended up passing out sometime after

three in the morning. His last thoughts were of Noel. He hoped, if she wasn't speaking to him, she at least had a good friend with her. He'd figure out a way to get her the money if that's what she really wanted, but he wanted to talk to her first, make sure she understood what this could do to a girl.

He didn't want her going through this alone. It made him sick to think of what their relationship had become and how careless he'd been last night when she needed him. She undoubtedly was pissed at him, but no way was anyone more furious with him than himself. He'd find her. Tomorrow he'd find her and they'd work it all out.

CHAPTER 1

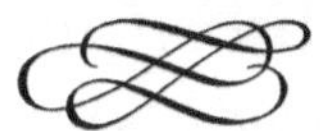

$\mathcal{M}$ay

"No, I'm definitely in. I just gotta run home and change. I'll meet you down at Bailey's in about an hour." Shane drove his truck down the dusty main road of Sunny Acres toward his trailer.

Duce's voice came over the phone. "Sims is already there. He said that girl, Sue, with the big lips is there."

Shane grinned. "Oh, yeah? Is she asking where I am?"

Duce laughed. "Not from the way Sims made it sound. You better get there quick if you want a piece of that. He sounded like he was moving in for the kill."

Shane shifted the phone to his other shoulder as he took the turn. "You tell Sims I said back off. I've been trying to get in her pants for a month now. I don't need him cock blocking me."

"Better hurry, bro. Clock's a ticking and she's probably already tipsy and doing that pouty drunk face she does."

Shane groaned. "Goodbye."

He tossed the phone onto the passenger seat of his truck and whipped into his driveway. A cloud of dust coated his trailer. It hadn't rained in ages, but he was okay with that. No rain meant plenty of work.

He shut off the truck and headed into his home. His shirt was off before he cleared the front door. Tossing it onto a pile of crap lying on his couch, he shucked his pants and hit the bathroom.

Five minutes and he was showered and looking for something to wear. As he sorted through the bag of clothes from the Laundromat he berated himself for being lazy. Everything was fucking wrinkled.

There was a knock at the rickety front door. "Hold on."

He shoved his legs into his nicest jeans and zipped the fly. When he opened the door he stilled. A uniformed officer stood on the other end. Shane quickly took inventory of his civic duties. All tickets were paid. He had no issues that he knew of with the IRS. He hadn't been summoned for jury duty. "Yeah?"

"Are you Shane Martin?"

"Yes."

"The brother of Noel Rose Martin?"

Fuck. Cold knifed through him like razorblades in his veins. It had been eight months, nine days, and roughly sixteen hours since he last saw his sister. Unable to catch his breath he stared, fighting back his hope, at the officer on his property. He'd be grateful if she was in jail. At least that meant he could find her.

The past eight months had been filled with the worst worry he'd ever known. For nearly three months he'd spent every free minute searching for her. She'd vanished. Her phone eventually turned off and no one, not even Tracy, knew where she'd gone.

Shane toyed with multiple scenarios. Maybe she ran off with the baby daddy. Maybe the guy was married and that was their only option. Maybe she'd gotten the money, taken care of the pregnancy, and didn't want to face those that knew. Maybe she hated him. The latter was his greatest fear. He'd never forgive himself for letting her think he wouldn't ultimately be there for her when the anger wore off.

His life became focused on finding her. When six months had passed, his boys sat him down and told him he needed to let her go. They said she'd come home when she was ready. Some days he was furious with her for putting him through this. He probably had an ulcer the size of the Grand Canyon from worrying about her. Her selfish actions affected him and she was wrong to punish him like this.

Adrenaline coursed through him as he eyed the officer. This was the first possible trace of her whereabouts he'd had since she left. He couldn't talk fast enough. "Yes. Do you know where my sister is? Did she do something wrong? I'll get a shirt and follow you to the station and—"

"Sir, that won't be necessary. May I come in?"

Shane frowned. Where the hell was Noel and what did she do? "Uh, sure. The place is kind of a mess, but..." He waved the officer inside.

The constable remained by the door while surveying the mess.

"The maid called out sick two days in a row," Shane joked, but the cop didn't crack a smile. Rather, the man looked at him with something akin to pity. Dread made a slow crawl up his spine.

"I'm sorry to have to tell you this, but your sister's body was identified two nights ago in Belmar, New Jersey."

Cold heaviness tingled at his nerve endings as he blinked. The cop's mouth continued to move, but no noise broke through the pounding in his ears. The tips of his fingers stung and a knot formed between his shoulders.

Oh God, that pain…a pain he hadn't felt since he'd received news about his parents death. No. His body wavered and he gripped onto the first solid object his hand could find. His heart accelerated as breath sawed in and out of his lungs. He was going to vomit.

Swallowing back the bile in his throat, he breathed. "What?"

"Your sister, her body was identified—"

"You're wrong," he snapped. "Noel…" He swallowed, his larynx scraping painfully as though something heavy was wedged inside his throat. His legs shook and suddenly he was sitting on the pile of crap on his couch, the officer handing him a glass of water. He hadn't even seen the guy move, let alone hear the water running.

"I know this is a lot to take in, son, but I need you to contact the Belmar morgue in order for them to release the body. The only records we could find on your sister identified you as her next of kin. Is there anyone else I should be contacting? Parents? Other siblings? A spouse?"

"No," he rasped. "It's just us." All this time… all this time she was alive and well, and now she was…dead? No. This couldn't be happening.

The officer's hand settled like a foreign object on his shoulder. "I know this is difficult, son. I'm going to leave this information here for you..." The officer continued to talk, but Shane heard nothing over the white noise ringing in his ears.

Noel was dead. Impossible. It simply couldn't be. He'd tried to contact her countless times over the past few months. Once her phone was disconnected, her friends began calling him, looking for her too. No one knew where she'd disappeared. What was in Belmar?

When he looked up again, he was alone. A pile of yellow forms sat on the counter beside an empty can of Bud and a bottle of drain solution. He briefly considered drinking the drain cleaner rather than dealing.

He sat for a long time debating the benefits of suicide versus a life on earth all by himself with no family. The drain cleaner was looking pretty good when his phone rang.

With numb fingers he brought the phone to his ear, his eyes never leaving the blue gallon of sudden death sitting on his counter.

"Yeah," he answered.

Noise and shouting from the bar filled the background. "Yo, man, where you at? Sue just left with Sims. I think you lost your chance."

Shane tried to formulate an answer, but his mouth wouldn't work. Who was Sue? What was Duce talking about?

"Shane? You there?" Duce's voice echoed in the phone. "Hello? McFly? Bueller? Bueller?"

"I'm not coming," he finally grated.

The noise cut away as though Duce were stepping outside to hear him better. "Shane? You all right?"

"It's Noel," he offered by way of explanation.

"Noel? Your sister? You found her? Where the fuck's she been? Where is she?"

There was only one reply. He choked on it, but somehow forced the answer out, needing to hear himself say the words to know they were true. Pain lanced through his chest.

"She's dead."

There was an eerie silence. When Duce spoke, his voice was as serious as the grave. "I'll be right there."

~

THE DRIVE to Belmar was impossible to catalog. It would be filed away in the back of his memory under moments he never wanted to visit again. If not for Duce, he never would've made the trip to see his sister for the last time.

It was Duce who drove. It was Duce who held him up when he had to identify Noel's pale body on the slab. It was Duce who filled out the required paperwork to have her body brought home so she could be buried in the same cemetery as their parents. And it was

Duce who hugged him for countless moments as he cried and totally fucking lost it in the parking lot.

He had no idea what to expect, but the additional disappointment that accompanied the pain of seeing her nearly knocked him to his knees. He hadn't wished for the baby to die. Subconsciously, he'd convinced himself she didn't go through with the abortion. But seeing her slender waist under that draped sheet on the slab in that cold, clinical room told him otherwise. She'd gone through with it and the morbid irony of her circumstances triggered a deluge of emotions he couldn't make sense of. Everything was lost.

When they returned home it was dark. Shane hadn't eaten in over twenty-four hours and had no appetite whatsoever. The thought of food, of sustaining his shitty life in any way, only made him want to vomit. Stumbling into the trailer, he went straight to his bed where he collapsed and slept for two days straight.

When he woke up his trailer was tidied up and Sims was waiting for him on the couch. Shane couldn't bring himself to look his friend in the eye.

"I am so sorry, man," Sims said as he patted him on the back in a manly hug. "Duce said it was a hit and run?"

"Yeah." Shane's throat burned as if gravel

and shards of glass had been churning there for days.

"Do they have any suspects?"

"Not since we left. I don't know if anything's changed. All I've been doing is sleeping. I'm so fucking tired."

"Have you eaten? You want me to go get something?"

"Not hungry," Shane said as he dug in the fridge for something to drink. When he came up empty he went to the kitchen faucet and leaned over the basin, drinking straight from the tap.

"When's the service?"

"What's today?"

"Thursday."

Shane rubbed his head. Jesus, he'd almost missed it. How pathetic would that be? "Tomorrow. It's just gonna be small. I could barely afford the plot."

"Aw, man, don't beat yourself up. No one could have seen this coming. You did what you could."

There wasn't enough breath reaching his lungs. Emotion strangled him and he hunched over the counter as dry sobs wracked his body. The pain was fucking unbearable. Sims awkwardly rubbed his back and offered well-intentioned words of comfort that did absolutely nothing to ease his grief.

But it wasn't his friends' fault they didn't

understand death. None of them had ever lost anyone close. Shane, however, had lost both his parents in a train accident and now his sister…

Fuck! He needed to reach a point where he could cope, but he didn't see that happening. His heart felt like it was being ripped from his ribs. He was drowning. He needed air.

Flashes of Noel ran through his head, clouded and tainted by their last interaction. Why had he been such a prick? This was his fault. He should have taken her aside, talked to her, listened, been there like he was supposed to be.

God fucking damn it!

His jaw tightened and he held his breath until he was dizzy and the room swirled. He couldn't do this. He couldn't go through this again. Not with her.

Forcing out a staggering breath, he rasped, "I think I want to be alone, Sims."

His friend hesitated, but nodded. They were probably concerned, but he was too overwhelmed to think about that.

Clapping him on the shoulder, Sims said, "Okay. You call me if you change your mind and want some company."

No company. He wanted to be alone. Forever. Maybe go to sleep and never wake up. "All right, man."

After Sims left Shane fell onto the couch and moaned through the pain that never eased.

The coarse cushions abraded his damp face, but he couldn't bring himself to move. Eventually, he passed out.

When Shane awoke it was dark. Fumbling to his feet, he stumbled into the kitchen. His stomach ached for sustenance. Hanging like dead weight from the door of the fridge, he scanned the shelves and found nothing appealing. The light coming from inside the fridge was excruciatingly bright. He shut the door and rummaged through the cabinets. When he spotted a bottle of Jack he grabbed onto it like a lifeline.

His belly burned when the first swallow settled in his gut. He drank until he was ill and then he passed out again.

Shane woke up to banging. His face was fused to the rough carpet covering the floor of his trailer. Wincing, he peeled himself off the ground and weakly forced his body into an upright position.

"Shane, open up."

On shaky legs he wobbled toward the front door, but took a minor detour to puke in the kitchen sink. Spitting into the basin, he wiped his mouth on the back of his arm. His head pounded as the incessant knocking continued. When he opened the door, Duce stood on the other side holding a bag of dry cleaning.

"Whoa, you look like fucking shit."

"Fuck you," Shane mumbled as he stumbled

back to the sink to dry heave. There was nothing left in his stomach to purge. Shutting his eyes, he blindly reached for the faucet and caught some rushing water in his mouth. He swished and spit until his mouth felt somewhat normal.

Duce hung the dry cleaning bag on the latch to the kitchen cabinet and grabbed his shoulder. "Okay, buddy, into the shower you go."

Shane was shoved in that general direction. The shower kicked on and the door shut as Duce backed out of the tiny room. He needed to shower. He needed to shower for his sister's funeral.

As the warm water rushed over him, his mind slightly cleared. Problem with a slightly clear mind was that it left room for his other thoughts to play. His fingers gripped his hair, tugging fistfuls of the wet knots over his eyes, trying to force back reality. His groan reverberated off the shower walls as he slumped to the side and slid to the cold ground.

Nothing was real. His toe scraped over the drain as he wept, wishing he'd drown there. Anything was better than what lay ahead.

Somehow he managed to pick himself up, but not until the water had run cold, leaving him shivering for well over ten minutes on the floor. Once dried off, he wrapped the towel around his waist, and headed into the kitchen. Opening another cabinet, he grabbed the first bottle to hit his fingers. Twisting the cap off he tossed it aside and tipped his head back, letting the fire burn its way down to his empty stomach.

"Whoa, dude, you think that's wise?"

His lips smacked together as he pulled the bottle away from his mouth. "I don't really fucking care. It's necessary."

Duce looked concerned, but made no further comment. "Tucker loaned you his suit. It should fit. Everything's there, shoes, tie, shirt…"

Shane intended to say thank you, but all he managed was a weak nod.

"Why don't I run down the street and grab you a coffee and something to eat while you get dressed?"

"Sure," Shane said quietly. He eyed the suit hanging in his kitchen as though it were the Grim Reaper. He'd acquired a buzz by the time he was dressed.

When Duce returned Shane was fumbling with his tie. His fingers trembled so severely the simplest task seemed impossible. "Never did learn how to tie one of these things."

His friend handed him a coffee and sighed. "Good thing I brought reinforcements then. One of those fucks should know how." He opened the screen door and yelled, "Any of you guys know how to tie a tie?"

Shane peeked out the door. Damn, it was

bright. All of his friends, dressed like a bunch of derelicts preparing to rob a Sunday school, stood in the tiny lot between their cars and his trailer, awkwardly waiting.

Tucker, the only other one wearing a tie, stepped forward. "Lisa can do it. Here, give it to me. She's waiting in the car."

He took the tie and disappeared into his vehicle. Shane stared at his friends. "Hey."

"Hey." They said as one.

Shane nodded. No one said another word. What was there to say? Tucker returned with the tie in a loose knot. It looked like a noose. Perfect.

Shane slipped it over his head and tightened it. "Does that look okay?"

"It looks fine," Tucker said, patting him on the shoulder. "You ready to do this?"

"No," he answered honestly.

His friend took a long breath. "It'll be over soon. Then we'll get wasted. How's that sound?"

Shockingly, even getting wasted didn't appeal to him anymore, yet that seemed to be the only thing he was capable of doing properly.

The guys somberly made their way to the various cars. "Come on, I'll drive," Duce said, pulling the trailer door closed behind him. Shane followed in a trance.

The funeral home was the same one they'd used for his parents years ago, but this time it lacked the flowers and flare their friends and life insurance had provided. The director said a few short words that were appropriate. As they followed the hearse, Shane shut his eyes and pretended he was somewhere else.

The sun was hot on his back when they reached the cemetery. He stood motionless beside the open ground. His sister's casket was suspended on metal beams over his parents' plot, disguised by a sheet of green Astroturf.

He should have been listening to the words being said, but all he could think of was what his parents' bodies now looked like. It had been ten years since he'd been there to bury them.

He recalled a young Noel gripping his hand as they'd cried over their graves. He didn't remember what was said that day either. He did recall the roses they placed on the coffins, but only when the funeral director handed him a yellow one to place on Noel's. Odd, that he found funeral procedures familiar.

In the distance he took note of another funeral taking place. A pang of guilt for not being able to provide something nicer for his sister stabbed redundantly into his conscience. The funeral in the distance was made up of a crowd shrouded in black. People comforted each other and hugged as they wept over the deceased.

He surveyed their motley crew. Everyone wore an expression of utter shock. No one touched anyone. The only person who didn't appear deeply affected by the situation was Lisa, who stood stoically beside Tucker. Shane wished he had a girl like that, someone to lean on other than Duce acting as his pillar of strength.

He dropped his yellow rose on the polished casket and stepped back. There should have been music playing, but the only sound was the press of grass beneath their feet and the occasional throat being cleared.

The others placed their roses. Shane looked around as if playing an inappropriate game of I-spy. There were his parents' names. Soon his sister's would be there as well—once he got the money. Fuck, he couldn't even afford to mark her damn grave. He failed her in so many ways. Turning, his gaze settled on the pile of dirt that had blanketed his mom and dad and would soon do so again, his sister tucked in with them.

Flowers decorated various tombs. His family wouldn't have flowers because he'd never visit this place again until it was his time to join them. Strange, how he hoped that was soon.

Duce placed a hand on his shoulder. "How you making out?"

He shrugged. The service was over and the guys were heading back to their cars parked along the path.

"I'll give you a few minutes," Duce said. "Whenever you're ready. Take your time." He turned and joined the others by the cars. Sims lit a cigarette in the distance, the scent carrying over the May air. He'd quit for a while, but apparently started again.

Shane stared at the ground. What was he supposed to do? Should he be thinking something? He stepped forward where the ground was soft.

His eyes closed.

You shouldn't be here, Noel. This shouldn't be you. It wasn't your time. God damn it, where have you been? I looked for you. I called.

He'd gone to the police the week she disappeared, but they'd only taken the basic information. Noel was an adult and not required to check in with him. His chest tightened as his breath ceased. He didn't want to breathe anymore. Could a person force himself to suffocate? Emotion clogged his throat, tightening to a point of acute pain until his mouth reflexively gasped and he sucked in a lungful of air.

I wish it was me. At least you have Mom and Dad wherever you are. I have no one. Why didn't He take me? What the fuck do I have to offer this world? You had so much ahead of you. College. A career. God damn it, this wasn't supposed to happen.

His thoughts repeated and repeated as the funeral in the distance dispersed. Where were her friends? Their absence only confirmed his opinion of the types of people they were. Even Tracy wasn't there. The others, he expected as much from, but Tracy…

He sighed aloud. "Right."

When he turned a woman waited a few feet away. Staring at her, he waited for some sort of recognition to strike. There was nothing. Was this a friend of his sister's? He didn't have the energy to talk so he headed in a detour to the cars where his friends lingered, hoping to avoid any commentary from the woman.

"Shane?"

Damn it. He paused, bracing himself, and faced her. "Yeah?"

"My name's Tabitha Laramie. I'm sorry for your loss." She held out a card. "I know you're grieving, but we really need to speak. It's about Noel. I'd like you to call me at some point to-morrow. The earlier the better."

He took the card. It was plain white and simply said her name and listed a number. "Were you a friend of Noel's?"

He hoped she was. If she was, then maybe she could explain what his sister had been up to over the past eight months.

"I'm afraid not. I'm from the Department of Public Welfare." She looked about to say more, but hesitated. "I don't mean to intrude. There was a mix up with the paper work and I didn't know how else to find you. If you could call me tomorrow I'd be more than happy to explain more."

Confusion knitted his brow and he nodded. She gave him a sad smile. "My condolences." Silently, she turned and walked away.

The woman cut through the cemetery and climbed into a black sedan parked at a distance from the other cars. He squinted, watching her as she made a note in a booklet before driving off.

His friends were waiting inside their cars. He slowly ambled past the graves to join them. Duce was in the back of the line waiting to drive out of the cemetery.

Their caravan meandered through the narrow road lined with statues and mausoleums. He didn't like leaving her here alone. His parents were dead, but he had yet to accept she was. It felt wrong, like he was abandoning her all over again.

By the time they made it around to the other side, workers had already converged on his sister's plot, making quick work of the burial. Gazing through the sad, faded reflection of himself in the window, he watched the workers press the plow of the backhoe into the earth and move the dirt toward his family. They were all in the ground and he was going somewhere else. Nowhere.

Blinking back some unnamable emotion, his finger pressed into one of the button's on the door. His eyes shut as warm air blew into his lungs. Breathing seemed all he could manage at the moment.

This was what life amounted to, dust to dust and nothing but bullshit in between. Every monotonous move seemed worthless. He'd been swimming upstream against hard currents all his life and he was fucking tired. For what? To die like everyone else? He'd prefer God to just get on with it. Save him the hardships that came with all the pointless crap intended to waste the irrelevant time toiled away on earth.

CHAPTER 2

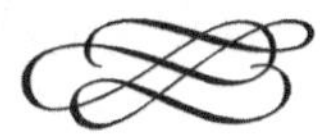

His friends' intentions to get him wasted failed miserably. They returned to his trailer and sat in a somber row, milking bottles of domestic beer waiting for someone to break the ice. Turned out, there was no way to break that sort of ice.

One by one they'd made their apologies and goodbyes and left him on his own. The following morning he woke up abnormally early. However, he had zero ambition to start the day.

He sat on his couch for a while staring at the ceiling, waiting for motivation to strike. He was still in his friend's suit pants and dress shirt. The crap from his pockets rested in a messy pile on the coffee table. When he spotted the business card from the woman at the cemetery he reached for it.

He fished out his cell and dialed. The phone

rang twice and switched over to a recording, which threw him into a bunch of automated prompts. What the hell was this crap? Did Noel owe money to the government? Was that what this was? Would he have to clear up some debt?

He looked at the card and found the woman's extension and entered it when prompted. It went directly to voicemail.

"Uh, yeah, this is Shane Martin. I was told to call here." He rattled off his number and waited, thinking of something else to say. When nothing came to him, he hung up.

A while later he found the motivation to shower. Hunger gnawed at his insides, but there was no food in the trailer aside from pickles, questionable Chinese, and beer. He got dressed and headed out to find sustenance.

He was in the deli department of the local grocer when his phone rang.

"Hi, Shane? This is Tabitha Laramie. Is this a good time?"

Shane stepped out of line and went to the bread aisle, which was less crowded. "Yeah."

"Thanks for getting back to me. I have some things we need to discuss regarding your sister's case. Her caseworker was actually out of town last week, but she's back today. Would you be able to come down to our office in Lakota? Joanne, Noel's caseworker, would have to travel from Belmar, but she would be able to make it here by three. Once everything's sorted out we can reassign the case—"

"I don't understand. Caseworker? Is this about the hit and run?"

"Uh, no. This is about your sister's living situation. We need to allocate guardianship and decide if the state should intervene as soon as possible. She didn't have a will, but as her next of kin you're automatically on our list of contacts in the event of a death..."

As the woman went on Shane frowned. Whatever she was talking about was going right over his head.

"...It would really be best to sit down with the caseworker and discuss all of this in person. As you can imagine, in cases like this, time matters quite a bit. We try to keep things as co-pasetic as possible for all involved. Would you be able to come down to the office today?"

"Uh, where did you say you were located?"

She gave him directions to the Welfare branch in Lakota. When the call ended, Shane was more confused than before it started. Had his sister been on welfare? She could have called him. He'd waited eight months for her to call, but of course she hadn't. Nothing made sense.

He was suddenly too exhausted to think. Abandoning the grocery store without making a purchase, he drove home in a daze. When he arrived at the trailer he was painfully hungry and tired. Lying down on his bed, he considered texting Duce to ask him to go with him that afternoon, but it wasn't Duce's problem.

He fell asleep and dreamt of screeching cars and screaming women. When he awoke in a cold sweat it was quarter to three. He quickly jumped out of bed and grabbed his keys, rushing out the door.

Following the directions the welfare lady gave him, he found the office. Parking was a bitch. By the time he walked into the building it was three-twenty. He'd probably missed the people he was supposed to meet.

There was a grumpy looking woman behind a glass window. Everyone in the place looked miserable. A line of citizens snaked here and there and he couldn't figure out the beginning from the end. A red ticket dispenser stood beside a police officer who apparently enjoyed too many donuts.

He eyed the officer as he pulled a ticket. Number two-four-eight. He looked around for any indication of what number they were currently servicing. On a black board with red pinhole digital numbers he found the number two-twenty-seven. *Great.*

He crumpled the ticket in his palm and took a seat beside someone who looked fairly clean. His stomach was a mess and his nose seemed overly sensitive. If this person was one of the better smelling people, he dreaded to think what the lady with the stained hat smelled like.

The numbers ticked onward about one digit every ten minutes. He found a vending machine and grabbed a bag of chips. He was starving. By four o'clock he was ready to bash his head against the wall. Instead, he tossed his ticket in an empty coffee cup sitting on the floor and stood to leave.

"Shane?"

Turning, he spotted the woman from the cemetery. About fucking time.

"Have you been waiting here all this time? We thought you didn't come. You should have told the clerk you had an appointment."

Like he was supposed to know that. Would have been helpful information an hour ago. He kept his mouth shut when she smiled apologetically at him. "Please, come with me."

He followed her through a set of double doors and what looked to be a metal detector. They entered a small room with a plain wood veneer table and four folding chairs. A woman with black hair and severe, red painted lips smiled at him.

"Shane, this is Joanne. She's from our Jersey branch. Joanne, this is Shane, Noel's brother."

Painted Lips stood and extended a hand. He briefly shook it taking note of her soft palm and flowery fragrance.

"Have a seat, Shane."

He sat down in the cool metal chair and waited for someone to explain what the hell was going on.

"I've already said my part to Shane. Why don't you go over what you need to, Joanne? You're more familiar with the case."

Joanne's painted smile was replaced with a much more serious expression. She perched a pair of half moon glasses on the bridge of her nose that hung from a chain around her neck, and withdrew a manila folder with Noel's name on it.

"Well, Shane, let me first begin by offering my sincere condolences. Noel was a sweet girl and although I only helped open her case, I do regret hearing what happened to her. However, being that I worked on setting up her assistance, the county thought it best I familiarize you with the proceedings. Although, you will eventually be reassigned to someone local to your district if you choose to proceed."

She glanced at him expectantly. Was he in the wrong room? He was missing something and decided it was time he 'fessed up.

"Uh, not to sound like a complete ass, but I have no idea what this is about."

The women frowned. Tabitha smiled nervously. "It's about Shane of course."

What? "I'm Shane."

"Well, yes, you're Shane, but this is about Shane, your nephew."

He stilled. "My what?"

"Your…Shane, were you not aware your sister had a child?"

"A child?"

Joanne nodded, a look of confusion on her face. "Yes, Shane Logan Martin."

"My sister had a son?" It had only been eight months.

The women both stared at him. What they were saying sunk in slowly.

"She had the baby?" he whispered. Jesus, she hadn't gotten rid of it. Him. Shit. It was a he and he was his nephew. And she fucking named him Shane after him and Logan after their dad.

"I hadn't realized you were unaware of the situation," Joanne said apologetically. "I just assumed… During the short period I spoke with Noel she mentioned you often. She said if anything were to happen, in the event of an emergency, you were to be contacted as Shane's next of kin. I assumed you knew you had a nephew."

"Shane," Tabitha intervened. "If this is an issue for you, we need to know now. As of the past week your nephew's been placed in state custody. We were under the impression you'd apply for guardianship. If that isn't the case we need to know in order to make arrangements for foster care."

"Wait," he mumbled, shaking his head

dumbly. "Wait just a goddamn minute. You expect me to be in charge of a baby?"

"Of your nephew. You'd first have to go through the placement process with a caseworker, but once you proved a caring and capable caregiver, you would go before a judge and request sole guardianship."

"Where's the dad?"

"You're sister never provided a name for Shane's father."

"How old is he?"

Joanne smiled kindly. "He's two months. I have a picture if you'd like to see him." She sifted through the file.

Two months old? She was gone for eight months. Pregnancies usually lasted nine. That meant she might have been a lot further along than he expected. Maybe coming to him was her last resort. *Oh, Noel. I'm so sorry.*

Things were moving so fast he didn't have time to process the oncoming guilt. "Wait, where is he now? You said he's in state custody. What exactly does that mean?"

"He's currently in an age appropriate cottage at an orphanage in Altoona, Pennsylvania where orphans are given temporary housing and care."

"My nephew's in a fucking orphanage?" Both women drew back. Shane quickly apologized for his language. "Well, can I go get him?"

"I'm afraid it isn't that easy. You first need to

fill out the required paperwork and have the proper background checks completed. We can expedite things, but then a notary of republic must authenticate your request for guardianship. You'd need to make an appointment with the district court. If everything checks out, you'll go before a judge, agree to the allotted time, in which a caseworker will be assigned to report on your progress, and then an advocate from Children and Youth will advise you regarding permanent guardianship."

"Do I have to call him that?"

The women appeared confused. "Shane's his name."

"But it's also my name. You said his middle name's Logan. That was our father's name. Can I call him that?"

"I suppose you could call him whatever you want," Joanne said slowly.

"But will he answer to that?"

The women were frowning again. "Mr. Martin, Shane is nine weeks old. He's at a developmental stage where he's just learning to open and close his fists over objects and can barely see beyond a foot in front of him. Have you ever been around babies before?"

He bristled. "Not really. But how hard could it be?"

The women exchanged worried glances. "You'll be required to take parenting courses. However, due to the urgent nature of the situation and the space issue among the state facilities, the court will likely waive the prerequisite nature of those courses, allowing you to complete them during the time frame in which you already have custody. But might I suggest a few books you could read over the next two days?"

Books? Shane hadn't read a book since he was in school and even then he was more of a Cliffs Notes kind of guy. "Yeah, I guess some kid books wouldn't hurt. So, uh, what do you need me to do?"

"Are you willing to apply for custody? This isn't a simple process, Mr. Martin. Your entire life over the next several months will be under the scrutiny of the state. You'll have a caseworker who will be assigned to you and act as an advocate for Baby Shane. He or she will be required to report back to the judge on everything that happens between now and your final custody hearing sometime next fall."

"Well, what other choice do I have? I'm not going to let some stranger raise my nephew."

Joanne smiled, appearing proud of his decision. "Your sister did say you raised her after your parents passed on."

"I did. For a few years until she came of age. After that she sort of started doing her own thing."

"How is it you didn't know she was pregnant?" Tabitha asked tentatively.

Shane shifted in his seat. "We, uh, sort of

had a falling out. Last I knew she was pregnant, but planned on getting an abortion."

"Well, I'm glad she didn't. From what I hear, Shane is a joy. The women at the orphanage said he sleeps like an angel and eats like a little piglet."

He was glad to hear that. From what he could guess, all kids that age did was sleep and eat. He could manage that. It would be cool when it got bigger and they could play sports together. *He*—he corrected. Not an it. *He.*

He grinned at the women. "Where do I sign?"

Around five o'clock, just as the government building was closing down for the weekend, they finished their meeting. Joanne gave Shane a picture of the baby who looked like every other baby he'd ever seen, and a list of reading materials he was supposed to study by Monday.

As he climbed behind the wheel of his truck his face eased into a smile for the first time in days. He was getting a piece of his family back. He didn't have a fucking clue what to expect or what babies needed other than sleep and food, but how hard could it be?

When he pulled into his lot, the roller skate sat outside his trailer. He walked inside and found Duce playing the game station and eating a pizza. "Hey, man, where you been?"

Shane shut off the game.

"Aw, man! I almost had Sims score beat!"

"You're never beating Sims's score, Duce. The guy doesn't have a life for a reason."

Duce eyed him critically. "You look better. Where'd you go?"

Shane popped a beer and plopped on the couch. "Did you see that woman at the funeral yesterday?"

"The one in the black sedan? Yeah."

"Well, she said she had something for me, something to do with Noel. You'll never guess what it was."

"From the look of your face I'd say it was something good. Did your sister have some money hidden away?"

"Nope."

"A car? A new ride would be sweet. Your truck's on its way out."

"Nope, not a car."

"What?"

"Prepare yourself." He waited a beat. "She left me… a baby."

Beer sprayed from his friend's lips across the table. *"A what?"*

"A baby," Shane repeated.

"Dude, tell me you're talking about a baby hermit crab or a baby chia pet or something, not a living, breathing, pooping human being."

"Oh, I forgot about the pooping."

"Dude, are you fucking nuts? You cannot have a baby!"

"Why not?"

Duce shook his head as if all the reasons were obvious. He held up his hand, a slice of pizza balanced between his thumb and fore-finger as he ticked off the reasons. "One, you're a glorified child yourself, except you can buy beer and get drafted. Two, you know nothing about babies. Three, you know *nothing* about babies! Four, this is a human being you're talking about. I got you a plant for a housewarming gift and you killed it in a week."

"Sims killed that plant by using it as an ash-tray. No one's going to put ash on the baby. Come to think of it, there probably shouldn't be any smoking around the baby at all. Their lungs are all miniature and shit."

Duce smacked his head. "Oh my God, this is worse than when they found Carlos in *The Hangover*. I can just see it now. You've to give it back!"

Shane smiled and snatched a slice of pizza from the box. "Nope. I'm keeping it. Noel said if anything happened to her she wanted me to raise it. *Him!* Damn it, I have to stop calling it an it."

The door swung open and Tucker walked in. "What's up, ladies? I got us some sweet salad greens for tonight." He held out a fist and a bag of weed miraculously appeared. "Who's mixing?"

"You see? This is exactly why you can't have a baby!" Duce yelled.

"Whoa, who's having a baby?" Tucker asked, his color slightly paling.

"Shane is!"

Tucker's head tilted quizzically. "You preggers, bro?"

Shane laughed. "Yes. I'm due Monday. I think you guys should throw me one of those parties girls have and buy my son some cool shit. I'm pretty sure he's gonna want a sweet Powerwheels SUV and some hockey equipment."

"Okay, now you're freaking me out, because I'm not sure you're joking," Tucker said. He faced Duce. "What the fuck is he talking about?"

"Noel had a baby."

"*What?* Like a real baby?"

"Yes, a *real* baby! And Shane here thinks he's gonna raise it."

"I am gonna raise it," Shane said then cursed. "Damn it, *him*! I'm going to raise *him*."

Tucker wasn't breathing. He stared at Shane as if he had a dick growing out of his eye. "What?"

He still didn't move. Duce jumped back in. "Where are you even going to put a baby in this dump?"

Shane frowned. "I'll put it in the bed."

"Babies sleep in cribs, genius. My cousin

just had a baby. You should see all the crap they require. There are swings and bouncing vibrating things, and cribs, and cradles, and netted box things to trap them in so they don't run—"

"Dude, you can't have a baby!" Tucker finally squealed, a petrified expression on his face.

Shane tossed down his crust and grabbed another slice. Standing, he took an exasperated breath. "Why the hell not?"

Tucker shook his head rapidly. "Be serious! You have beer and questionable mayonnaise in your fridge. The other day I killed some bug in your bathroom that was a cross between a tarantula and a pterodactyl. People with kids don't have shit like that in their homes. They have doilies and Dijon mustard."

"So I'll upgrade my condiments and do a little decorating. The only reason I don't have that sort of shit is because I've never needed it before. Having this baby will be good for me. It'll give me something to stand for."

"You called it an *it* again," Duce mumbled under his breath.

"Damn it! *Him*! *He* will give me something to stand for."

Tucker looked highly concerned. "Why don't you stand for doing the right thing and let someone who knows what they're doing raise this kid?"

All joking aside, Shane looked at his friends. "Because he's mine. He's my nephew, not some stranger's. I have no one. I lost my parents. I lost my sister. He's all I have left. The other day I actually considered drinking drain cleaner because I had nothing to live for. Today I have a purpose. It's him. He needs me and I need him and I'm going to do whatever I have to do in order to keep him."

They were quiet for several minutes. When they spoke again it wasn't in exasperated tones, but in pure curiosity.

"What about chicks?" Tucker asked. "Having a kid around is going to majorly cramp your style."

Shane shrugged. "He's gonna be a part of me. If some girl has a problem with that, then she isn't someone I want in my life. He'll be like a filter for crappy women. I'll only let the good ones in. Besides, women dig babies. For all I know he may be a total chick magnet."

"What about work?" Duce asked. "Who's gonna watch him when you're working?"

Fuck, he hadn't thought about that. Living paycheck to paycheck didn't really allow for much of a savings. He needed to work. "I don't know. I'll figure something out."

"You know you can't take him on the job," Tucker said.

He tossed a piece of pizza crust at him. "No shit, wise ass. Look, I know I don't really have a clue what I'm doing, but I'll learn. This is what Noel wanted. I need to do it right. For her."

Duce sighed. "Jesus, this is like our last Goonie weekend. Everything's going to change."

"I need a change," Shane admitted. "Maybe we all do. Losing Noel was the last straw. I can't keep letting life slip through my fingers."

Duce held up his beer. "To Noel. May this tiny part of her grow to be a piece of us all, so we never truly have to say goodbye."

Shane smiled. His friends were good guys. He held up his beer. "To Noel."

Tucker joined them. "To Noel."

CHAPTER 3

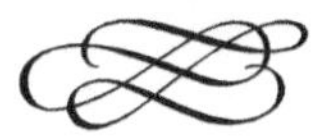

Shane was a master of procrastination. "I gotta call out of work tomorrow," he told Sims who sat like a relentless addict playing the game station on the floor.

"Yup."

"Are you even listening to me?"

"Nope."

Shane sighed and stood. He still had to straighten up his place, go to the library, skim over the books. He looked at his watch—twelve forty-five—he should probably get moving.

"You're gonna have to go," he told Sims. "I got shit to do."

"Aw, man, just do your shit around me. I'm on level eighteen."

Shane didn't really care if he stayed, but he knew so long as Sims was sitting around doing nothing, nothing would get done on his part either. He shut off the TV.

"Fuck! Why'd you do that?" It was a rather dramatic response to having a video game shut off, but Shane had been there before. Sadly, he understood.

"Seek help. You're addicted. I gotta run to the library so you need to leave."

Sims stood and collected his phone from the table. "Library's closed on Sunday."

"What? No, it's not," he argued, but feared his friend was right.

"Oh, okay," Sims said easily, telling Shane he didn't need to argue because he was certain the library was closed.

Fuck!

"Shit. I gotta get those books about the baby. I'm supposed to read them before tomorrow."

"You can go to the bookstore."

"I can't buy all those books. I already have to miss work tomorrow and lose a day's pay. I'm gonna need to buy diapers and stuff."

"Just read them there. People do it all the time. It's part of that new liberal-literature-coffee-generation thing stores are doing."

"What the fuck are you talking about?" He checked his pockets for everything he needed and picked up his keys.

"Trust me. Go to a bookstore and you'll see tons of people sitting around reading books and drinking enormous cups of coffee. It's weird. I think a bunch of hippies are trying to phase out bars with cafes. It'll never work."

Their conversation had gone on about twice as long as it should have. "Okay, well, I gotta go. I'll catch up with you later." They walked outside and got into their separate cars.

The only bookstore Shane knew of was far, so he drove past the library first. Sims was right. It was closed. He was also right about the coffee and books thing. Nobody seemed to have any hang-ups about reading a book that wasn't paid for, so he found the first book on the list, *What to Expect-Baby's First Year*.

The book was huge, bigger than the Bible. Shane thumbed through it and saw a bunch of words he didn't understand. He'd need to read a dictionary alongside it. Within twenty minutes he was completely overwhelmed.

He looked at the back of the book. Twenty bucks! He really didn't want to buy it, but it seemed like there was a ton of shit to know about babies. The smell of caffeinated drinks and paper was giving him a headache so he took the book to the register.

The cashier rang him up and smiled. "Would you like a gift receipt?"

"No, it's for me," he said as he slid her his debit card.

"Oh." She swiped his card and lowered her face, eyes wide. What was that look about?

Shane looked around and spotted a father and son. That dad wore a sweater vest and khakis. His hair was short and spikey in a totally manicured way. Shane looked down and took in his own appearance. Jeans, work boots, a worn cotton T, coupled with his thick, dark hair hanging past his shoulders—he was definitely not meeting society's standard of fatherly figures.

He frowned. Was there some rule if you were a dad you had to look like a Circuit City sales associate? He didn't fit that bill, nor did he want to. There was no way he was going to change to meet some social standard. He'd be a cool dad and little Shane would be a cool kid. End of story.

Once his purchase was bagged, he headed back to the truck. Did two month olds crawl? If so, he probably should clean up his place a bit. He should probably do that anyway. He headed home and began doing the usual Sunday bag up of trash.

As he worked his mind went to thoughts of his sister. What kind of mother was she? Did she like having a child? Was it hard? Was she good at it? He wanted to be a good dad. His father was a good dad, always making him feel safe and confident.

Shane remembered being a little kid and thinking his dad could do anything. Shane was seventeen when the train derailed, and his first thought was why didn't his dad do something to stop it? Thirty some people injured, four dead, and his parents were half of the casualties.

In terms of the accident, he'd been able to think of his father, but never his mother. She was so delicate and soft. She always smelled like cookies and sunshine. Her hugs were the best and what he missed most. Even at twenty-seven he missed his mom's hugs.

Did Noel give good hugs? Shane decided he would hug little Shane as much as he could since his little counterpart probably missed his mom's hugs too.

It was nine o'clock by the time he got the trailer somewhat clean. By the door was an enormous pile of laundry, but he didn't have the energy for that. Shane grabbed a beer and the remote and settled onto the couch.

Sniffing the air, his lip curled. There was a silent but deadly smell coming from one of the cushions. He really needed to get new furniture.

Before he forgot, he texted his foreman and told him he'd be out tomorrow. His eyes drooped as he stared at the television and, before he knew it, annoying infomercials were waking him up. He shut off the television and curled onto his side, wincing and gagging when his face brushed against the unidentified smell on the couch.

The following morning was strangely anti-climactic. He dressed like he always did, wondering if there should be some sort of flare to a wardrobe when one was picking up a child. He opted for his normal, jeans, a t-shirt, and boots.

His hair was tied back and his face freshly shaved. He grabbed his keys, his phone, and his book. Something told him that book would be his bible over the coming months.

It was strange that babies were exchanged at the same courthouse he paid his parking tickets. The waiting room smelled like stale coffee. Various civilians sat in the blue plastic chairs along the wall. The paneling needed updating and there was a watermark on the ceiling.

Phones rang on the other side of the glass divider as women efficiently went about filing paperwork. A man was called up to the window and Shane watched as he discussed an agreement advised by his parole officer.

A young pregnant woman came to the window. "Shane Martin?"

He stood. "That's me."

"You need to sign in. Joanne and Tabitha from the DPW are already here. They asked that I send you back."

He scribbled his name on the clipboard and looked expectantly at the girl. This was it. His gut pinched with a cross between excitement and anxiety. Aiming for nonchalance, he wiped his clammy hands down the front of his jeans.

The pregnant woman came around the counter and led him to a door marked Room C. Inside sat Joanne and Tabitha. No baby.

His head was clouded with too many thoughts. He'd been on a two day adrenaline rush and was crashing hard. He was stuck somewhere between hyper and exhausted, which caused his pulse to beat rapidly no matter if he was moving or sitting still.

"Hi, Shane. How are you today?"

They exchanged niceties as he awkwardly lowered himself into the chair across from them and waited. Finally he asked, "Where's the baby?"

"Oh, the baby's with one of our advocates. You need to speak to the judge first."

Was there a chance he'd be shot down? "Should I have brought anything?"

"No, we have all your paperwork," Tabitha said.

"Tabby's going to speak on your behalf. You just need to answer any questions the judge directs to you. It's basically everything we already went over. Don't be nervous. Everything will be fine."

He didn't think he was nervous, just unsure of what to expect. He was anxious to get to the next stage of the game, whatever that might be.

There was a knock at the door and a uniformed officer stepped in. "The judge will see you now." In such a stuffy office setting, the officer's holster and guns seemed obtrusive.

He followed the women into the courtroom. It was smaller than Judge Judy's court, which he found disappointing because he was ready to blow this shit up like Johnnie Cochran.

There were four rows of wooden chairs, two on each side. A meager railing divided the floor from the onlookers, but there were no onlookers—just them.

The entire room was carpeted. It was basically a glorified office with a fancy flag and the big desk for the judge. They shuffled behind one table and stood there. A beaten Bible rested forgotten on the surface.

A man with a shiny bald head and a black robe walked in. "Good morning."

"Good morning," they echoed.

The judge sat at his desk and sifted through papers hidden by the lip of his table. "We're here to discuss the custody of a Shane Logan Martin, son of Noel Martin who is now deceased?"

"That's correct," Tabitha said.

"You're Shane Martin, uncle to the baby?"

"Yes, sir."

"Place your hand on the Bible."

Shane did as he asked. How did the judge

know if he believed in that Bible? Maybe he followed the Koran.

"Do you swear to tell the truth, the whole truth, and nothing but the truth, so help you God?"

"I do."

"Be seated."

They sat and Tabitha gave a detailed explanation of his situation. The judge made very little eye contact as he scribbled down notes. When she finished her exhaustive synopsis the judge asked, "Has a new caseworker been assigned?"

"Yes, Your Honor. A woman from our Lakota office. She'll be making her first visit this week, once Shane's had a chance to get settled."

The judge nodded. "You understand you're being charged with the responsibility of a human life? This child will be at the mercy of your good judgment. Do you feel capable of handling such a responsibility?"

Shane nodded. "I want to be a good parent. I don't have any family left. My nephew's it. I want to do this."

"Plenty of people do it, son. It's a matter of doing it well."

"I intend to do my best."

The judge nodded. "Then let's hope that suffices. I have here your child abuse clearance papers and criminal record report. Thank you for that, Mrs. Laramie. We'll reconvene in three months with an update, at which point I'll hear from the caseworker assigned to Mr. Martin and he may petition for a more permanent arrangement."

He tapped the gavel and Shane was childishly satisfied. Everything was so much more casual than what he'd anticipated and some juvenile part of him feared the judge wouldn't use the gavel. Dear God. Could he actually be a parent? He was pretty much a man-child himself. Well, the time for self-scrutiny had passed.

"Congratulations, Shane," Joanne said, holding out her hand. "I'll go get Shane."

She left and he looked to Tabitha. "Do we just wait here?"

She nodded. "She'll only be a minute."

The judge left and they were alone. He fidgeted anxiously. When the doors opened again, he turned. Joanne carried a mint green car seat. All he could see was soft blue blankets and a plush bumblebee dangling from the handle.

She hefted the seat onto the table and his heart stuttered to a stop. Like a sleeping cherub, his nephew rested, swathed in what looked like the softest blanket in the world.

He had dark hair like him. The lids of his eyes were so fair they seemed almost translucent, darkening to deep pink at his perfect lashes. What color were his eyes? Were they brown like his? Blue? His cheeks were rosy and his mouth was pursed as if sucking an invisible thumb. Suddenly his lips moved in quick suckling motions.

Shane backed up. "What's he doing?"

The women smiled affectionately. "He's just sucking. Babies do that in their sleep sometimes."

The women gently touched the baby's head and doted over him. Women were so natural with babies. Shane was suddenly terrified. He'd thought the baby would have been more... sturdy.

"While he's asleep let's go over some things," Tabitha said in a soft voice. She slid him a pamphlet. "Here's some information on SIDS—

"SIDS?"

"Sudden Infant Death Syndrome."

His stomach bottomed out. What the fuck was that?

Tabitha, luckily, didn't seem to notice his panic. "It briefly explains about how the baby should be put to bed, always on his back, never on his belly, where his soft spots are, and how to handle him. I'm sure after going through the reading material this weekend you're familiar with the basics, shaken baby syndrome, testing the temperature of baths and bottles. Babies are basically fragile little eggs. So long as you're gentle, you'll be fine."

The collar of his shirt seemed to be choking

him. He swallowed and pulled at his neckline with his fingers.

Tabitha slid him another pamphlet. "This is about car seats. Your local police station can help you install one if you have trouble."

She slid another brochure to him. How many fucking brochures did this woman have?

"This informs you about medical assistance and Shane's eligibility. This one's for supplemental nutritional assistance—"

"What?" He was on overload.

"Food stamps. You'll be eligible for a lot of government programs being that Shane isn't legally identified as your child yet. Once we get to that stage, your income will have to be considered, but for now he qualifies automatically."

Food stamps? They wanted him to go on welfare? Fuck that. He worked hard and supported himself for over a decade. He could do this without government aid.

"This is the help line for Care Works. They handle childcare assistance. They'd be able to help you place Shane in the right daycare for your situation…"

As she went on, Shane nodded dumbly and took each paper she handed him. He'd barely read the first book on the list. How the hell was he supposed to memorize all this other crap? These women were intimidating the shit out of him. He wanted to grab the baby and bolt. He'd figure this stuff out on his own.

Finally Tabitha reached the end of her spiel. "You have my number if you need anything. There's also a list of numbers on the back of the DPW sheet I gave you. Katherine Mc-Alester is the caseworker assigned to you and Baby Shane. She'll be in touch this week at some point. She'll be able to answer any questions you have. She's your advocate for the next few months. Don't be afraid to depend on her for help when it comes to doing the best we can for Shane. Good luck."

She smiled pleasantly and shook his numb hand. Joanne did the same. They left the room and he sat staring at little Shane. They made it seem so much more complicated than it really had to be. He had time to figure it all out. Babies slept. While the little guy was sleeping he'd read up on all this crap and be a pro in no time.

He grabbed the big baby purse Joanne had left and lifted the car seat. It was awkward to carry and he was terrified he'd drop him. No dropping the baby. That would be very, very bad.

Once he had a handle on the carrier, he left the room and headed to his truck. This was it. A strange self-consciousness set in. He felt like he was stealing a person.

CHAPTER 4

Shane hefted the baby purse on his shoulder and carefully shifted the carrier in order to open the passenger door of the truck. What seemed incredibly light moments ago was becoming awkward and heavy. What the fuck was in this purse? Bricks?

He stared at the interior of his truck. He probably should have cleaned it up before he got there. The carrier holding sleeping Shane looked pristine and clean while his truck resembled a dumpster. He swept his hand along the seat, toppling the many empty soda bottles and coffee cups to the floor.

His shoulder tingled with relief when he put the carrier down. He sat the baby purse of bricks on the pavement and stared at Shane. He was a cute little bugger. He wanted to wake him up, get to know the little guy, but figured he should get him home first.

He analyzed the seat. There was a tall handle, two red buttons, an awning, and tiny plastic hooks on the sloped bottom. It didn't seem too complicated. As a matter of fact it seemed too simple. This was supposed to keep babies safe?

He pulled out the seatbelt and fed it through the open brackets next to the handle. That didn't look right. He frowned, undid the buckle, and turned the seat around. That didn't look right either.

Angling the seat, the baby squinted and cooed. The sun was in his eyes. He extended the awning. Something still wasn't right.

"Do you need help with that?"

Shane turned and found an older woman was watching him. "Uh, I'm sort of new at this," he explained lamely.

She stepped closer and frowned at his handiwork. "A baby this age really shouldn't be in the front." She peeked behind his seats. It was a small S10 truck with no back seat. She sighed. "Car seats like this face backward. That way if you're in a collision the baby's protected. Do you have airbags? If so, you'll have to shut them off."

Shane opened his glove compartment and found the manual for his truck. He quickly looked in the appendix for air bag controls. Locating the button on the dash, he disengaged the airbags. "Wouldn't the airbag protect him?"

"No. He's too small. Airbags can crush a child of this size."

She finagled the belt around the carrier and locked it into place, tested the security of her work, and appeared satisfied.

"I have four grandbabies and three kids. I'm an old pro at this," she told him proudly.

"Thank you. I'm sort of out of my element here."

"You'll learn. He's a cutie. What's his name?"

"Shane."

She smiled and ran a hand over the baby's head. Women were always touching him. He hadn't touched him yet, but he looked soft, too soft. He didn't want to dent him.

He thanked the woman and stuffed the baby purse on the floor next to all the trash. He definitely had to clean out his truck.

Driving home was an ordeal. Had there always been so many maniacs on the road? People were doing forty in a twenty-five. To play it safe he drove a measured fifteen miles an hour the entire way home. It took him over an hour, but he made it there safe and sound, precious cargo still sleeping peacefully.

When he pulled up to his trailer the roller skate was out front. Exiting the truck, he carefully undid the seatbelt. Baby Shane stirred a bit, but didn't wake. He carried him inside and placed the carrier on the floor by the coffee table.

The toilet flushed and Duce came out of the bathroom. "You're back. How'd it go?"

Shane tipped his chin toward his nephew. "I got him."

Duce cautiously stepped closer to the baby. In hushed tones he said, "Dude, I can't believe they actually gave you a kid. What are you gonna do with it?"

"I'm gonna take care of *him*."

They both silently stared at the baby. "He doesn't do much," Shane informed. "This is basically it."

Duce reached forward with a pudgy finger. "Coochy, coochy, coo…"

Shane yanked his friend's hand back. "Don't touch him. You'll wake him up."

"Oh, sorry."

They stared some more.

"You wanna get something to eat?" Duce finally asked.

"Uh, getting him in the truck's sort of a pain. And I don't think he's supposed to be in the front. I may need to get a new car."

"How you gonna afford a new car? You can barely afford to keep this one."

He shrugged. "I don't know. I'll figure something out."

"Well, I'm starved. I'm gonna run down to Chung Luck. You want something?"

"Yeah, get me a few egg rolls."

Duce pulled out his keys. "What about for the little guy?"

Shane frowned. "Babies don't eat Chinese food, dumbass. They eat baby food."

"Oh. Right."

"Wait, stay here with him for a sec. I forgot that big bag in the truck. There's probably food in there."

When he returned Duce was exactly where he'd left him.

"Did he do anything?"

"No."

Shane put the bag down and Duce snickered. "What?"

"Nice purse, dude."

Shane grimaced at the mint green bag with ribbons around the straps. "I didn't pick it."

"The kid's gonna have a complex with accessories like that. You gotta get him some manly bags."

"I will."

When Duce left, Shane sifted through the bag. There were tiny diapers, wipes, some sort of yoga mat thing, a bunch of creams. He laughed when he saw something called Butt Paste. That was self-explanatory.

There was something resembling a miniature turkey baster. He found clothes, itty-bitty socks, a knit cap, a few rattles, two containers of formula, some bottles, and a small booklet with doctor's visits listed in it. He recognized the writing as his sister's and a strange, sad nostalgia settled over him. Was she here watching him now?

"He's beautiful, Noel," he whispered. "I'm gonna do this. Don't worry. I'll figure it out and I'll take good care of him for you. You'll see."

By the time Duce returned Shane was reading the bottle of formula. "What's that?" his friend asked as he plopped down the paper takeout bag of food.

"Formula. I didn't find any food. Do you think I should wake him to eat?"

"Uh, isn't there some rule about never waking a sleeping baby?"

Shane shrugged. "Maybe I should make up a bottle so it's ready when he does wake. He's been sleeping for two hours. He's gotta be hungry."

Shane wished he had Internet. He wasn't really computer savvy, but people were always talking about finding shit online. Duce was staring at him with a peculiar look. "What?"

"I think you should give him back."

"Give him back? There *is* no back. I'm it."

"He's just all perfect and small. What if you fuck him up?"

"Hey, don't curse in front of him. And I'm not going to mess him up. I just need some practice. I'll figure it out."

"Maybe you should ask someone who has kids what to do."

Shane reached for an egg roll. "I don't know anyone with kids. I have to take a class and I have a crap load of reading material."

"When do you take the class? Maybe that was something you should have done beforehand."

"It starts tomorrow night. I'll be fine."

They ate and zoned out to some reality TV. Baby Shane was so quiet they'd almost forgotten about him. Then Duce's face began to twitch. "Dude, what's that smell?"

Shane sniffed and choked. Whatever it was, it was powerful enough to make his eyes water. "Aw man, did you fart?"

"Wasn't me."

In unison, they slowly turned to the baby who still slept soundly. He leaned over and sniffed, almost gagging as he jerked back. "Holy crap! How could something so pintsize smell that bad?"

Duce covered his mouth and went to the window, quickly opening it to let some air in. The little guy made a tiny nook-nook sound and his miniature fist curled up by his chin in a dainty stretch. He looked like the fighting Irish.

"It's moving," Duce whispered as though the baby were a bomb about to detonate. And suddenly an explosion happened.

Baby Shane's face screwed up tight, turning

an unnatural shade of red. His mouth opened wide, showing nothing but pink gums, and an unholy squawk roared out of him.

They jumped and stared as the baby screamed, his little chest working in quick breaths as he drew in only enough air to force out another shrill, squawking cry.

"Do something!" Duce demanded.

Shane panicked. He reached for the book and began to thumb through, not sure what he was looking for.

"Don't fucking read! Pick it up!" Duce snapped.

Shane tossed the book on the couch and quickly kneeled in front of the angry baby. He wailed and Shane began to freak. Was he in pain? Ugh, the smell coming off of him was burning the back of his throat. "Sweet Jesus, he stinks!"

He quickly removed the soft blanket. Shane was strapped down with some sort of five-point harness a person needed a degree in engineering to unravel. He pressed buttons and undid latches, shaking with the urgent need to make him stop screaming.

Sweat seeped through the baby's tiny cotton jumper. The closer he got the worse the stench became.

"I thought babies were supposed to smell good?" Duce said, fanning the front door to let some air in.

"So did I. I can't figure out how to unbuckle him!"

"Hit the red buttons on the side. You gotta get the handle out of the way."

Sweat trickled into his eyes as he tried to dismantle the carrier. Finally he had the harness undone. "Now what?"

"Pick it up!"

"He stinks!"

Duce scowled. "So, my ear drums are about to burst. You gotta get in there. Tough it out. Take one for the team!"

Shane carefully picked up the screaming baby. He held him in front of his chest like a potted plant. He was so incredibly light. "What now?"

"I don't know. You're the one who's supposed to be Mr. Mom. Comfort it. Pat its back. Sing or something!"

Shane stood and awkwardly turned, swaying slightly. He didn't want to shake him and break him. He sang the first song that came to his mind, wincing at the lyrics about loaded guns.

Duce's mouth fell open. "*Teen Spirit*? Really? How about *Rock-a-bye Baby*?"

"I don't know *Rock-a-bye Baby*. Nirvana's the first thing that popped into my head."

"It's not really appropriate, Shane," Duce said coolly as if he were suddenly more qualified than him with babies.

"You wanna try?"

"No, I'm set."

He continued to sing *Teen Spirit* and eventually Baby Shane quieted. Blue eyes stared back at him and slowly the world began to settle.

Shane was sweating and Duce looked petrified.

"Hi," Shane said. The baby blinked. "I'm your Uncle Shane."

"I don't think he can talk."

"No shit, Sherlock."

Shane's arms were getting tired. He glanced over to the couch. It seemed unsanitary, although whatever was causing that stink was nothing close to clean. "Grab that yellow yoga mat thing so I can lay him down."

Duce spread the mat out on the floor. He really needed to vacuum. He ran out of vacuum bags like four months ago. He should probably start a shopping list.

Squatting down he attempted to lower the baby. "Support his head. He's all floppy."

Duce squatted across from him and carefully formed a bowl with his hands, cupping the back of the baby's head as Shane lowered him to the mat. Once he had him safely on his back they each released a tense breath. Now what?

Shane rummaged through the baby purse for a diaper and the box of wipes. He searched for rubber gloves, but couldn't find any. He was gonna have to go in bareback.

Taking a deep breath of shitty air, he carefully unsnapped Baby Shane's jumper. His pink thighs were pudgy and caked with what looked like avocado.

"Aww man!" He and Duce both looked away.

"His ass exploded! I don't think some little wet nap is gonna handle that. You may need a hose."

Shane pulled the Velcro fastens of the diaper, which was puffy and full of warm pee. Lifting the front flap, he unveiled a puke green nightmare.

"It's a boy," Duce declared.

Shane rolled his eyes. The smell was ungodly. "Hand me one of those wipes."

Duce handed him a wipe and he began to dab at the mess. Before long he had a pile of soiled wet naps on the mat and poop under his nails.

"That isn't right. Nothing this small should be able to do that much damage," Duce stated.

When he finally had the explosion cleaned up, he quickly stood and ran the trash outside to the can. He came back and washed his hands then returned to the floor with a clean diaper. It was then Baby Shane shivered and shot a stream of pee straight up in the air like Old Faithful and across Shane's shirt.

Duce fell over laughing. Shane growled at him, wiped off the baby and awkwardly folded the diaper around pudgy thighs and pulled the Velcro tabs down.

"There." He smiled triumphantly.

"If babies poop as much as I do, you're screwed."

"Thank you, Captain Obvious." Shane stared down at the baby. He seemed better. He was doing a form of the jagged Bill Cosby pudding dance. "Do you think he's hungry?"

"I don't know. It looked like he had a pretty serious breakfast."

Shane rolled his eyes and reached for the book. Thumbing through, he found a section on feeding.

"*During the first three months breast milk and formula will provide all the nutrition your baby needs.*" He skimmed ahead. "*Baby will consume more milk during each feeding as he develops.*"

He turned the page. "Here we go. *During the second month infants might consume between four and five ounces.*" He frowned at the container of formula. "How much is an ounce of formula?"

"Tucker's the ounce expert, not me."

Shane pursed his lips and turned back to the book. Baby Shane was still doing the Cosby on the yoga mat and now blowing raspberries. It was cute.

"Here's a warning about bottle feeding. It says it's easier to overfeed from a bottle nipple than a human nipple because the hole's bigger and I should never use a prop. Okay." He put down the book and rubbed his hands together. "I can do this. Ready to eat, little guy?"

The baby babbled up at him. He took that as a yes.

At the counter he opened a container of formula and filled the bottle, then he noticed the measurements on the side. Four ounces was nothing, only about a third of the bottle. Dumping some back in the container, he stuck the extra in the fridge next to a six-pack. He needed to go to the grocery store.

He placed the bottle on the coffee table and stood over the baby. With extreme care, he scooped him off the floor, supporting the back of his fuzzy head. He was warm and soft.

A string of drool dribbled down his chin. "Okay." Shane sat on the sofa and adjusted Baby Shane in his arms. Something expanded deep in his belly as if he just rolled down a steep hill. Baby Shane's slight weight settled into the curve of his arm. "Does this look right?"

Duce shrugged and stood back as though afraid to get too close.

"Hand me that blanket." The baby's jumper remained undone like the tails of a tux.

Duce handed him the soft, blue blanket and he carefully wrapped his legs. Staring down at his nephew, he smiled. He was looking back at him.

Shane saw a world of trust in those small eyes. Faith. If he tried to talk in that moment he would have failed miserably. Emotion welled up inside of him. The baby had Noel's nose.

Shane nodded. "The bottle," he said in a soft, hoarse voice. Duce handed it to him. Leaning back, he tilted the nipple to the baby's mouth. A few drops of white sprinkled on his porcelain skin.

It only took a second for Baby Shane to latch on. His lips pulled with a tight force he wasn't prepared for. Shane laughed. "You're hungry."

Suddenly the baby opened his mouth and cried. Shane looked at Duce in a moment of panic. He tried to coax the nipple back into his mouth, but Baby Shane wanted nothing to do with it. "I don't know what I'm doing wrong. Look in the book."

He gently bounced his knee as Duce flipped through the book. Baby Shane continued to cry, growing more upset by the second.

"Did you warm it? It says some babies prefer the formula slightly warm."

"It was room temperature. I don't know. Should I have put it in the microwave?"

Duce turned pages frantically as Baby Shane worked himself into a shrill scream. "No, it says not to microwave it because of hot spots." He read silently then went to the sink and turned the water on high. Within moments it was steaming out of the spigot. He grabbed a plastic cup and filled it. "Here, give me the bottle."

Shane handed him the bottle and tried to soothe his inconsolable nephew. Duce dropped the bottle in the cup of hot water and they waited. He worried he was failing, failing his nephew, failing his sister. He needed to get this right. Feeding was part of passing Baby 101. He'd already conquered the poop fiasco.

"There, try that," Duce said, passing him the bottle.

"Wait, squirt some on your arm. Moms do that."

Duce shot a line of white up his arm and stared at him. "Now what?"

"I don't know. What does it feel like?"

"It feels like someone just squirted me with milk. What's it supposed to feel like?"

"Lick it. Is it hot?"

"I'm not licking that! It's imitation boob milk."

Shane rolled his eyes. "What's the difference between that and milk from a cow's udders?"

"I don't fantasize about cows. You're gonna ruin boobs for me. You lick it." He held out his arm.

"I'm not *licking* your hairy arm. Does it feel

hot? I think that's supposed to test the temperature."

Duce grew frustrated and shouted over Baby Shane's angry squalls. "It feels fine. Plug that kid up. He's giving me a migraine."

Shane took the bottle and tipped it toward his nephew's mouth. The baby shivered and latched on. He waited. The baby began to suck and continued this time. Shane smiled triumphantly at Duce.

"The cup is key. Remember that next time."

They both sat, transfixed, watching little Shane guzzle down the formula. He made quiet clicking noises as he drank.

"Are you going to change his name?" Duce whispered. "It's kind of weird calling him Shane. Maybe we should call him Junior or something."

"His middle name's Logan, like my dad."

"Logan's a badass name. I think we should call him that."

Shane looked down at his nephew. His eyes were getting heavy and he was sucking less and less. "Logan," he whispered.

As Logan fell asleep Shane wondered if he should pull the bottle away. He gave it a little tug, but Logan's mouth immediately tightened on the nipple, greedily sucking it back inside. He laughed softly. "The boy can eat."

Duce chuckled. "Imagine if he was drinking

out of the real package. What guy wouldn't want some?"

When the bottle was filled with nothing but air, Logan's lips went slack. A small stream of white tinted slobber dribbled down his chin. Duce handed him a napkin and Shane carefully wiped it up.

At some point they began communicating in charades. Duce motioned toward the car seat and Shane nodded. He placed it on the floor in front of him and Shane carefully tucked Logan inside. He considered the harness. He should be fine just sitting there. The kid couldn't hold up his head. It wasn't like he was going to leap out of it.

He tucked the blanket around his sleeping face and they both sat back to admire their handy work. They turned at the sound of a car pulling up. Putting his finger to his lips, Shane stood and went to the door. It was Tucker and Sims. They went out front to meet them so as not to disturb Logan.

"What's up, Daddio? We got you a present," Tucker said as he went to the trunk of his car.

Duce joined them. The three of them pulled out a huge box.

"What is it?" Sims went to the back seat and removed a bag that said Baby Bugaboo. "You guys bought baby stuff?" No way.

"My mom said we should all chip in and get

you something. Lisa helped pick it out. It's a crib. Turns into a little person bed then somehow turns into a real bed, like a transformer," Tucker announced.

"I prefer to call it Decepticon Crib," Sims stated.

"Why not Optimus Prime's Crib?" Duce asked. "Logan's definitely one of the good guys. His crib should be an Autobot."

"You guys bought me a crib?" Shane repeated, shocked.

"Who's Logan?" Tucker frowned.

"The baby," Duce answered.

"Either way, I'm pretty sure the crib was manufactured in Cybertron," Sims said.

"I thought the baby's name was Shane," Tucker said, confused.

"We changed it. Logan's his middle name. Less confusing that way," Duce explained.

"Can you do that? Just change the kid's name?" Tucker asked as he dragged the box to the door.

"I can't believe you guys bought me this." Shane was beyond touched.

His three friends smiled. "Dude, that's what friends do. You were in the 'family way', so we got you some kick ass kiddie swag. Wait until you see the blankets," Sims said.

They shuffled into the trailer and dropped the crib on the floor. Shane and Duce immediately shushed them. Tucker went to the fridge and popped a beer. The four of them gathered around Logan's carrier and stared.

"He's so small," Tucker commented.

"Maybe he's part hobbit," Sims said.

"You think he's small, but don't be fooled. The kid can scream like a banshee and shits like a goose on laxatives." Duce informed.

They all looked at Shane who knew he was smiling stupidly. "What?"

Tucker laughed. "You're all glowy and shit."

Sims went to the fridge and grabbed a beer. "Where are we putting the Autobot crib?"

"I guess in the bedroom, but we should probably put it together out here."

They all went about opening the crib and assembling it. Within an hour they were proudly admiring their work. Sims reached into the bag and said, "Check it out."

He revealed a crib set made of blue, yellow, and brown patchwork. There were little guitars stitched in the center and the word ROCK STAR emblazoned across the front. "No way! You guys are awesome. Thank you."

They carried the crib into the bedroom. Surprisingly, it took longer to dress the thing than it did to build it. They tried to make it look like the picture, but their bows were flat and it just didn't seem to come out as pretty.

"Shane, the kid's doing something," Tucker

announced as he returned to the bedroom with another beer.

Shane turned and bolted into the living room. Logan was doing his Bill Cosby. "Hey, buddy." He carefully lifted him out of the seat and something fell to the ground with a splat. "Oh my God, what was that?" He looked down in a panic, thinking something fell off the baby.

Duce used the hind hooks of a hammer to scoop up a soggy diaper. "His diaper fell off. Must be all that milk weighing him down."

The blanket fell to the floor. "Aw, look at his little junk," Tucker said.

Shane scowled. "Don't look at him. Give me a diaper out of the baby purse."

"What the fuck is a baby purse?"

"That bag over there," Shane tipped his chin in the direction of the bag.

"This is definitely *not* Autobot cool like his crib," Sims said as he dug for a diaper.

Shane settled Logan on his yoga mat and went to work on securing a clean diaper.

"Check you out, all domesticated and shit."

Duce slapped Tucker in the chest. "Stop cursing in front of the baby."

"Ow, sorry."

When Shane had his diaper back on, he turned and balanced Logan on his knee, cradling him in the curve of his arm. "Guys, this is Logan. Logan, this is the guys."

Logan cooed and then immediately burped,

a stream of white puke projecting onto Shane's arm.

"Aw, gross!" Tucker said, stepping back.

Sims shook his head. "I had the same reaction when I met them."

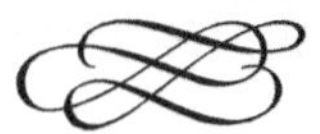

The following morning Shane was exhausted. Apparently, someone forgot to inform Logan that nights were for sleeping and days were for exorcisms.

After the guys took off Shane fed Logan his supper, which he proceeded to spew all over the couch. Shane was running out of t-shirts and the little guy was down to those one-piece things. He was also on his second container of formula. *Four ounces his foot.* He wondered how much that stuff cost, because as much as Logan drank, he only kept about a quarter of it down.

He woke up with poop around two in the morning. That was a trial. He acted hungry, but every time Shane fed him he puked. Sending a text to Duce, he asked him to come over first thing. Shane needed help.

At ten o'clock he heard the roller skate pull

up and breathed a huge sigh of relief. Duce came in with a box of donuts and some coffee, looking as well rested as ever. Logan slept, deceptively quiet in his crib.

"How was the first night, Ward?"

Shane narrowed his eyes. "I'm fucking exhausted," he hissed, taking a sip of coffee. "He didn't sleep at all."

Duce peeked at Logan and gave Shane a doubtful look. "He looks like he's sleeping fine now."

"I guess so. He partied his ass off last night. He's a total lightweight though. Can't hold his formula for shit."

Duce chuckled. He gestured to the book on Shane's lap. "Studying?"

"Yeah. I think Logan has this condition called co-licky."

Duce frowned and stepped back, his hand subconsciously going to the back of his neck and scratching. "Co-licky? What the fuck is that? Is it contagious? I just got over that weird stomach thing. I can't afford to get sick again."

"I don't think so. You have to be less than three months old to have it. It's something to do with spasms of the intestines and inconsolable crying."

Duce, ever the hypochondriac, continued to itch his skin. "Sounds horrible. Maybe you should take him to the doctor's."

"Well, he's calm now. I don't think he likes the formula, though."

"Well, I ain't no wet nurse so he better learn to like it. What did you need me for?"

Shane handed him a list. "I need you to go to the store for me. I'd go myself, but I don't want to wake Logan and I'm pretty sure you don't want to babysit."

Duce took the list and read over it. "I don't know what half this stuff is."

"Just go to that kid store in Lakota and ask someone there to point you in the right direction. It's all basic stuff. I only have a hundred bucks and I need food for myself too. Shit. I need to figure out something to do with him during the day. I can't keep missing work."

When Duce left for the store, Shane climbed back into bed and dozed for a bit. He awoke to the baby screaming and quickly jumped out of bed in a panic. How long had he been crying?

Frantically he went to the crib. Logan was beet red and angry. He also smelled terrifying. "Oh, no. Not again," Shane mumbled. He went to get the baby purse and the box of wipes, which was getting very light.

He rolled the yoga mat out on the floor and reached for Logan. Shane turned away and gagged at the smell coming off the little guy. "Okay, let's get you cleaned up. I know, I'd be crying too if my butt smelled like that."

He placed him on the mat and unsnapped his onesie. This time it was yellow like mustard. He'd only wiped away half the mess when his fingers touched the bottom of the wipe box. "Oh, no."

He looked in the box and turned it upside down. "Shit!"

Logan screamed, his cries coming faster and faster. Shane frantically looked around for something he could use to clean him up. His hair kept getting in his eyes, so he grabbed a hair tie and pulled it into a bun on top of his head.

When he picked up Logan, yellow crap smeared down Shane's shirt. "Oh, man!" He went to the kitchen and started the sink. That's when he heard someone knocking at the door.

He fished an old Zeppelin t-shirt out of the laundry pile and wrapped it haphazardly around Logan like a loincloth. "Don't do too much damage, little buddy, that shirt's vintage."

He opened the door and frowned. Who the hell was this? Avon calling? A prim blonde woman with a yellow cardigan stood on the other side.

"Can I help you?" he shouted over Logan's screams.

She looked startled. "Mr. Martin?"

"Yes," he said impatiently, sensing Logan's poop settling into the fibers of his favorite t-shirt.

"I'm Katherine McAlester."

"Who? I'm sort of busy right now. Could you come back later?"

Her frown turned into a scowl. "Mr. Martin, I'm from the DPW. I'm your caseworker. I'm afraid these appointments can't be scheduled. We like to see the caregivers in their natural environment to get an understanding of how they're handling things."

"Oh shit, you're the caseworker?"

She gave him a completely disapproving look. Great. This woman did not like him. "Yes. May I come in?"

"They said you wouldn't be here for a couple of days." He backed into the trailer and she stepped in after him, her eyes landing on the pile of laundry, then conveniently settling on the stack of empty beers on the counter.

"Sorry, I haven't really had time to clean up."

She reached in her bag and withdrew a folder. "May I sit down?"

"Sure."

She considered her options long enough to appear rude. Finally, she settled on the chair beside the sofa, which was probably the safest choice.

Her body perched on the edge of the cushion and he could read the disgust in her posture. She clearly thought his place was gross. Her little feet encased in tiny blue shoes pointed at him accusingly, all prim and proper. She was a snob. Great.

"Is the baby okay?"

"What?" he looked up from her feet. "Oh, yeah. I ran out of wipes. Also, I think he has co-licky."

"Co-licky?"

He stood, rocking Logan who finally began to settle. "Yeah, it's a condition some infants have that makes them cry inconsolably."

She raised an eyebrow. "Do you mean the baby is colicky, Mr. Martin, as in he suffers from colic?"

So he was pronouncing it wrong, so what? "Yeah. That."

She made a note in her paperwork. When she looked up, she sniffed and blinked.

"Uh, we were sort of in the middle of a bomb when you knocked."

"Your faucet's running."

"What?" He turned to the kitchen. "Oh!" He quickly stood to shut the water off. When he came back she was standing. She hadn't really moved far, but he could tell she was snooping.

"How are you adjusting so far, Mr. Martin?"

"You can call me Shane. I'm learning. It's a lot more demanding than I expected."

"Do you mind showing me where the baby's sleeping?"

He smiled. "Are you asking to see my bedroom?"

Her expression fell and she gave him a cool, unimpressed stare. Okay, no sense of humor.

"This way," he offered and led her to his room.

A pile of soiled wipes littered the floor and the entire room now smelled like the dirty diaper he'd left on the yoga mat. "Watch your step," he warned, pointing out the mess.

Her brows lowered and she stepped back. He followed her to the living room and waited as she made more notes.

"May I look around?"

He assumed that was normal. Tabitha and Joanne had warned him he'd be under a bit of a microscope. "Sure."

He watched as she nosed around his home. She stopped in front of the pile of empty beer cans and made a note. She made more notes after opening his empty fridge. When she looked in his cabinets and found the many bottles there she turned and faced him.

"Do you have a drinking problem, Mr. Martin?"

He drew back at her audacity. "Uh, no."

"You barely have any food."

"My friend just ran to the store. If you're hungry I can heat you up some of that Chinese in the fridge." *The three-week-old Chinese.*

"No, thank you."

He forced his lip not to curl. She was judging him hard and he had to take it. She looked like a total bitch. He'd wanted to ask her about the child care situation, get some more details on that, but there was no way he was asking this snob for any help. He'd figure it out on his own.

"Clearly you weren't prepared for my visit."

"I told you, my friend's at the store. I've barely had time to adjust to all this. It hasn't even been a week since I found out about my sister and learned I have a nephew. You'll have to excuse me if I'm not doing a stellar job yet."

She looked like she was about to offer condolences, but then dropped her gaze and scribbled more notes. "I'll take you at your word and overlook what I've seen here today, because honestly, Mr. Martin, it's not good. I'll give you another day or two to adjust and then I'll be back. Hopefully you can pull it together by then. But be warned, the *only* reason I'm giving you a little more time is because I can appreciate how you're able to soothe the baby. If it weren't for that…"

He was speechless. Not since he was a kid had someone talked to him like that. He wanted the lady gone and he wanted to see about getting another caseworker. Logan suddenly ripped a juicy fart and heat seeped through his Zeppelin shirt. Shane winced.

See, Logan doesn't like her either.

Her nose crinkled. "I'll let you handle that."

He watched her leave, calling her a hundred

unkind things as she went. Duce, of course, pulled in right after she pulled out. Figured. He climbed out of the car, arms filled with bags of baby paraphernalia, and turned back toward the caseworker driving away.

"Who was that?"

"My caseworker. She's a stuck up brat."

Duce shrugged and Shane stepped aside so he could come in. "Holy crap, it stinks like shit in here."

CHAPTER 6

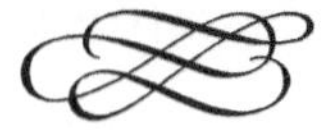

Shane traded cars with Duce in order to go to his first parenting class. The roller skate had a back seat and that made it safer than his truck for Logan.

After Duce's trip to the store, Shane felt more in control. He had a stockpile of wipes, diapers, and Logan had a few new duds. He was currently rocking a pair of button up jeans and a Rolling Stones baby-T for their first day of school.

He flipped the front seat forward and smiled at his nephew. "You ready, little man. Now, no pooping in class. There might be other girl babies there you'll need to impress."

He carried Logan into the building, baby purse slung on his side. The class was being held at the local YMCA. Shane went to the registration desk and a young girl directed him.

"You just head down that hall there and the classroom's on your left."

"Thanks."

"Your son's real cute."

"Thanks, but he's not..." He looked back at the girl and smiled. "Thanks."

He found the classroom right where she said it would be. It was a simple white room with a dry erase board and a conference table. Three women sat at the table with bored expressions on their faces. Self-consciously, he pushed himself through the door. None of the other women had kids with them.

"Is this the parenting class?"

The three women glanced at him and nodded. Where were their kids?

He found a seat at the end of the table and stowed Logan's seat on the floor. At the moment Logan was having a love affair with the dangly bumblebee rattle attached to the handle of the carrier, so he left him there.

An older woman entered and smiled. "Hello. I'm Dr. Haughenschlaugger."

Wow, that was a mouthful. Shane tried not to laugh. *Seriously, who has a name like Haughenschlaugger?*

She dropped a binder at the head of the table and went to the board where she wrote the date and Baby Basics. She returned to the table and pulled out a sheet of paper. "You all are going to have to sign in for the courts."

The paper came around and he signed. The teacher took a seat and folded her hands. "Okay, gang. I'm here to teach you the basics of caring for a baby. How are ya'll making out so far? Any major debacles?"

She looked at each one of them. The girls seemed to avoid eye contact. Shane was there to learn. He'd set another goal that afternoon. He wanted to prove to that stuck up caseworker that he knew what he was doing.

Dr. Haughenschlaugger glanced at the sign in sheet then back at him. "Shane? Any issues?"

"Uh, we had some diaper problems earlier, but after a serious talk Logan's agreed to try to keep his movements to a minimum."

She laughed. "Negotiating with an infant, you let me know how that works out for you."

She sat back. "The first thing I want to tell you about child rearing is that it's ninety percent common sense. If baby is happily cooing he's likely healthy. If he doesn't appear himself, seems sick, he's likely not feeling well. You know your child best, so trust your instincts. Do y'all have a pediatrician for your babies?"

The girls nodded and the doctor zeroed in on him. "Shane?"

"I haven't gotten to that step yet. I just met Logan yesterday."

"Oh, well, congratulations. I can give you a list of pediatricians I refer new parents to after class if you'd like. You can call and see if they accept your insurance."

"Thanks."

She nodded. He liked this teacher slash doctor. It was a shame she wasn't also a caseworker.

"It's very important your babies see their pediatricians on a regular basis for check ups and immunizations. Your child's pediatrician is there to answer your questions and, as new parents, I'm sure y'all have lots of questions.

"Next let's talk about a routine. How many of you have managed to get the baby on a schedule? Darla?"

The girl who looked about ready to pass out sat up. "She's started sleeping through the nights."

"Good. It's important you get your sleep too."

Shane listened as the doctor went on about how to establish a healthy routine. He wished he had a piece of paper to take notes. He was getting tons of good tips, but was afraid he'd forget what he learned.

They discussed the benefits of clean water versus wipes, the dangers of talcum powder, and the fact that creams were sometimes nice, but not necessary. She discussed how easily babies got sick and recommended not taking the baby around crowds of people in the beginning unless absolutely necessary, and if it was necessary, ask friends to wash their hands and not touch the baby's face.

At the end of the class Dr. Haughenschlaugger asked for questions. The girls had none. Maybe he had so many questions because he was a guy. He asked about bathing the baby, heating bottles, which he found out he'd done right, and about the vomiting. Apparently Logan was spitting up because Shane hadn't been burping him.

The doctor complimented his determined attitude and assured him he'd be fine with some practice and confidence. When he left his confidence *had* improved. He stood and shook the doctor's hand and smiled on his way out. He could do this!

"Shane?" Dr. Haughenschlaugger called as he left the classroom.

He looked back. "Yeah?"

"Forget something?"

Shane frowned and then saw Logan sleeping in his carrier by the chair he'd vacated. "Oh crap!" He flushed and quickly went to retrieve his nephew. The doctor laughed. He gave her a pleading look. "Please don't tell anyone I did that," he begged.

She tried to hide her smile. "Your secret's safe with me, Shane. I'll see you next week."

～

THE FOLLOWING morning he took Logan to the Laundromat while he still had the roller skate. Logan really got a kick out of the spin cycle.

Shane read up on what to expect during the second month. This was the month the book said Logan would be showing signs of his own personality. Shane got that. If someone tried to explain to him a week ago that a two-month-old baby was more than a drooling blob, he would have told them they were full of crap. But he was starting to recognize signs of Logan's personality.

For instance, he really liked his bumblebee rattle. He also preferred the blue blanket to the green one, which wasn't as soft. And he really liked to suck on his fist, which he was going to town on at that very moment.

According to the book, he should be doing something called tummy time with the little guy to strengthen his muscles. "We're gonna buff you up, big guy," Shane informed him. Logan babbled back at him. Shane wasn't sure if he was agreeing or arguing. *Sass.*

When they left the Laundromat Logan was sound asleep. Shane took time to make a few necessary phone calls. First on the list, finding a pediatrician. He referred to the program Logan was enrolled in and found a doctor right near Sunny Acres. He scheduled a check-up for the following month.

Next, he called the Care Works people and

asked about childcare. That was when his mood dropped. Even with assistance, childcare would take a huge chunk of his paycheck. He'd barely have enough money for food after he paid his lot rent.

He considered how expensive formula was. In two months Logan would be on solids too. Between the costs of groceries, gas to get to work, childcare, and rent, there'd be nothing left. He calculated how much he usually spent on beer and take out. His life as he knew it was over.

He needed to work out a serious budget. The more he crunched numbers the more impossible it seemed. He wasn't even taking into account how hard it would be when there wasn't work. When he thought about the three days of work he missed that week he grew sick to his stomach.

If he believed things couldn't get worse, he was wrong. There was a knock at the door. He stood and frowned when he saw the little Volkswagen bug. *Great.*

Shane opened the door and faked an unconvincing smile. "We meet again."

"Hello, Mr. Martin. Is this a better time?"

"Sure." He turned and let the caseworker show herself in.

She frowned as she glanced around his place. What now?

"Where's the baby?"

"Logan's napping in his crib. Babies do that."

"I'm aware babies nap, Mr. Martin. How are you managing today?"

"Fine."

"May I sit down?"

He waved an arm toward the sofa. She grimaced and chose the chair again. Today she wore a black pencil skirt and a turquoise cardigan, with simple black slippers on her feet. She was pretty, but in a stuck up kind of way. Nothing like the girls he was attracted to.

"Did you attend your parenting class last night?"

"Yes."

"And how did that go?"

Aside from almost leaving Logan there… "Great. Logan's top of the class."

She jotted down notes, but didn't smile. "Have you selected a pediatrician?"

"As a matter of fact, I did."

She looked surprised, but said nothing, only jotted down more notes. "Have you been shopping?"

"Yes, would you like to look around?" *Go ahead. I dare you.*

She glanced around, but didn't get up to look in his cabinets. "What do you plan to do about work, Mr. Martin?"

His expression fell. She'd found his kryptonite. "I, uh, I have a job."

"Doing what?"

"Construction."

"What sort of hours do you work? Every time I've come by it's been the middle of the work day and you've been home."

He shifted uncomfortably. "I took a few days off to get Logan situated."

"When do you plan on returning to work?"

I don't know. "In a few days."

"And when you return, who will be caring for Logan?"

"I'm looking into various options now."

"What kind of schedule do you work?"

"I usually go in around six and I'm home by four. I also play a few gigs each month for some extra money."

"Gigs?"

"I'm a musician."

She frowned and jotted down more notes. He really was developing a strong dislike for this woman.

"Have you filled out the paperwork for food stamps yet?"

His jaw locked. "I don't think that will be necessary."

She eyed him and his pride smarted. "Mr. Martin, with all due respect, yesterday your cabinets consisted of dust and Wild Turkey. A baby requires more sustenance than that."

"With all due respect, Ms. McAlister, I've

been to the store and I'm more than capable of filling the pantry."

"How much is your annual income, not including your gigs of course," she asked patronizingly.

Who the fuck did this broad think she was? Talk about kicking him right in his manhood. "I make decent money when there's work." There was no way he was reporting his income.

She pursed her lips and narrowed her eyes. She had very pretty lashes, golden almost. The fact that he noticed only made him dislike her more. "These programs were recommended to you for a reason. I could summon the court and request proof of your wages."

"Be my guest," he called her bluff.

She scowled at him. Suddenly Logan began to cry. He stood. "Are we done?"

"If you don't mind, I'd like to stick around for a little while and observe."

He did mind, but he couldn't force her to leave. Why couldn't he have been assigned to someone like Joanne or Haughenschlaugger? They liked him.

He turned and went to get Logan.

"Hey, big guy." He reached down and scooped him up. He was already becoming more comfortable with holding him.

Logan immediately settled once in his arms. Shane carried him to the living room and sat him in his car seat while he heated up a bottle he'd had on the ready from that morning.

"Aren't you going to latch that?"

Shane stilled. "I'm coming right back."

"It only takes a moment for a baby to get injured, Mr. Martin."

He scowled at her. She was really starting to piss him off. "Maybe you weren't aware, but Logan's two months old. At his age, he's just learning to hold up his head. I think catapulting out of car seats is a little advanced for him—even if he is at the top of his class."

"Do you think you're funny, Mr. Martin?"

What. A. Bitch.

He gave up. Sighing, he went to the car seat and removed Logan. Collecting the bottle, he sat on the sofa and proceeded to feed him. Mentally, he asked his nephew, if he had to puke to please project it in the bitch's direction. Logan blinked and Shane took that as corroboration he understood the plan.

Her gaze weighed on him. How much longer would she be there?

"Did you get a new car, Mr. Martin?"

"What?"

"Your truck, it's gone."

"Oh, no, I just traded with a friend for a day or two."

"Perhaps you'll consider purchasing a vehicle with a higher child safety rating."

Did this woman have an off switch? Like he

hadn't already considered that. Unfortunately, the money tree was dead, so he had no fucking clue how that would ever happen. "I'll consider it."

"I'm sure on your salary, what with your gigs and all, you could afford it."

His gaze jerked to hers. That was it. "Are you new?"

"I beg your pardon?"

"Are you new? I was wondering if we were maybe your first case or if your social skills were just this bad all the time. If it's a disability of some sort I'd be willing to overlook it, but if it's something personal you have against me, maybe I should ask to be reassigned."

She stiffened. "I'm afraid it doesn't work that way. You get who you get."

"So I guess at social work school they don't really teach a social graces class."

"Mr. Martin, I'm sorry you find my presence so insufferable, but truth be told your feelings are not my concern. I'm only concerned with the well being of that little boy."

"Well, this little boy's well being is just fine. He's usually rather pleasant when he isn't being hassled by stuck up harpies."

She jumped to her feet. Her mouth opened and closed. He was done being intimidated by this shrew. "I'll be talking to my supervisor about this." She marched angrily to the door.

"Go right ahead. Be sure to tell her that you don't like babies."

She stilled and turned on him, her eyes furious. "I love babies! It's you I can't tolerate. Good day!" She left the trailer and let the screen door slam behind her.

"Shit." This wouldn't end well. Gritting his teeth, he went after her.

CHAPTER 7

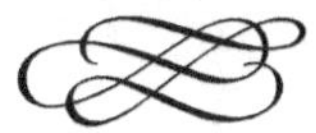

Shane popped the bottle out of Logan's mouth and stuck it on the table before he followed her outside. She was sitting behind the wheel of her little lime green bug, looking overly frustrated. Incidentally, she looked cute when she was knocked off her high horse. He held Logan to his shoulder and knocked on the driver's window.

She ignored him, obviously aware of his presence, so he knocked again. Her lips formed a thin line as the window lowered. "What?"

Shane patted Logan's back. If the kid wound up going through with their puke on the caseworker plan, things would only get worse. "I'm sorry. That was rude of me to talk to you like that."

Her chin quivered. She still wouldn't look at him. Fuck, was she crying? "Are you crying?"

"No!" she barked then sniffled.

Shit, he really fucked up. "Look, I'm apologizing. Please come back inside."

"No, thank you."

"I didn't mean what I said."

She turned on him. "Didn't you?" Her eyes were red and glassy. Definitely crying.

"No, of course not. I just—"

His truck came barreling in at that moment, cutting off his words. He faced Logan away from the dust and she took advantage of the interruption to pull out. Shit.

Duce jumped out of the truck and looked after her. "That the social worker snob?"

"Not anymore. I made her cry."

His friend's eyes bulged. "Dude, you made your caseworker cry? Why?"

"Because I'm an idiot."

Logan took that moment to belch, which Shane interpreted as complete agreement. Great.

Later that night after Duce left, Shane put Logan to bed and pulled out the food stamps information. He'd always put down people on government assistance programs, believing he was better than that. But tonight, after looking into Logan's eyes and fearing there might come a time when he couldn't put food in his belly... well, that was much more intolerable than his wounded pride.

When he realized he could get between two

hundred and four hundred dollars a month in food vouchers, he called himself an idiot for sticking up his nose at such a program. He decided to apply, but he'd be filing out the paperwork himself. No way would he willingly let Little Miss Fancy Shoes know he was that tight on money.

By midnight he had all the forms filled out and was ready to pass out. He heated up a bottle and quietly lifted Logan out of his crib. This was part of the building a routine thing Dr. Haughenschlaugger suggested.

He barely woke up, but drank at least four ounces. Shane softly worked a burp out of him and laid him back in his Autobot crib then fell into bed. He was completely wiped out, the past few days seemingly catching up to him all at once. How would he ever manage all this and working at the same time?

On Friday, Shane and Logan borrowed the roller skate again and went to visit daycares. "One day we'll be looking at colleges for you, too, if you're anything like your mother," he informed a gurgling Logan. "She was real smart."

They first visited one place that was okay, but it was pricy. *Really* pricy. For the cost, Shane wasn't very impressed. However, as they worked their way through the list he became more and more discouraged. They returned to the first place, Kiddie

Academy, and requested the enrollment paperwork. Logan would start there on Monday.

"Now, make sure you don't let the kids who've been there longer push you around. You don't take any lip from anybody. And I don't want to hear about you being distracted from your studies by any pretty girls, you hear?"

Logan farted…possibly more than a fart.

Shane scrunched up his face as he pulled into Sunny Acres. "You keep that up and you won't have any problems keeping the bullies *and* the girls away."

The following Friday night the guys came over as usual, but Tucker was coughing and Shane asked him to leave.

"You're kicking me out?" Tucker asked, shocked.

"You're coughing. I don't want Logan getting sick."

"But I'm not sick," Tucker argued.

Sims chimed in from the floor where he was playing the game station. "Lisa was sick. You had your tongue in her mouth. You're probably a carrier of whatever funk she had."

Duce held his cheesesteak mid-air and froze, hypochondriac at full alert. "You better go."

"Shut up, Duce."

Shane stood his ground. "Seriously, Tucker,

Logan can't get sick. Dr. Haughenschlaugger said—"

"Wait," he laughed. "Doctor who? Hasphenpepper?"

"Haughenschlaugger." They all cracked up, but Shane was being serious. "I'm serious. You need to go."

The mood chilled. Tucker was insulted. "Whatever, dude. You act like I have the plague." He grabbed his keys and left.

"He's pissed," Duce commented, spraying crumbs over the table.

"Use a napkin," Shane snapped. "I just vacuumed."

Sims kept his eye on the television, but didn't miss a beat. "Uh, Shane, how long do you plan on being on the rag? Because you're sort of a buzz kill like this."

Shane stiffened. "You can leave too. I'm sorry if I don't feel like dealing with a bunch of bullshit tonight like I have every Friday night for the past decade."

Sims paused the game and stared at him. "Are you serious right now?"

Defensively, he glared back. "What? I can't have boundaries? You guys come over here every week, trash the place, use my game station, drink my beer—"

"We come here because you invite us!" Sims snapped.

"Well, I need to consider Logan now."

"You sound like a woman."

"*You* sound like a woman all the time. Get over it."

Logan's cry filtered from the bedroom. Shane stood. "Great, you woke the baby."

He switched on the lamp in the bedroom and went to the crib. Logan cried softly, but quieted the moment he saw Shane. "Hey, bud. Did we wake you?"

He stilled, staring up at Shane as though considering his question. His head slightly raised then dropped onto his *ROCK STAR* sheet as he cooed. Shane laughed and scooped him up.

"You wanted to come hang out, didn't you?"

He stepped back into the living room and Duce sat at the table. Sims was gone.

"He leave?" He should probably feel guilty for being a dick, which he sort of did, but he needed to establish some ground rules now that Logan was living with him.

"Nah, he just went out to smoke."

Well, that was an improvement. At least Sims knew he couldn't light a cigarette inside the trailer with the baby there. The door snapped open and shut as Sims stepped in smelling like second hand smoke. "Sorry, man," he said.

"Me too," Shane mumbled. They didn't need to hug it out, but Sims, always the sensitive one, gave him a pat on the back anyway.

"Hey, big guy," he said, greeting Logan.

Logan babbled out the funniest stream of syllables and they all laughed. As if this were the norm, Sims settled back into his game, Duce plopped on the couch and absentmindedly flipped a rattle in his hand, and Shane spread a blanket on the floor to change Logan's diaper.

Tucker should have been there too, but not if he was sick. Logan arched and kicked like a cricket as Shane undid his diaper. Once he was all fresh, Shane turned him on his tummy.

Duce laughed, observing from the couch. "What's that, his army crawl?"

"This is his work out. Baby push ups," Shane joked.

Logan worked to lift his head, straining to see where the voices were coming from. It looked incredibly draining for the little guy. They all made moaning sound effects as if they were doing the work too.

Shane dropped his chest to the carpet and rested his chin on his arms, watching. When Logan's bright blue eyes met his, he gave a gummy smile. He smiled back. Shane had been doing that a lot lately, smiling. Logan did that to him. He liked having him around.

～

SUNDAY, Shane, Logan and Sims drove over to Clayton to visit a used car dealership. When they pulled up Logan was babbling away so Shane decided to carry him rather than lug the car seat around the lot.

"Can I help you find something, gentleman?"

They turned to find the quintessential car salesman waiting for the kill. Ten bucks said his name was either Eric or Carl. He had an oiled appearance and likely a case of Napoleon syndrome.

"We're just looking right now," Sims said.

The salesman's gaze fell on Logan then back to him and Sims. "Well, my name's Carl if you have any questions." Bingo. Car and suit salesmen always had the same names. It was sort of like how if someone named a kid Barry he had an eighty percent chance of becoming a dentist or doctor. He wondered what Logan's usually became.

They walked around the lot and Carl stayed to the shadows doing that creepy salesman slinking stalker thing. The selection was disappointing. After they made a full circuit of the lot, Carl reappeared. He reminded Shane of an eel.

"Were you looking to trade in that Celica?"

"The DeLorean?" Sims whispered, offended for his car. "Back off," he hissed under his breath.

"Uh, no. I have a truck I'm thinking about trading," Shane said, giving Sims a calm down look. It was a shame Sims didn't have a cooler car. He *so* wanted some nerd trophy to drive.

"What kind of truck is it?"

"Ninety-five Chevy S10."

"How many miles?"

"A hundred and eighty thousand."

Carl whistled through his teeth and Shane swore he might have seen a forked tongue slither past his lips. "Not gonna get much for a truck like that with that many miles. How's your credit?"

Shot. When he was younger he hadn't realized how badly he was screwing up his future when he let the bank take his parents' house. He was a kid. How was he supposed to know that shit stuck to you like a rash?

"Not so great."

"Well, we have a program here that helps people with low credit scores get loans. If you bring the truck in we could give you a price on it and go from there."

Shane knew that was what he'd end up doing. He'd likely be financing a piece of shit for three times its worth and losing his nuts in the process on interest and everything else. But he didn't really have any other options. He needed a safe car for Logan. Bumming rides wouldn't cut it forever. He just hoped he got a fair deal on the S10.

They rode home and Sims petted his car's dash for a good part of the way. Logan fell asleep just before they pulled in.

"Whose car's that?"

Great. The green bug sat beside his truck. Sims shut off the DeLorean and they watched as Katherine McAlister got out. Sims jaw dropped.

"Who is she?"

"She's my caseworker."

"Dude, you said she was a shrew."

"She is."

"I think our definitions of shrews are way different. She's like…Smurfette cute."

Shane turned and narrowed his eyes at Sims. "Smurfette's a cartoon."

"So? She's still hot."

"She's blue!"

"I'd do her."

He shook his head. "You're an idiot." He climbed out of the car and flipped the seat up to lift out Logan.

Sims came around the car. "Come on, are you saying you wouldn't bang a girl just because she's animated? What about the Little Mermaid or Jessica Rabbit?"

He stepped up to the door and hissed. "I am not having this conversation."

He smiled at the caseworker. "Hello."

"Hi." She fidgeted with the button on her

cardigan. This one was Kelly green. "I didn't think you were home. I was about to leave."

"We went car shopping," he explained. She looked different today. Softer somehow. "Uh, this is my friend Sims."

"Sheldon Simpson," Sims introduced, holding out his hand. "It's a pleasure to meet you."

Shane rolled his eyes and unlocked the door. "Come on in. I just gotta put Logan down and I'll be right out."

She eyed Sims as though he were some odd life form then nodded and followed him inside. Shane carried Logan into the bedroom and put him on his back in the crib. When he came out, Sims was explaining the various methods of cloning and Katherine wore an expression like she needed to be rescued.

"Do you want something to drink?" Shane asked as he headed for the fridge and pulled out a bottle of water.

"Is it Wild Turkey?" she asked.

He stilled and turned to face her. Was that a joke? Her lip twitched nervously. Sims gazed at the two of them and frowned.

"No, I have water, juice, and formula if you're interested, but the formula's a little thick for my liking."

She smiled. "I'll take a water. Thank you." She had a nice smile. Was she wearing lip-gloss today?

He handed her a water and signaled for her to sit down. They cracked open their bottles and she asked, "Did you find a car?"

He drew in a hesitant breath. There seemed to be an unspoken truce going on between them. He didn't like the way she'd spoken to him before and he hadn't been nice either. She was his caseworker and he didn't want to make waves, so he was willing to work with this new *let's pretend we're friends* thing. "Not yet, but I'm looking. Hopefully I can work something out soon."

The room grew quiet as Sims' gaze bounced between the two of them like he was watching a tennis match. Usually Shane would be glad for having him there as a buffer, but at the moment he sort of wanted him to leave. Was she still upset with him?

"I go back to work tomorrow," he said, trying to make conversation.

She didn't have her notepad out. "I was wondering," she said. "Good. What did you decide to do for daycare?"

He sipped his water. "Kiddie Academy."

"Good."

There was an extended moment of silence. Her gaze shot to Sims and she quickly looked down at her feet. She was wearing jeans today and little tangerine colored slippers. She seemed more casual than usual.

"So you just come here to check on Shane and Logan and make sure he isn't doing anything stupid?" Sims asked.

Shane frowned at him and Katherine opened her mouth. "Um, yes, basically."

"Do you like your job?"

She hesitated. "Yes."

"Shane says you're a hard ass."

Shane winced and shot Sims a look to shut it. Nice going, douchebag. Katherine glanced at him accusingly. "I'm only looking out for the baby's best interests."

"Sims, didn't you have somewhere to be?" he asked pointedly.

"No." He frowned and caught Shane's look. "Oh, *uh*, yeah. That's right." He stood. "It was lovely meeting you. What did you say your name was?"

"Kate."

Shane tilted his head. Kate? He liked that better than Katherine.

"Well, I'll probably see you around," Sims said as he stood to leave.

"Nice meeting you," Kate said.

They watched as he left. The silence expanded as the sound of the DeLorean drifted away.

"Is he one of your friends?"

"Yeah. Don't mind him. He isn't around pretty girls much. He's a closeted *vidiot*." When she didn't get it, he explained, "Video game idiot."

"Oh." She folded her hands on her lap and looked down. Her reserve wasn't the hoity sort he'd come to expect. Today she seemed nervous.

"I didn't think you guys came by on the weekends."

She looked at him guiltily. "We normally don't. I mean, we can pop in whenever necessary, but we try to keep it to the weekdays. I, um…wanted to come by and apologize for my behavior the other day. It was very unprofessional."

He took a moment to mask his surprise. Forcing his eyebrows back down, he said, "It's already forgotten. I wasn't very nice either."

Her knee bounced and he wondered if she was anxious. "I'm not usually so…harpy-like."

He smirked. "I'm sure."

She gazed at him, her shoulder length blond hair forming a curtain over her one eye. He'd never seen it down like that. It was pretty, shiny.

"Most of my caseloads are women."

He nodded. That made sense. All the other parents in his class were women.

"If, um…" She fidgeted. "If you really wanted to be reassigned I could talk to my supervisor."

Did she want to reassign *him*? It was one

thing to be the dumper, but no one liked being the dumpy. Plus, that might reflect negatively on him. He gentled his expression. "I don't think that'll be necessary," he said softly and she looked at him. When she wasn't interrogating and insulting him, she was actually quite adorable.

Her shoulders lifted as if relieved. "Are you sure?"

He nodded. *This girl* he could deal with. It was her alter ego that scared the crap out of him.

Her gaze lowered again. She looked chastised and guilt weighed on him. She shouldn't take all the blame for the way they started off. "Look, Ms. McAllister—"

"Kate."

"Kate," he amended. "I'm not a nasty guy. I'll admit, I'm kind of out of my element here, but I'm trying."

"I know you are."

"Why don't we start over?"

She nodded. "Okay."

He smiled, tipping his head, waiting for her to meet his gaze. When she did, her pink lips slowly curved into a matching smile. Good. This was better.

Logan squawked and the moment of shy smiles was broken. She stood. "I should go and let you get him."

For some reason he didn't want her to leave. Logan's squawk turned into a cry. He was probably hungry.

She grabbed her bag. "Thanks for accepting my apology."

He tried to come up with some way to stall her, but Logan was screaming and she was already at the door. "Thanks for accepting mine. When will I see you again?" He winced. That sounded like a completely inappropriate question to ask his caseworker.

She glanced at him and flushed, her eyes darting away in a show of vulnerable softness. Appearing flustered, she shifted her purse on her shoulder. "I'll probably be back in the next two weeks to check on things."

That long? "Oh." He tried to hide his disappointment, which he didn't understand. Her presence made him tense and uneasy, yet this seemed different this time and it felt...nice... having her there. Weird. "Okay. Well, I guess I'll see you around."

She nodded then awkwardly slipped out the door. He watched her walk to her car, a jolt of satisfaction hitting the pit of his stomach when she looked back before she climbed into her little green bug.

She pulled away and he sighed then frowned. That was unexpected. It was like dealing with two totally different women. Shaking his head he contemplated how he could suddenly like someone he hated two days ago. He didn't want to get his hopes up. This could be a fluke and the harpy could return at any time. Turning, he went to get his bellowing little man.

CHAPTER 8

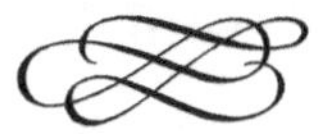

The next few weeks were a trial in adulthood. Shane showed up late for work four times. His foreman actually said something, which was uncomfortable and embarrassing.

It seemed there was always something delaying him. Either Logan needed to eat or had an accident or the damn car seat was giving him trouble. One day he forgot the baby purse and had to drive all the way back to the trailer for it.

Logan's teacher, Miss Jill, was very understanding. She looked about his age, but was cute, bubbly. She loved Logan and that made it easier to leave him there each day. It was insane how hard it was to trust him in the care of strangers when he and Logan had been strangers only a week ago.

There'd been a rain out early in the week and he used the time while Logan was still at daycare to visit the dealership again. Carl the eel ran his credit and appraised the S10. The dealership had a small, gunmetal gray, 2005 four door Kia on the lot he could live with. It had a ton of miles and was clearly a girl car, but the color made it less so, or so he told himself.

Carl offered sixteen hundred for the truck. With the special financing, Shane would be looking at a payment of about one hundred and eighty dollars a month over the next five years.

He knew he was getting ripped off, but it was the best he could afford. Hopefully the car would last that long. It already had ninety thousand miles on it. But it had good safety ratings and as things stood, it was the best he could provide.

When he signed the loan papers and handed over his keys he felt like he was making a deal with the devil. Carl handed him his new set of keys and gave him a reptilian smile. He was doing this for Logan. That's what he kept telling himself. It was all for Logan.

The upside was that paying for a loan over five long years should straighten out his credit. Having a kid meant having expenses. He needed a line of credit in case there was ever an emergency. So, no matter how much he understood a forked tongued car salesman named

Carl was raping him, he believed he was doing the right thing.

When he drove Logan home that day the little guy seemed unimpressed with his investment. What did he know about cars anyway?

They went to the grocery store and stocked up on some necessities. It was the first time he actually used his government card. Swiping it through the scanner made him self-conscious, like he was on display. He stood so the people in line couldn't see what he was doing.

He hated knowing he was on welfare. His pride stung every time he admitted he couldn't do things on his own. It didn't matter that times were tough and the economy was in the shitter. He was a man and as such he should be able to provide for himself and his boy. Still, his gratitude for such assistance was immeasurable. Logan was already humbling him in uncountable ways.

When the number on the register dropped from a hundred and ten dollars to thirty-seven he almost jumped out of his skin. Holy shit! Seeing the results of assistance programs in black and white made it somewhat easier to tolerate, but he still wanted to get on his feet as soon as he could and get off welfare. There was just some part of him that demanded he try harder and do this for Noel and Logan...and himself.

He was unloading groceries while Logan

cooed from his blanket on the floor when the phone rang. Shane pulled his cell out of his pocket and frowned when he didn't recognize the number. He watched Logan doing his workout and flipped the phone open.

"Hello?"

"Hi, is this Shane?"

"Yeah."

"Shane, this is Arty, down at the Moosen Grill. I got your number from Steve Wallace. I'm looking for some live entertainment over the next few weeks and Steve suggested I give you a call to see if you're interested."

Shane mentally pictured the Moosen Grill. It was a decent place. Sort of had a dinner crowd thing going on the weeknights. "Yeah, I'm definitely interested."

"Great. I can pay you two hundred a night on the weekends and one hundred on week-nights. I'm looking for four-hourly sets. How does that sound?"

"That sounds great. How many nights were you thinking?"

"Well, as of right now I was hoping for Wednesdays, Fridays, and Sundays."

He quickly did math in his head. Holy shit, that was an extra five hundred dollars a week! "How far in advance did you want to schedule?"

"Well, let's agree to the next two weeks and renegotiate from there, see how you mix with the crowd. Steve says you do a lot of classic rock."

"That's right, but I could add stuff to my list if you were looking for something more. I'm happy to take requests if I'm familiar with the song."

"Sounds good. So I'll see you this Friday? Say you start around seven? You can show up earlier to set up."

"Okay, I'll see you then. Thanks, Arty."

He hung up the phone. "Yes!"

Logan startled and Shane went to the floor, a grin splitting his face. He scooped up the baby and rolled to his back, holding him above his chest like an airplane.

"Sorry, buddy. Guess what! We're gonna make some money. Baby needs some new shoes and he's gonna get them. That's right! Maybe even that neat bouncy thing I saw you eyeing up at the store the other day."

Logan stared down at him and smiled. As he babbled, a string of drool fell from his mouth onto Shane's face.

"Ugh, gross. When are you going to get some teeth and learn to control the spit?" He laughed and wiped away the drool. Sitting up, he crossed his legs and propped Logan in his lap. He opened the phone and dialed.

"What's up, dick breath?" Tucker answered.

"Nice. Hey, what are you doing this Friday night?"

"Nothing. Probably coming over to nag your pansy ass."

"What's Lisa doing?"

He could hear the confusion in Tucker's voice. "Why?"

"Well, I sort of have a gig and I need a sitter."

"You want my girl to babysit?"

"Well, it's either her or one of you guys and I don't know if that's a good idea."

"You don't trust us? I'm hurt."

Shane rolled his eyes. "Is this something that really bothers you?"

"Nah, not really. I could ask her, I guess."

"She likes kids, right?" Shane didn't really know Lisa. She was nice. She didn't drink a lot or ever smoke pot. And she was going to college for nursing or something. But mostly she was qualified, because she was a girl. Sexist or not, girls had natural know-how when it came to babies.

"I guess. She wants kids some day. She's always oohing and ahhing and shit when she sees babies."

"Okay, could you call her and let me know what she says? I'd need to leave around six and wouldn't be back until after midnight."

"Sure."

He hung up the phone and waited. A few minutes went by and Tucker called him back to say that Lisa agreed to watch Logan. Luckily he saved money on groceries that week, because he'd need to pay her, but it would be worth it once he got money from the bar.

Things were actually working out better than expected. Whenever Kate showed up again she'd be pleased with his progress. He hadn't seen her since that Sunday two weeks ago.

Shane hoped she might come by this week. He wanted to tell her about all the things that were happening.

~

THURSDAY, a buddy from work brought in an old highchair. It was pink, but Shane accepted it gracefully. Logan was currently sitting in said chair, apparently unaffected by the liberal statement he was making.

Shane flipped his grilled cheese and was stirring the tomato soup when there was a knock at the door. It'd been nearly three weeks since he'd seen Kate and his gut tightened at the thought of her possibly coming by.

He put down the spatula and went to the door. Kate stood on the other side and smiled. He held open the door. "Hey, stranger." He winced, realizing his greeting was inappropriate.

She lowered her gaze and followed him in. "How are you?"

"Good. How are you?"

She glanced around and smirked when she spotted Logan banging a rattle on the tray of his pink highchair. "I'm good. Is that new?"

Shane's neck heated. He rubbed it self-consciously. "Yeah. A friend of mine from work gave it to me. Logan's cool with it. He likes pink—refers to it as more of a salmon bisque."

She giggled and he stared at her. The soft melodic sound hung in the air stealing his attention.

Her gaze returned to his and her mouth twitched self-consciously. "What?"

A strange chill tightened his gut. "I never heard you laugh. It's nice."

Her golden lashes lowered and a salmon bisque tint colored her cheeks. Nice.

He headed to the kitchen. "Are you hungry?"

"Oh, no, thank you," she said quickly. She sidled up to the highchair and ran a hand over Logan's fuzzy brown head. Staring at her with curiosity in his blue eyes, he gurgled. Show-off.

"Well, have you eaten? It's just grilled cheese and soup. It's no problem for me to make more. Eat with us." He told himself he was only being courteous to prove his competency.

She hesitated. Maybe it was against the social work rules for them to share a meal. Slowly, she nodded. "Okay."

Her agreement pleased him. He hid a smirk

over the fact that Little Miss Goody Two Shoes might be a rule breaker—liked knowing she wasn't always rigid.

He went about making another sandwich and pulled out two bowls. Ladling out the soup, he finished the grilled cheese while Kate quietly whispered words to Logan. Logan performed for her, doing his best Bill Cosby and, his newest trick, singing the "Ah, ah, ah, ah, ah…" song.

He carried their plates to the table and got silverware. Kate smiled gratefully at him as he handed her a napkin. "Dig in."

He watched her dainty fingers part her sandwich, the golden strings of the melted cheese giving ground reluctantly. She nibbled at the corner and blushed when she noticed him watching.

"Sorry," he mumbled and bent to take a swallow of his soup. She'd somehow gone from annoying and intruding to pleasing and fascinating.

"You got a new car?" she asked quietly. She was wearing a soft pink cardigan and a pale yellow sundress. It was a dress, but not professional attire. She looked…pretty. There was that chill again. It wasn't a bad chill. More like a soft tug that made his blood pump.

"Yeah. I'll be paying for it until Logan's driving, but it's safe and it runs okay."

She nodded and looked back to her plate,

taking another bite of her sandwich. She was being a lot shyer since they argued. Something changed and he wasn't sure what. She seemed a lot more approachable this way, but he wondered what happened to the feisty little firecracker who first came to interrogate him.

"So, what do you do when you aren't social working?"

She paused and considered his question. Shit. Should he not have asked that? She asked about anything and everything regarding his life, so it seemed natural to ask some questions back.

"I like to go to the movies and I read a lot."

"What do you read?" He wanted to ask who she went to the movies with, but that was definitely none of his business.

Logan dropped his rattle on the floor. Shane leaned over to pick it up and gave it back to him. He blew bubbles and babbled his thanks only to immediately drop it again. Picking it up, Shane handed it over again. This was one of his nephew's favorite pastimes—fetch.

"I, um, read a lot of romances, some young adult stuff."

She looked fresh out of college, but was definitely more mature than him. "How old are you?"

She dabbed the corners of her mouth with the napkin—*right there*—maturity. He searched for his own napkin, and noted he hadn't used it once. "Twenty-five."

After wiping his mouth, he asked, "How long have you been a social worker?"

"A little over a year. I'm planning on going back for my masters in psychology."

"To be, like, a doctor?" The thought had him drawing back and doing some inner assessments on his own success. Maybe he overestimated her approachableness.

She nodded. "Eventually, but that's a long way off."

She must be really smart. He didn't know why this made him feel uncomfortable about himself. "Wow."

"How about you? How long have you been in construction?"

Hearing her talk about getting a big fancy degree made his job seem small and meaningless. He shrugged. "Since I was eighteen."

"Oh." She looked like she had more questions, but rather than ask them she went back to her dinner.

He had a sudden urge to explain his situation, so she didn't think he was a loser. "My parents died when I was seventeen. We had a house with a mortgage. I needed to take care of Noel, so I dropped out of school and started working. I planned on going back, but… life sort of got away from me."

She looked at him. He expected her to criticize his lack of ambition, but rather she said, "You took care of your sister all those years on your own?" There was something soft in her gaze, compassionate, and it soothed his bristling pride.

He exhaled, relieved she wasn't judging him harshly. "Yeah. We eventually lost the house. It was too much for us, but we got an apartment and I think we did all right. Well, until..."

The room quieted and he regretted bringing up his sister, still struggling to face reality head on. Softly, she whispered, "Do you miss her?"

He stared at his soup. Those hollow aches of loneliness had faded since he'd met Logan, but if he actually thought about the family he'd lost, the pain came right back. "Yeah. We weren't really close in the end. I said some things and she took off. I tried to find her, but I never did." His voice grew quiet. "I'd give anything to take back those last things I said to her."

Kate's small hand softly pressed into the top of his and he mentally jerked at the unfamiliar, yet pleasant, feel of her touch. "She knows." He stared at her perfectly manicured fingernails, wondering if such an impeccable hand had ever touched him.

She was just being polite, but it felt personal, more than just common manners. He continued to stare at her hand on his. Her nails didn't appear painted, but under closer inspection there was the faintest gleam of pale shell pink.

He met her gaze and she blinked, her lips parting the slightest degree. "Thank you."

When she pulled her hand back he drew in a breath. He wanted to hold it there, but that would be wrong. Did most people get this attached to their caseworkers? Maybe it was a subconscious need to convince this woman he was a good parent. Yeah, that was it.

"What about your music?" she asked, her voice slightly breathless.

He smirked, glad for the distraction of lighter topics. "You mean my gigs?"

Her cheeks flushed as a contrite expression took over her face. How had he missed these vulnerable signs before? The more he watched her the less intimidating she became and the more tempting it was to prove he wasn't anyone she needed to fear. Was she afraid of him?

"Sorry I was such a bitch that day." Her dainty fingers flew to her mouth. Eyes wide, she glanced at Logan apologetically.

His mouth opened, shocked at her language —shocked and sort of impressed. "It's okay. When you're not around he curses like a sailor."

She tried to hide a smile as her cheeks darkened. His attention snagged on the slight lift of her shoulders. Her breast pressed against her dress with each breath and he suddenly wanted to see her shoulders hidden by her ever-present cardigan.

He pushed his plate away and sat back. What they were doing felt more like a date than a visit from his social services. Did she realize that? Did she have dinner with her other people? Part of him wanted to believe he was special, but Kate's dates were probably way more fancy than canned soup and grilled cheese.

Clearing his throat, he grasped for the qualities most women found appealing. "I've been playing guitar since I was a kid. Mostly rock and stuff." He shrugged. "I used to have big dreams, but now my priorities have sort of changed."

She smiled softly, approval in her eyes. "Because of the baby?"

He nodded. "Because of Logan."

Standing, he carried the dishes to the sink. She folded her hands and said, "You're very good with him. If someone didn't know better they'd think he was yours. He looks like you."

He grinned. "You think so? He has Noel's nose, but his hair's definitely all mine." He yanked on his ponytail.

"He's a cute baby."

He stilled. Was that some sort of sideways compliment? He stared at her and she nervously lowered her gaze then stood. He stepped closer, not wanting her to leave and sensing she was about to do just that.

"I should go," she quietly said.

"You don't have to." Logan was watching them from his chair, oddly quiet for a change.

She looked up at him, her gaze studying his face. She glanced at his arm where he had a sleeve tattooed. Her scrutiny made him uncomfortable.

He stepped back. They were too different and she was hired to report to the courts on him in two months. Turning, he scooped up Logan, giving her the opening she needed to leave.

"Thank you for dinner."

"Sure." He avoided direct eye contact. He couldn't screw this up.

She slowly walked to the door, but looked as though she was forgetting something and couldn't think what. She hadn't taken any notes again. Weird.

"Oh, how are the classes going?"

A burst of relief hit him as she asked the question, but he hadn't even processed what it was. Classes. Right. "Good. My last one's this Monday. The teacher says we're graduating top of our class," he joked.

She smiled and nodded. "Good. I look forward to reading her report."

His smile fell. Dr. Haughenschlaugger reported back to Kate?

With nothing left to say, she grinned and left. He was thrown by her announcement that the doctor would be giving her a report, so he let her leave without further delay.

He didn't like being talked about when he wasn't there. What did they say? Would Kate laugh when she found out about all his stupid questions?

His brow creased with worry as she shut the door. Shaking off his uncertainty, he headed back to the kitchen. It was bath night and that was always an ordeal. Babies were extremely slippery when wet.

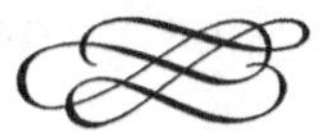

CHAPTER 9

"His diapers are in here and extra wipes are in the bedroom. I usually give him a bottle around eight and sit with him with the lights turned down. That way he knows it's time to sleep. You want to lay him down before he totally drifts off—on his back —so that if he wakes he isn't startled and wondering where you went. He should be in the same place he was when he fell asleep."

"Dude, take a breath!" Tucker said.

Lisa smacked him in the arm. "Shut up, Tucker. This stuff's important."

Shane should have smiled, but he was too nervous. "I made up bottles. They're in the fridge. Use the cup by the sink to warm them up. Fill it with hot water and let the bottle sit in it for about a minute to get rid of the chill.

Shake it and test it before you give it to him to make sure it isn't too hot."

"And just the one bottle?" Lisa asked. She seemed calm. Shane liked that, because he was a total basket case.

Maybe he should call and cancel the show. No, it was good money.

"Well, he usually eats again at midnight," he said. "But if he doesn't wake up just hold off and I'll do that feeding when I get home." For some reason he wanted to be the one to do Logan's midnight feeding.

"Okay."

Shane picked up Logan and pressed his forehead to his. "You be good, my man. I'll be home in a few hours. No friends over and stay out of the liquor cabinet."

Logan grabbed Shane's nostril and tried to pull his nose off his face. It was one of their secret handshakes. He hesitantly handed him to Lisa and picked up his bag. Anxiously, he looked around.

Logan was tugging on her hair and cooing happily. "My number's on the fridge and the bar number's there too. If anything happens—anything at all—or if you have any questions, call me. Unless it's an emergency, then call 911."

"Shane, you bringing that pretty bag with you to the show?" Tucker asked, grinning.

Shane looked down. The baby purse was

hanging from his shoulder. "Shit." He put it down and picked up his guitar case. "Okay. Call me if you need anything."

"We'll be fine, Shane. I have three younger sisters."

Reluctantly, he left. Once he was behind the wheel he needed to do some deep breathing to calm his nerves. It was only for a few hours. They'd be fine.

The bar was semi-crowded when he got there. People were finishing up their dinners and moving on to cocktails. Drafts were a dollar until nine, which usually led to a pretty decent crowd.

Shane went directly to the stout wooden stage and checked the wires as he set up his speakers and microphone. He put his acoustic guitar on the stand and went back to the car to get his electric bass.

Once he was set up, his mind calmed and he was on autopilot. This was familiar. This was who he was before his life was overhauled with diapers and wet naps.

A few minutes before seven, Arty came out and introduced himself. They shook hands and he slid Shane an envelope of money.

"One of the waitresses'll bring you a beer. Just let them know what you want."

"Water's fine."

He sat on the stool on the stage and turned on the microphone. "Hello. I'm Shane Martin and I'm here tonight for your entertainment. If you have any requests don't be shy."

His fingers struck the chords and he fell into a riff he'd been practicing for a few weeks. It was a little softer than what he usually opened with, but this was the first time he'd played since losing his sister.

He leaned into the microphone. "This is for Noel." His knuckles curled over the strings and he began singing his cover of *Dust in the Wind* by Kansas.

He didn't expect his voice to seize at the bridge, but the words got to him. He played through it, imagining Logan, wondering what his sister would think of how fast he was growing.

As he sang his eyes settled on a girl in the crowd watching him. She twirled the straw in her drink and smiled sweetly at him. He smiled back and her eyes softened.

When he finished his opening song the bar erupted with applause. The girl who'd been watching him so raptly appeared almost breathless. Sometimes he had that effect on women when he played, but it never panned out to anything more than a quick fling. Once he was off the stage, they saw he was just an average guy and the appeal wore off.

His first set ended around eight fifteen. He called Tucker to check on things. Logan was asleep and he and Lisa were watching a movie.

Breathing a sigh of relief, he took his bottle of water outside to get some air before his second set. He was standing at the curb when a voice startled him.

"Hi."

He turned as saw the girl from the bar step out of the shadows. "Hi."

"I really like your voice. You're good."

"Thanks."

She stepped close and batted her eyes. She was sending off signals she was interested, but he wouldn't be able to hang out afterward like he usually did after a show. He wanted to get back to Logan in time for his feeding.

"Do you play here often?" When she stepped close, her breasts rubbed against his arm. "Ooh, I love your ink. I just got a tattoo last week. Wanna see?"

"Sure."

She lifted up the bottom of her shirt, exposing a flat, tanned belly. Around her pierced navel was one of those dandelion wish things with all the seeds flying off as if caught in a breeze. It was actually decent work. Nice to see something other than a tramp stamp on a girl. She definitely had the body to pull it off.

"Pretty."

She grinned and shifted even closer. Her fingers ran over his triceps. "You got other tattoos?"

"A few."

"I bet." Her eyes stared up at him. "You wanna go over there and show me?"

His dick twitched. Sometimes women made it so simple. "I got another set to do in five minutes."

"Five minutes is all I need."

He stared at her for a moment, considering the offer. She was hot—a little easy—but definitely hot. He nodded and she wrapped her small hand around his arm and dragged him around the corner and his mind was distracted with visions of pale pink fingernails, unlike the ones touching him now.

Next thing he knew his back was against the brick exterior wall of the bar and she was against his front, tongue in his mouth, hand stroking his chest.

"Mm, you're a good kisser."

So was she. His hand cupped the back of her neck and he deepened the kiss. Her hand coasted down his abs and over his belt buckle, settling at the bulge in his pants. He pressed his hips forward, filling her palm. She giggled and squeezed.

Her hair smelled like flowers. He reached for her small waist and glided his palm up until he found her breasts. They were firm, too firm to be real, but he squeezed them all the same.

She moaned into his mouth and draped a leg over his hip. A door opened and the sound of bottles falling had them jumping apart. They were both breathing heavily. He looked at his watch. "Fuck. I gotta go back in."

She nodded. "What time are you playing to?"

"Midnight, but I have somewhere I need to be afterward. I have another break in about an hour."

"Wanna meet here then?"

Did a bear shit in the woods? "Sure, cutie." He turned to head back in and paused. "Oh, what's your name?"

She giggled. "Kate."

And just like that his whole mood faltered. Guilt, for some strange reason, surfaced inside of him and he felt dirty as if he'd been doing something wrong. Images of Kate his social worker filled his head. She'd never be caught making out with a musician she didn't know behind a bar.

That's because she's stuck up. He mentally frowned at himself. That wasn't true. It was because she was respectable.

He went back to the stage and started his second set. Kate the barfly sat watching him with imploring eyes. He tried to look anywhere but at her.

When his next break came he called Tucker again, then went to the men's room in an attempt to lose his little groupie. She'd moved on by the time he started his third set, flirting with some guy in a hat by the bar. When he wrapped up for the night, thankfully she was gone.

The whole way home he berated himself for being a pussy. He was fucking horny and could have gotten laid tonight if he wasn't being such a bitch. The more he thought about Kate the barfly and Kate the social worker the angrier he got.

He didn't owe his social worker anything. She was reporting on him for Christ's sake. For all he knew she could wind up being his enemy in all this. Out of everyone involved in his current situation, she posed the greatest threat to his custody of Logan. She could totally screw everything up if she wanted to. But she wouldn't do that. Somehow he knew she wouldn't. He really was starting to believe Kate wanted to see him succeed at parenting. But no matter what he thought, there was no guarantee and he had to play it safe.

Something changed over the past few weeks. There was something about the way she looked at him that was new. She didn't talk to him like a loser anymore. Was that because he stuck up for himself and showed her he wasn't going to be treated like crap and kiss her ass just so she would give him a good report? Or maybe it was the way he was with Logan that impressed her. Either way, he was really digging the new Kate—maybe a little too much. He doubted he even crossed her mind when she wasn't working, yet he couldn't stop thinking about her.

He wondered when he'd see her again. The other Kate from the bar was nothing but fake boobs and a blurred face in his mind. Kate the social worker, however, was clear as day.

As he drove, he thought of her shiny blonde hair and her brown eyes. She had great lashes. He liked that she didn't wear a lot of makeup. But he also liked when she wore that shiny stuff on her lips. It made him want to kiss her.

Whoa! Okay, yeah, he wanted to kiss her. So what? He could fantasize. It wasn't like she'd ever know.

She was a petite little thing, but also not a stick. It was hard to get an idea about her body when she always wore cardigans. They sort of hid her curves. She had tiny feet and tiny hands, but a nice set of hips on her. She was built like a real woman, not one of those bobble head, starving-to-death girls that may as well be boys with breasts.

What would it be like to fuck someone like Kate, all prim and proper? Would she want it gentle or kind of rough? It was always the quiet ones guys had to watch out for. Mmm, imagining a kinky Kate was a shit load of fun.

When he pulled into Sunny Acres he was totally hard. Fuck. He thought of baseball, solved a few math problems, but nothing helped. He should've never let his imagination get away from him. He hadn't even jerked off since bringing Logan home. It just felt wrong. Which was stupid, but he couldn't bring himself to do it, not even in the shower, knowing the little guy was in the next room.

He pulled into his lot and the trailer was dim. Blue flashes from the television flickered on the other side of the blinds. Everything looked under control.

He grabbed his guitar and headed to the door. As he entered, Lisa and Tucker jumped apart. Oh, come on! Not on his couch!

"Hey, man, what's up," Tucker said all too fast.

"Hey."

Lisa busied herself by looking for her shoes and straightening her clothing. Shane gave her a moment by going into the bedroom to check on Logan. He approached the crib and his heart plummeted.

Jesus! Logan was face down. Shane quickly lifted him and turned him in his arms. He was going to kick someone's ass!

Logan startled then sighed and nestled into his hold. He went to the bedroom door. "You put him to bed on his stomach," he hissed. "He could have died!"

They both turned and frowned at him. "No, I didn't," Lisa said defensively.

"Well, that's how he was lying!"

"She put him on his back, Shane. I watched her."

"Maybe he rolled over. When I went to check on him he was on his back. He must have turned."

Shane stilled. "He doesn't know how to flip over."

"Yes, he does. He was doing it all night when we had him on the floor."

A humongous sense of loss washed through him. "What? He rolled over and I missed it?"

"You never saw him do that?" Tucker asked.

"No." Shane looked at Logan who was sleeping soundly. He wanted him to do it now so he could see. What did this mean about the sleeping on the back rule? Was he supposed to watch him at all times and continuously move him off his belly when he fell asleep like that?

His last class with Dr. Haughenschlaugger was Monday. He'd ask her then. But what was he supposed to do in the meantime? He'd have to keep an eye on him.

He placed Logan back in his crib—on his back—and went to say goodbye to Lisa and Tucker. He gave Lisa thirty bucks and told her thank you. Then he heated up a bottle and went to feed Logan. The little punk was back on his belly again.

CHAPTER 10

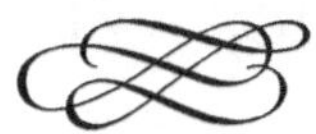

"Yo, Shane, you got a call!"

Shane removed his earplugs and walked away from the jackhammer pounding a few feet away. "What?"

His foreman pointed to the general call box indicating someone was on the other line. He headed in that direction, through a cloud of cement dust and picked up the red phone.

"Hello?" he shouted over the sound of construction and traffic passing.

"Mr. Martin?"

"Yes?"

"This is Miss Jill from Kiddie Academy."

He plugged his gloved finger in his other ear as anxiety stiffened his limbs. "Yeah?"

"Would you be able to come pick up Logan? He's hasn't been himself today. He feels a little warm, but doesn't have a fever. I didn't know if he might be coming down with something, but I figured I'd give you a call so you could come get him."

"He's sick?" Panic welled up inside of him like erupting lava.

"Well, he isn't his typical, happy self. You might want to call his pediatrician and see about getting him in there."

The world fell away as his brain quickly organized. Logan's appointment with the pediatrician wasn't until next week. Technically he didn't have a doctor yet. He had to go get him and make sure everything was okay. Dr. Haughenschlaugger said go with his gut.

"I'll be there as fast as I can."

He hung up the phone and didn't return to what he'd been working on. Instead he went right to his general foreman and told him he had to go—family emergency.

The ride home took forever. He hit every red light and got stuck behind every geriatric driver on the road. Forty-five minutes passed between the time he hung up with Miss Jill and the time he pulled into the school.

The secretary at the desk buzzed him in. "Hi, I'm here to pick up Logan."

"Sign here and I'll go get his teacher."

He scribbled his name quickly and waited for Logan. His patience was beyond frayed. What if something was really wrong? Dr. Haughenschlaugger said him sleeping on his belly was fine so long as he was able to lift his head and turn himself back over, but what if she was wrong?

Miss Jill appeared carrying Logan who was nuzzling her shoulder. Shane immediately saw what she was talking about. He didn't look like himself. He held out his arms and she handed Logan to him.

Shane checked over his little body. "Hey, big man. You not feeling too well?"

"He's been a bit off today."

Shane looked at the teacher, waiting for her to tell him what was wrong with his baby, but she didn't. "What do you think it is?"

She tilted her head and ran a hand over Logan's forehead. "Babies have their ups and downs. It could be gas. He could be coming down with something. He may even be cutting some teeth."

"But the book says that doesn't happen until around six months." The book was the Bible. Why would it say six months if in reality kids started getting teeth at three months?

"Well, six months is the norm, I think, but I've seen teeth break around this age plenty of times."

Shane peeked down at Logan's tiny, flushed face. He looked sad. "Does your mouth hurt, buddy?"

"If he isn't feeling better by tomorrow I'd call his pediatrician. Keep an eye on his temperature and if you feel any teeth beneath his gums or see an abnormal amount of drool, you may want to give him some Tylenol or a cool washcloth to suck on."

Shane nodded and gathered up Logan's things. He packed him in the car and continuously felt his little head. Logan fell asleep on the way home. When Shane carried him in he didn't stir, so he put him down for a nap.

It was already four o'clock, but he called the pediatrician anyway. They also said it could be teeth, but if he didn't seem himself by morning they suggested he call back and bring him in for a check-up.

He hated the sense of helplessness. As Logan slept he paced the trailer, unsure what to do. He watched some television and when dinnertime passed, he made a bottle. The little guy had to eat.

He went in his room and woke him, but Logan didn't seem to have an appetite. His eyes were glassy and his cheeks were flushed. He looked tired. When he fell back to sleep Shane carried him to the crib, but as soon as he laid him down he started crying so Shane held him.

They watched a few episodes of *Hoarders*. Around nine o'clock Shane was sweating. He touched Logan's head and cursed. He was burning up.

On instinct he went to the bathroom and soaked a washcloth in cool water. After wringing it out, he gently wiped Logan's brow. He whined and fussed, but Shane didn't know what else to do.

He looked in the baby book under fever. It said a fever was a sign that the body was fighting an infection. It suggested not over-dressing your baby when his temperature was high and the book was very adamant about keeping him hydrated.

Shane undressed Logan. His little legs were on fire. Even his tummy was hot. When he checked his diaper it was bone dry. He really started to panic the more he read.

The book said a fever should be permitted to do its job so long as the child didn't appear listless, uncomfortable, or unable to eat. If the baby wasn't taking in fluids, the fever needed to be brought down. The book suggested Tylenol like Miss Jill had recommended.

He tried to get Logan to take a bottle again, but he wanted nothing to do with it. He also tried a bottle of cool water. Logan drank a few swallows, but then lost interest.

He needed to get to the pharmacy and get a thermometer and something to bring down his fever. Rather than dress him back in his clothes, he only put him in a t-shirt and a diaper.

When he put him in his car seat he screamed like Shane never heard him scream before. It was horrible, hearing him cry like that and not knowing what to do. Should he call 911?

He quickly went to the folder with all Logan's papers while trying to calm him down. He screamed, sobs coming out in quick succession in between cries. Shane accidentally dropped the folder and all the papers fell out. A huge crocodile tear rolled down Logan's cheek and a piece of Shane's heart broke.

"It's okay, buddy. It's okay. I'm here."

His gaze fell on a card. Katherine Mc-Allister.

He bopped his knee up and down, soothing Logan as he dialed. He looked at the clock. Fuck, it was late.

Kate answered on the second ring. "Hello?"

"Kate?"

"Shane?"

He was startled that she knew his voice. Maybe she programmed her clients' numbers in her phone. "Yeah. I'm sorry to bother you, but would you be able to come over here? Logan's sick and I'm scared he might need a doctor. He has a fever and I don't know what to do." The admission fell from his lips without a moment's hesitation. Who cared if this looked bad to the courts? He needed to help Logan.

"Sure. I can be there in twenty minutes. What's wrong with him?"

"I don't know. He wasn't feeling good today so I picked him up early from daycare. He slept all evening then woke up cranky and now he's burning up."

"Did you give him anything?"

"I don't have anything here. I know. Stupid. I—"

Before he could finish, she said, "I'll get something on my way over. I'll be right there. Try dabbing his neck with a cool cloth."

"I did that."

"Good."

He ended the call and paced. Logan was completely inconsolable. He'd stripped him down to a diaper and held him with a thin receiving blanket wrapped at his hips. When Kate finally got there he wanted to collapse. He held open the door as she climbed out of her car.

She was in flip-flops, a vintage Madonna t-shirt, and sweats. She looked totally different. She looked young and…cool.

Stepping inside, holding a bag from the pharmacy, her hands immediately went to Logan's back and she winced. "Here, let me take him for a minute. You're frustrated. Babies can sense that."

He handed him over and took the bag from her.

Her arms cradled him naturally as she slowly swayed. "I also brought my humidifier in case you needed it."

He sorted through the items in the bag. She'd bought a lot of stuff. "A humidifier?"

"In case he's stuffy."

Shane nodded. Logan screamed, and Kate rocked him on her hip. Her ass looked great in those cotton pants, but now wasn't the time.

He cracked open the box of Tylenol and read the label. "How do I get him to drink this?"

"There's a syringe."

"Where am I injecting it?"

She laughed, her mannerisms so calm compared to his frantic mood. "Into his mouth."

Shane measured out the dosage and went to Logan. He was still crying, but now with quiet, shivering sobs. His little body shook with tremors every few seconds as each big snuffle hit. Shane had never seen anything sadder.

"Here, buddy. This is going to make you feel better." He brought the tip of the medicine injector to his mouth and Logan turned away.

"Come over here," Kate suggested, heading for the couch.

She held Logan on her lap so that he couldn't squirm. Shane quickly injected the medicine in his mouth. He swallowed thickly and screamed again. Kate turned him to her shoulder and soothed him.

"Shh…" she whispered softly, her dainty hand rubbing slowly over his back. "I know you don't feel good." Even he found her tone soothing.

Shane sat back and dragged a hand over his head. He needed a minute. He sat, simply watching Kate's foot bounce. She had blue nail polish on her toes. That was unexpected.

When Logan quieted again she asked, "Do you want to try to give him another bottle? He might take it now." How was she so calm?

Shane dumped the bottle he'd been using and made a fresh one.

"Maybe not heat it up since he's so warm already."

He shrugged and carried it over. He expected Kate to hand him the baby, but instead she gestured for the bottle. He handed it to her.

She turned Logan in her arms and softly whispered as she angled the bottle. Tension unraveled in his shoulders as Logan began to drink. Shane stood idly to the side as she fed his nephew. His mind went blank at the vision. There was something so incredibly…beautiful about watching Kate feed Logan.

Her gaze skated to his and a smile trembled to her lips. "What?" she whispered.

He blinked. "You're good at that."

She smiled and stared down at Logan who was drinking with his eyes closed. "I have two nieces."

"Do you spend a lot of time with them?"

"I'm twenty-five and single. According to my sister that makes me the best babysitter in the world."

He swallowed, something akin to gratitude

and awe taking his breath away. "What are their names?"

"Keira and Kiley."

He stared a while longer. Logan finished the bottle and remained asleep. They probably shouldn't move him just yet. Shane sat beside her on the couch.

The awkwardness of her presence settled in and he realized how inappropriate it had probably been for him to call her. She didn't seem to mind, but he knew this went beyond her job description. However, seeing his little man calm and no longer suffering, he had no regrets. "Thanks for coming over."

She smiled, her gaze tilting away from Logan and finding his. "No problem." Damn, she was pretty.

She probably thought he was totally incompetent. "I'll give you money for the things you picked up."

Her mouth opened as if to object, but she said nothing, only turned away to gaze at Logan. Her hand gently touched his head. "He feels like he's cooling down. I bought a thermometer that goes in his ear. We should probably take his temperature now, so we know if it changes."

"Good idea."

He opened the thermometer and returned to the couch. She turned her body so that he could place the tip of the device in Logan's ear.

Shane kneeled and waited. Logan's face rested along the soft curve of her breasts, which filled out her worn t-shirt to perfection. The thermometer beeped.

"One hundred point one."

"That's good," she said.

"It is?"

"Yeah. Anything over one hundred point four is cause for concern. Hopefully the medicine will bring it down. We'll check again in about a half hour."

Relieved she'd said *we,* he tried to relax. If she stuck around a little longer he'd probably be okay, but the idea of her leaving was slightly terrifying. What if his temperature spiked? What if the medicine didn't help?

She was so composed. He didn't know who her presence was soothing more, Logan or him. Shane glanced back down at Logan, peacefully sleeping on her chest. Probably Logan.

He sat awkwardly waiting for her to say something. Finally, he decided to break the silence. "What were you doing when I called?"

She blushed.

He laughed. "What?"

"Watching *Teen Witch.*"

For some reason he could totally see her doing that. Not the woman who'd first come to interrogate him in her cardigan, but this chick in the Madonna shirt...yeah, he could see that. "*Teen Witch,* huh?"

"Yeah, there was an eighties marathon on television. *Goonies* was next."

"I love *Goonies*!"

She looked at him with a dead serious expression and said, "Goonies never say die."

Dear God, he was in love. "What channel?"

"Twenty-eight."

He grabbed the remote and switched the channel. It was right at the beginning, Cyndi Lauper was still singing. Perfect. He glanced over his shoulder, seeing if she was okay with his choice. Her smile expressed approval and he placed the remote on the table settling back on the couch. Maybe she'd stay for the whole movie. That would be good.

They watched quietly for a while and then she admitted, "I used to love Brand."

"Really?" He gazed at her, noting that her flip-flops now rested on the floor and her legs were crossed, making a nest for Logan in her lap. The casual pose put him at ease.

She giggled and nodded.

"I was always a chunk fan myself."

"He's skinny now," she told him.

"I know. His wife's hot!" Her expression froze. Probably not the right thing to say. "Sorry."

He faced the television and the silence grew. Why did he say that? Needing to break the silence, he said, "Here, I'll take him to his crib."

"Oh." She looked down as if she forgot she was even holding the baby. Logan had been sleeping so peacefully for the past while. She handed him over and he carried him to the crib.

When he came back out she was standing. "Are you leaving?"

She nibbled her lower lip as if debating. Her face turned, her gaze skittering to the floor. "You seem to have everything under control now."

"I…I thought you were gonna watch the movie with me." He didn't want her to leave.

"Don't you have work in the morning?"

"I'm not going." He decided in that moment. "I need to take Logan to the doctor's to make sure everything's okay."

Her face lifted. "Yeah, that's probably a good idea." As she looked at him his heartbeat seemed to get stronger. He couldn't think of anything to say.

Swallowing, he stepped closer. He wanted her to stay. "What time do you go into work tomorrow?"

Her shoulders shifted and he worried his nearness was bothering her, yet he didn't step back. "I only have one case to deal with tomorrow. I can do that whenever. My schedule's flexible. Why?"

He took another step closer and noticed the way her chest rose and fell slightly with each breath. "Stay," he whispered. "Watch the movie."

Her lower lip disappeared beneath her little teeth. A small V formed in her brow as she considered his offer. He held his breath.

"Okay," she finally whispered.

He smiled and they sat down on the couch. She sat at the far end so there was a whole cushion between them. They watched the movie in utter silence. Kate barely seemed to move. He kept glancing over at her and sometimes caught her staring at him. Whenever he found her watching him she blushed and quickly turned back to the movie. Little by little he made infinitesimal shifts closer to the middle of the couch.

He shifted when it came to the scene of Brand and Andy's kiss in the water. Out of the corner of his eye he caught Kate watching him again. She was sitting up straight, her breathing shallow.

Tension rolled around them. She had to feel it. It couldn't be just him. If he were just a client she wouldn't be this involved. Caseworkers didn't make night calls, did they?

"Fuck it." He turned and stretched, going in for the kill. His lips found hers and she jumped as his hand cupped the back of her head. At first her body tensed, but as his lips gentled she was all warm softness and smelled like the beach.

She sighed and her mouth slightly opened letting him in. He scooted closer and eased his body over hers. She slouched into the back of the couch. Her hand gripped his bicep, squeezing slightly. She tasted amazing.

His mouth pressed over hers as he slowly eased his tongue into her mouth. She made a soft hum of pleasure that seemed to vibrate all the way to his core. A rush of excitement tunneled through him as they found a more comfortable position. Sweet Jesus, she had an incredible mouth.

He hadn't kissed like this in so long. They were actually making out. He nudged her body down on the couch and her knees curled, lightly bracketing his hips. His body pressed into the cradle of her thighs and she moaned. She was all warm curves and sweet caresses.

Her hands coasted over his back, tickling him and making him arch like a cat. His fingers brushed over her soft blond hair and he stared at her, his own mane making a curtain around them. "You're so pretty."

She turned a delicate shade of pink and leaned up to press her lips to his. Still amazed she was letting him kiss her, he slowly lowered his lashes. The gentle weight of her fingertips on his skin was incredible. He was rock hard. Deepening the kiss, he pressed his body into the cradle of her thighs. Energy shifted to something hot and intensely intoxicating.

God, he wanted to have sex with her. He drew back, not wanting to spoil the moment.

Her lips were puffy and she was breathing fast. Did she feel it too? His fingers toyed with the edge of her shirt. "I like this," he whispered. "Your shirt."

Her hair was slightly disheveled as she lounged beneath him. "Thanks."

"Can I take it off?" Fuck. He shouldn't have said that. She wasn't like the girls he picked up at bars.

Her lips parted and she stilled. Just like that, he watched her grow very aware of where they were, and what they were doing. She broke eye contact and he panicked.

Shit. He didn't want her to wig out. "Don't," he whispered.

She blinked at him, her brow tense with something that resembled regret. "Don't what?"

Their mouths were still very close. "Don't say we have to stop."

She glanced at the television. "The movie's over."

"So?" Everything inside of him feared she'd bolt. He didn't want to be her client in that moment. He wanted to be the guy who was making her feel good, hopefully as good as she was making him feel.

"I said I'd stay for the movie."

He looked at the television. "*Breakfast Club's* coming on next."

Her eyes closed as a regretful expression tightened her mouth. He was losing her. He could sense it. He quickly pressed his lips to hers, begging her to stay.

She kissed him back for a moment then turned and gave him her cheek. "I should go."

He pressed his forehead into the curve of her neck as disappointment doused his mood. "I don't want you to," he admitted, breathing in the soft beach scent of her hair.

"But I should."

"Why?"

Her hands remained around his shoulders, holding him to her. "Because I'm your case-worker and this isn't right."

"Says who? It feels right." Desperate for her to stay, he slowly nudged her with his body, showing her how much he was enjoying her in his arms.

She whimpered as though she were having some major debate in her head. "Shane—"

"Stay. Please."

"What about Logan?"

He hesitated. What if this was a test? "He's too young to date," he joked and she silently laughed. He liked when he made her smile.

"You know what I mean. He's sick."

Yes, he was. Damn it. He didn't want her to think he was thinking with his dick and not being a good guardian. Maybe she was right and things were getting too personal.

Hesitantly, he sat up and she slowly followed, righting her clothing that had been nudged out of place. The flash of her stomach made him want to throw her back down and peel off her clothes.

He shifted awkwardly, painfully aware of his hard-on.

"Will you be okay?"

He looked at her, misunderstanding for a moment then realized she was referring to Logan, not his blue balls. "Yeah." He stood. "Thanks for tonight—the medicine, I mean. How much do I owe you?"

She shrugged. "We can figure it out later."

"I don't want you paying for that stuff. It's my responsibility."

"It's okay."

He stepped close and brushed her chin with the backs of his knuckles. "Kate, tell me how much you spent."

She drew in an unsteady breath. Good, she was as affected by his nearness as much as he was by hers. He didn't want her to act like nothing happened.

Leaning down, he brushed his lips to hers and whispered, "Where's the receipt?"

"It was twenty dollars," she breathed against his mouth.

He reached in his pocket and pulled out his wallet. She turned away. Why was she uncomfortable taking money from him? Logan was his responsibility, not hers. "Here."

Her mouth tightened as she took the bill. He followed her to the door. "Thanks for…having me."

"Thanks for helping with Logan."

She nodded and turned to leave. He caught her wrist and jerked her back. His body covered hers as he pressed her into the wall and kissed her deeply. She sighed and melted into him. He kissed her passionately. Giving her something unforgettable, so she wouldn't try to act like nothing happened, which he already sensed her planning to do.

When he pulled away they were both breathless. Her lips were nude and puffy. God, she was cute.

"Goodnight," he whispered.

"Goodnight," she mimicked. And this time, when she tried to leave, he let her.

CHAPTER 11

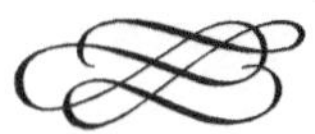

Shane dried off from his shower and combed out his hair. It was getting really long. He wondered if Kate liked long hair on guys. And tattoos. And did she like musicians for that matter? Tonight he'd seen a whole new side of her. His prim and proper caseworker was a little bit of a retro punk. He liked that.

After pulling on a pair of sweats, he checked on Logan, laying a palm gently on his back. Sometimes he was so still when he slept it was almost frightening. His body temperature felt good, normal.

Today had been terrifying. He was definitely taking his little man to the doctor's tomorrow to see what was what.

Quietly pressing the button on the thermometer, he reset it and pressed it to Logan's ear. 97.9. Shutting his eyes, he let out a breath of relief and thanked the gods his temp dropped.

At the closet he pulled out the soft quilt that belonged to his mother. When he was a little boy and didn't feel good, she'd cover him with it and let him rest on the couch all day. While his friends were at school he'd catch up on *Three's Company* reruns and *Gilligan's Island*. He always passed out during *The Facts of Life*.

He scooped Logan up and cradled him to his chest, shushing him when he started to stir. He told himself he was comforting his sick little man, but knew he was acting more for his own piece of mind.

Shutting out the hall light, he carried Logan to the couch and made a nest of pillows along the floor. He carefully reclined, curling his arms protectively around his boy, and faced the back of the couch. He needed a new couch.

Shane stared at Logan, experiencing a wonder of emotion welling up inside of him out of nowhere. He'd been scared tonight—really scared—more scared than he'd probably ever been. He'd be more than willing to admit at this point that babies were not as easy to take care of as they seemed.

Logan's small, rosy mouth puckered and he sighed in his sleep. He looked like an angel. So much so, Shane was tempted to check for wings.

He smiled. "You're my boy."

That night he rested on the surface of sleep, never really truly relaxing, tuned into every whispered breath or sound Logan made. It was a tense night, but at the same time, totally reassuring to hold him through the dark.

Somehow, Shane's rest didn't matter. He was exhausted, but found a reserve of usable energy to take care of Logan. He'd always take care of him, no matter what.

The following day, once they returned home from the pediatrician's, Shane cleaned. His place hadn't been tidied up like that since… ever. It desperately needed a good scrubbing.

He reorganized his medicine cabinet, assigning an entire shelf to baby stuff. He cleaned out the drawers in his bedroom, which were mostly jammed with CDs and crap. He actually folded his clothes and put them away. It was a novel concept, not leaving clothes out on the dresser or the floor or wherever. He even arranged two drawers for Logan's pint-sized wardrobe and blankets.

The doctor said Logan likely picked up a twenty-four hour bug. Shane had tons of questions and the other parents in the waiting room gave him the stink eye as he left, probably because he took up so much of the doctor's time. Well, tough shit.

By the following evening his little man seemed to be acting more himself. Shane vacuumed and spread a blanket out on the floor along with several toys. He didn't have much. There was a used baby toy store he passed on the way home from work he wanted to stop by next time he got paid. Right now Logan's favorite toy was a rubber spatula.

He compulsively checked his phone, but other than a few texts from the guys there was nothing. He didn't know why he expected Kate to call. She never had before, but for some reason he found himself wishing she would.

When he was done for the night he sat on the floor with his back to the couch and played his acoustic as Logan sang and gurgled along. Logan liked being serenaded so Shane sang him some Jack Johnson and rolled into a bit of *Somewhere Over the Rainbow.*

Logan's eyes grew heavy. He blinked slowly and rolled to his back. His hands balled into pudgy fists and played over his face. Shane quietly watched as he played, finding it therapeutic to observe his little man discovering new things at every turn.

As his fingers gently strummed the notes Logan grew more and more sleepy. He played on, singing softly, turning the riff into a soft lullaby. Logan was sound asleep by the time he crooned the verse about clouds being far behind.

Shane played out the song, ending on a slow harmonic pull of his voice. Grinning, he placed his guitar on the couch, and carried Logan to his crib.

~

"HOLY SHIT! You gotta come look at the steamer I just left in your toilet," Duce shouted from the bathroom.

"No thanks, man."

His friend peeked around the corner. "Seriously, my nickname should be The Riddler. It's a perfect question mark!"

"I'll pass."

The toilet flushed and Duce came into the living room. "Your loss. That was some impressive shit. Literally."

Shane flipped through the weekly saver and ignored his friend.

Duce plopped down in the chair and picked up the remote. "What's up with you today?"

Shane tilted his head. "What do you mean?"

"You're all quiet."

He shrugged. "I don't have anything to say."

Duce's phone buzzed and he glanced at it. "Lisa's having some friends over. Tucker wants us to go there."

"You know I can't do that. I have Logan." He spotted a coupon for formula and tore it out.

"You could bring him."

"I don't think so." On the next page there was a buy one get one free on diaper rash cream. It wasn't the kind he usually used, but the price was good.

Duce sighed. "I'm bored."

"Then go over to Lisa's."

A few minutes passed. "I bet Sue will be there."

"Then I'm sure Sims will too."

His friend's stare irritated his senses like little needles over his nerves. "I thought you were into her?"

"I'm not into girls my friends have been in."

He snorted. "No way Sims made it that far. He's a total ball bag around girls. Doesn't know how to talk to them. We should go over there just to see him make an ass out of himself."

"No thanks."

When Shane finished going through the circular he'd clipped about ten good coupons. He stacked them up and tossed the rest. In the kitchen he rinsed out his cup and made a bottle for Logan. He'd be getting up soon.

"Next month Logan's going to be able to have cereal. That's gonna be cool to give him actual food."

Duce frowned at him in confusion. "What, like Lucky Charms and shit?"

"No, it's like oatmeal sort of. He can't have real food for a while still." Duce continued to stare at him as if he had three heads. "What?"

"I think you need to get out."

"I went out last night," Shane reminded him.

"Yeah, to play a gig. When's the last time you went out just to hang?"

Shane shrugged and washed his hands. "I haven't felt like it. Besides, I already have Lisa babysitting three times a week while I'm playing at the Moosen. I can't afford another night of babysitting *and* the cost of a night out."

"But you're getting paid decent."

"Money's tight. If you want to go out, go. No one's holding you hostage."

Duce's lips pursed as he flipped through the channels. After a while he said, "Sims said your caseworker's hot."

"Sims can keep his fucking eyes and opinions to himself."

Duce faced him, a wide grin slowly crawling over his face. "Aw, you like her."

Shane pulled out a diaper and the box of wipes. Logan usually pooped around this time of day. "Shut up."

"I only saw her real quick one time, but she looked all right."

Shane shrugged, pretending he wasn't interested. She was more than all right. Anyone who didn't see how cute she was, had a vision problem.

"You gonna ask her out?"

"Dunno."

"You put the moves on her yet?"

"What are you writing a fucking book?"

"No. Just asking. Dude, what the fuck are you doing? The kid's sleeping."

Shane looked down at the artillery he'd set up on the coffee table. He had the yoga mat, a diaper, the wipes, the butt paste, and a bottle. "He's gonna wake up soon."

Duce shook his head. "I think you need a break from all this. You're clipping coupons, your place's clean, pretty soon you're gonna start jarring homemade applesauce and shit like that Diane Keeton chick in that *Baby Boom* movie. Where's the old Shane?"

He frowned. He hadn't changed that much, only in matters where Logan was concerned, which just so happened to touch every part of his life. So what if he'd been slightly overhauled by a three month old? He was becoming more responsible as a result of all of it. Nothing wrong with that.

Before he could formulate an answer Logan woke up. He stood and went to get him. When he returned he laid him on the mat and undid his diaper. Duce made a gagging sound. "What the hell is in that formula?"

"Babies poop," Shane said, as he went about changing him.

"Maybe *he* should be called The Riddler," Duce mumbled.

As Shane leaned back to feed Logan, Duce dropped the remote on the table and stood. "I'm gonna take off."

"All right."

He hesitated by the door, keys to the roller skate in his hand. "You should come. Lisa's not gonna let things get crazy. You could bring the kid."

"No. Were just gonna hang here."

"Suit yourself."

~

THE FOLLOWING day Shane stopped at the used baby toy store. There was a ton of stuff. It was all clean and in great shape. He couldn't wait until Logan was a bit bigger and could play on the big plastic slides and baby equipment. For now, however, he had his eye on a baby swing and a mat with all sorts of plush rattles dangling from two cross arches.

The mat was only ten dollars, but the swing was forty. He had about twenty dollars he could spare. He bought the mat and left, wondering if he should have held off and saved up for the swing.

That night he sat down and did the bills. Things were really tight. After his lot rent and car payment he had practically nothing left. He had to start shutting out lights and conserving water. His utilities were killing him. He'd cut back on personal bullshit, like beer, and also called the cable company to change his service package. But even after

those cut backs he was still barely getting by.

The following day he did something extreme he knew he'd catch a bunch of shit from
the guys for. With a heavy heart, he packed up
his game station and all his games and drove it
to the refurbishing place on Route 9. He
walked out with a hundred and seventy bucks
and that night he walked into his home with a
swing and a bag full of baby clothes. It was a
bittersweet feeling he decided was more sweet
than bitter.

It'd been a week since he'd seen or heard
from Kate. He debated calling her, but didn't
have a valid casework related excuse. He was
getting the impression she was going to act like
nothing happened. At one point he even called
the Children and Youth office to ask a question
about his court date, well aware his hearing
was scheduled for September first, but he
wanted a reason to call.

It was stupid. He didn't even talk to Kate.
Some receptionist asked for his social security
number and looked on a computer and gave
him the date, probably right before making a
note in his file that he was a forgetful douche.

By Friday he was pissed off. Wasn't she supposed to be doing a job? Shouldn't she be
keeping a better eye on them? He knew she
was only expected to visit every few weeks, but
he'd gotten used to seeing her. Logan even ad-

mitted he missed the nice woman with the cardigans.

The Moosen Grill was working out great for both him and the owner. He'd started drawing a crowd and Arty asked him to continue playing through the summer months.

Lisa agreed to continue babysitting until she started up her night classes again in August, at which point he'd have to make other arrangements. But he'd cross that bridge when he got to it.

He was just opening up his second set on Friday, the dinner crowd thick, when he did a double take. He was singing a cover of Crosby, Stills, Nash and Young's *Ohio* when his fingers slipped. Luckily the crowd didn't take notice.

His mind blanked and he quickly fumbled for the right note as his eyes set on Kate standing by the door. Not Kate the barfly, but Kate the caseworker. Dressed in a pristine white cardigan and a pale blue sundress, her golden hair hung loose around her face and she had that shiny stuff on her lips. Her shoes were little gold slippers with bows.

A slow grin split his face, making it difficult for his mouth to climb over the words. It was hard not to sing her name so she saw him. She worked her way through the crowd and his eyes followed her. It was awesome she was here. Did she come to see—

His face harden.

She smiled as she approached a booth along the far wall. A man with a blond buzz cut wearing a pansy ass pink polo shirt stood. When he leaned in to kiss her cheek Shane's jaw clenched.

Who the fuck was this tool bag?

Kate blushed and slid into the booth. Her blushes were supposed to be for him, not dweebs who wore pink button up collars. The waitress arrived at their table and he watched them order. Was she on a date?

Shane finished out the song and took a swig from his water bottle. Should he say hi? Maybe play her a song? Completely thrown, he referred to his list of songs and moved on to the next one. He tore into an acoustic version of Petty's *American Girl* and observed them.

She nodded and smiled and even laughed from time to time. His blood boiled. This was bullshit. She hadn't called or come to see him in over a week. Didn't she want to know how Logan was doing?

It usually didn't bother him to simply be background noise, but tonight it did. Not once did she look up to see who was playing. Instead, she was totally engrossed in whatever the pink panther was saying.

He finished out his second set and placed his guitar on the stand. Climbing off the stage, he headed to her booth. As he approached, her date was in the middle of some anecdote, probably about how gay he was, and she was smiling.

When he reached their table the pink panther stopped talking and looked up at him. Kate turned, following his gaze. Her eyes grew wide the second she recognized him.

"Shane."

"Hi, Kate."

"What are you doing here?" Her hand touched her hair in what he would guess was a sign of nervousness.

He tipped his chin toward the stage. "I play here." He stared at her and added, just to be a smart ass, "It's a gig."

"Oh."

"You look nice."

She glanced down at her outfit and blushed. *That's right.* My *blushes.*

"Um, Shane, this is Blake. Blake, this is Shane."

The date eyed him critically. It was clear he was trying to figure out how he and Kate were connected. Shane nodded, but didn't offer to shake the other man's hand.

"You never called."

She frowned and glanced apprehensively back at Blake. Who had a name like Blake? *Where's your tennis racket,* Blake?

"Shane and I have a mutual acquaintance," she quickly explained.

What? What the fuck? He glared at her. Was

that all he was? A fucking case? "Logan's doing better, by the way," he said snidely. He waited all this time to see her, never once expecting she'd be on a fucking date. He didn't mean to be a jerk, but there was no hiding his irritation.

Her expression looked relieved and guilty. "Good. I had wondered…"

"Had you?"

She narrowed her eyes at him. Was she wearing eye shadow? "Yes."

He shrugged, pretending indifference. "Oh, I couldn't tell."

Her eyes narrowed further and her tentative smile morphed into a thin straight line. He had no claim to her, but he wanted one. He at least wanted to know she didn't always go around kissing guys the way she had kissed him.

He was second guessing everything now. And on top of that, he was just standing there like creepy band guy intruding on their freaking date. Damn it.

The conversation was over. "Well, I gotta get back to work. Enjoy your *date*." He turned and walked back to the stage before she could say another word.

When he sat back down on the stool he saw her talking. She was probably making excuses to *Blake*. Her motions were flustered. He should probably feel bad, but he didn't. He hoped he ruined their night. Yeah, he was that immature.

His hand gripped his guitar and his fingers strummed the strings hard. The beat was quick and accusing as he pounded out Maroon 5's *Wake Up Call*. His gaze drilled into her as she frantically spoke to her date. As he sang he poured his anger into the lyrics.

Her gaze suddenly jerked to his. His eyes narrowed and he articulated each word, making sure she heard every cutting lyric.

Color rushed to her cheeks and she blinked quickly, her hand on her purse. His fingers strummed harder as he belted out the lines of betrayal and being a fool. She stood and her date followed. The pink panther turned and glared at him. The guy was taller than he appeared sitting in the booth. His pants were pleated. He was nothing like Shane and everything like the kind of man he could see Kate dating.

After some fast-talking, Kate put down her purse and went to the ladies room. The date glared at him again and finally took his seat. So they were staying.

Shane ended the song and went into some Beatles, his eyes never leaving the door to the ladies room. When she returned she resolutely kept her gaze away from the stage. She looked upset and that was when his guilt finally appeared.

Their waitress brought over more drinks. The date continued, but now without the presence of blushes or smiles. His anger subsided and shame settled heavy and unwelcome in his gut. He was a jerk.

She wasn't his girlfriend. She was his caseworker, his caseworker who let him kiss and touch her. He didn't want this douche bag putting his mouth where his had been. It occurred to him that his childish tantrum may have only increased the unfavorable outcome of Kate hitting it off with the pink panther, since Shane so easily shoved his lesser qualities into the light.

Here he was, a juvenile jerk, and there Blake was, all sympathetic and mature. Fuck. The guy probably had a really good job too.

He'd pissed her off and now this guy was going to swoop in and be all sweet and listen to her as she complained about him. He suddenly wanted to make her smile return, but not because she was on a date. *He* wanted to be the one to put a smile on her face.

He finished with the Beatles and cleared his throat. "This is something new I've been playing around with, so pardon me if it comes out kind of rough. It's an old throwback to the eighties. If there're any Goonies in the audience…this one's for you."

Her gaze turned to his. Whatever she'd been saying was forgotten. Mouth slack, she watched him, a slight crease between her tapered brows.

He concentrated on the rhythm, trying hard to find it. He'd played the song a few times for Logan, it having stuck in his head since the night they'd watched *Goonies*, but Cyndi Lauper was no easy talent to mimic.

Once he found the beat he rode it for a while, getting the feel. The intro was longer than it should have been, but it was working for him. He practically whispered the first few lines, wondering if he was making an ass out of himself.

The second line he sang a bit clearer. As he sung about unspoken expectations the audience's curiosity grew and their expressions told him they were trying to place the old tune. It was likely hard to recognize done unplugged like this.

When he rocked the chorus about being good enough and belted out the *ya, ya, ya, ya,* people whistled and clapped, finally placing the throwback. And there it was, her smile, worth more than all the tips in his jar.

They left before he finished his last set, but he believed he mended some of the damage. He'd have to wait until he saw her again to find out. When he packed up, his fingers were sore and his back tired. Driving home was a challenge and he had to be up for work in five hours.

Once he got home, Lisa whispered a goodbye and he went to check on his little sleeping angel. Shane was detaching from the man he used to be, sort of lost, but heading somewhere good. He was getting a feel for this parenting thing, doing the work the best he could.

He patted Logan's back and wished him sweet dreams. That night Shane dreamt of soft cardigans and dainty gold shoes. There were no pink shirts to speak of.

CHAPTER 12

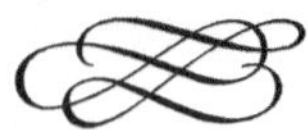

The following six days proved a trial in patience. Kate hadn't been to check on them in over two weeks, so with each passing day he knew she'd eventually show. She had to. Anticipation intensified until he was ready to burst.

On Thursday, when he heard the sound of her little VW bug pulling into his lot his stomach tightened. *Finally.*

He went to the door and waited as she climbed out. When she stood, she paused and stared at him for the briefest moment, her expression unreadable. She bent and retrieved her bag then stiffly walked to his trailer.

"Hey," he said as he held the door open for her. Excitement pummeled his gut.

She went in and waited. Logan slept peacefully in his swing as it rocked back and forth. He directed her to the kitchen table and she sat.

All business, she began pulling out her notebook and a pen. "How are you?" she asked.

"I'm good. How about you?"

"I'm good, thank you." She opened her book and scribbled a date in the top right corner of the page. "Tell me how things have been going?"

Okay, she wanted to get business out of the way first. He could do that. "Things have been good. I've been busy. Working. Logan's started sleeping a straight six hours through the nights which is good and bad."

"Why bad?" She made notes, her eyes never leaving the page.

"Well, not bad, it's just some mornings I have to leave for work and he's still sleeping. I hate having to wake him to get ready, but I can't be late."

"You've been back to work, still on the same job?"

"Yes, same job. I should be done there in a week or so and then my union rep will send me somewhere else."

"Same hours?"

"Usually."

Her pen moved. As she filled in a full page of notes she turned the page and continued writing. "Tell me more about Logan. Has he visited the pediatrician lately?"

"Yes. He was vaccinated last week. That sucked."

She scribbled, the sound of her scratchy pen abrading his nerves. "Has he moved to cereal?"

"Yes. He loves it. I think that's part of the reason he's sleeping better. He isn't as hungry as often as when he was only on formula."

"Did you get your certification in the mail from your class?"

"Yeah, a few weeks ago." He frowned. She still hadn't looked at him.

"There've been no other incidences I should know about?"

He raised his brow. "Like what?"

"Any accidents? Trouble with childcare? Injuries?"

"Are you asking if Logan's been hurt?"

Her mouth opened and closed. "I…no. I just need to know if there's been any incidences."

His eyes narrowed. She knew he'd never place Logan in a dangerous situation. Didn't she? "No. No *incidences.*"

She nodded tightly and placed her pen in her book and shut it. Looking to her left, clearly avoiding eye contact, she said, "I need to check the cabinets."

His molars locked down. He stood. "Go ahead."

He watched as she silently walked through his kitchen. The cabinets looked nothing like they had during her first visit. The shelves were stocked with canisters of cereal, bottles, and tiny plastic bowls. The drawers were organized with bibs and baby spoons. The fridge was filled with milk, eggs, and fresh deli products and other necessities.

"Are you using the food stamps?"

His lip twitched as his manhood withered. "Yes," he rasped. His hand coasted over his hair. Did she have to ask him about that?

She nodded and returned to the table. Her hair was in a low ponytail. She wore no non-sense brown pants and a coral colored sweater set. "Your court date's scheduled for less than two months from now. You're required to fill out this questionnaire. Next time I visit I'll get it from you. It talks about how you're adjusting to your guardianship and asks questions about various parts of parenting."

"Is it a test?"

"More of a survey. There are no wrong answers."

He found that hard to believe. She packed away her book and stood. Was she leaving?

"You'll be seeing me again sometime over the next two weeks."

Two weeks? That was bullshit.

She pulled the strap of her bag over her shoulder and headed to the door. He panicked but couldn't think of anything to say that would make her stay. *You're losing her, asshole.*

She paused without looking directly at him. "Do you have any questions?"

No way. She was not leaving like this. "How was your date?"

Her gaze finally met his. Her eyes narrowed. "Don't, Shane."

He stepped closer. Her hand fidgeted with her bag. "Don't what?"

"Don't do this."

"Do what?"

"You know what."

He stepped closer again, crowding her in his doorway. "Tell me. What is it I'm doing?"

She looked down, her chest rising as her breathing accelerated and she licked her lips. "You're making me uncomfortable."

He hesitated a second, but his instincts told him she was just scared, not of him, but of how he might make her feel. "How?"

She frowned, her gaze fused to the floor. She wore plain brown shoes. Was she trying to deter him by dressing down? Shaking her head she whispered, "We can't do this."

"What are we doing?" He lifted his hand and slowly traced his thumb along the delicate line of her jaw.

"Please don't," she whispered, voice trembling.

"Why?" If she didn't like him, fine. But he felt their chemistry. She had to feel it too.

"Because it's inappropriate. I could lose my job."

And he could lose Logan. If he had to choose, his loyalty was to his nephew, but they were just talking. No one else was there to report them. He needed to know what was going on in her head. "Do you feel nothing for me, Kate? Am I really just another case to you?"

Her throat worked as she swallowed. In a small voice, she repeated, "I can't lose my job."

But someone would have to tell on them for that to happen. He didn't intend to go bragging to the judge. Would she? If she could just trust him… "I have something on the line too."

"Exactly." Her face turned but he didn't back down. She licked her lips again and tucked a strand of blonde hair behind her ear. "It doesn't matter what we feel. This is wrong."

He understood there were rules, but sometimes people made exceptions. Was she using ethics as an excuse? Maybe she realized he was just a loser who could barely support himself. If this was about him, he wanted to hear her say it, but the last time they were together, he'd showed her how vulnerable he could be and she hadn't laughed in his face. He didn't believe she could suddenly be that superficial. "Tell me the truth."

"The truth is irrelevant. The only truth that matters is that I'm your caseworker and this can't happen."

"I'd never sabotage you. I like you, Kate. I like you a lot," he whispered, bringing his lips a breath away from hers.

Her chest rose and fell as her breathing became labored. Her eyes slowly shut. If he wasn't standing so close, he never would have heard her breathe his name. "Shane." There was so much longing in that one word. It was the plea, the confession he needed.

His lips pressed to the corner of her mouth and he kissed her softly, implying that he wanted more. He tried to coax her lips apart, but they didn't budge, despite her body softening. He continued to kiss her anyway.

"Please stop."

He stilled. He didn't want to manipulate her. He only wanted her to admit she felt a quarter of what he felt for her. She sounded as if she were about to cry. Easing back he looked at her. Her brow puckered, a pained expression weighing on her face. "Why?"

"I told you why."

"Give me a better reason."

Suddenly her lashes lifted and she glared at him. "I'm not interested."

His breath seized in his lungs. Her rejection stung more than it should have. He suspected she was lying, but he wasn't completely sure. It irritated him that she might lie to him, yet he didn't have the confidence to one hundred percent trust that a girl like Kate could actually like a guy like him. It made more sense for her *not* to be interested. That hurt.

Staring into her eyes, he saw nothing but certainty and stepped back. "Because you're my caseworker?"

"Because of a lot of things, but yes, that's the main reason."

He considered that for a moment, refusing to accept she had zero interest in him. Maybe it was complicated and that was tricky, but she had to feel something. Giving her some space, he said, "I think you're full of shit."

She gasped, anger flashing in her whiskey brown eyes. "You don't know me well enough—"

"I know you just fine." It wasn't fair she could judge him based on a few meetings and a peek in his cabinets and assume he wasn't making his own observations. "I see what you're doing. Coming in here all buttoned up like you did that first day. You never answered my question. How was your date?"

Her shoulders trembled as she silently seethed, her breath coming fast. "That's none of your business." Her nose tipped up and, though she was several inches shorter than him, it implied she was looking down at him.

"Was he everything you dreamed he'd be? I bet he was, in his designer polo with his parted hair. Let me guess, Ivy League graduate, probably majored in something dreadfully dull, but highly lucrative. He speaks at least one other language. Doesn't like spicy food and only does it missionary—on Tuesdays—with his socks still on."

He nearly shit himself when her palm collided sharply with his face. She slapped him. *She fucking slapped him.*

Her eyes burned with anger. "You're a pig."

He got in her face and growled, "I'm real, which is more than I can say for that Sears mannequin you went out with last week."

Moment over, she glared at him, shoving her finger in his chest. "Who I go out with or what I do in my free time's none of your business."

"What about when your tongue was in my mouth only a few weeks before you started playing bachelorette with Tobin County's most lame bachelor? Was it my business then?"

She shifted her bag and tried to get by. He blocked her exit. He'd obviously overestimated her affection. It hurt and he probably shouldn't provoke her, but if she was going to lay him out he was gonna call her on it.

"Just admit it, Kate. You think you're better than me. Well, you're probably right. You're also better than that douche bag you were out with the other night. But if you're going to act like you don't feel the chemistry between us, you're a liar."

She was stressing over her job security, but

in two months when he proved he was the right guardian to the courts and she was no longer his caseworker, none of that would matter. Couldn't she see that?

Her voice suddenly snapped, "I don't go out with guys like you."

He drew back. Okay, maybe it was more than her job security. "What's that supposed to mean?"

She was clearly exasperated and no longer choosing her words carefully. "You're a child. You sleep all day and play video games all night. Your balanced diet consists of Slim Jims, beer, and God knows what else. You have tattoos and long hair and work in bars singing and playing guitar."

Every word was like a punch to his manhood. "So fucking what? And half that shit isn't even true. I've changed since Logan—"

"But for how long? I've seen where you live. I've met some of your friends. We're too different, Shane. All this..." she waved a hand, encompassing his trailer. "This isn't me. It's you."

His lips pressed together. He could have said a million things to put her in her place, but the truth was the truth, and her words killed him. Rather than continue to argue, he quietly admitted, "I'm a simple man, Ms. McAlister. I don't go around pretending to be someone I'm not. All I want is my own quiet piece of this world. You come here and look in my cabinets and think that's enough to decide what kind of person I am, but you're wrong. When I was younger I did a lot of dumb shit, but I never hurt anyone. I just wanna live my life and not be judged for being who I am."

They were both shaking. Things had definitely taken an unexpected turn and he saw no way of reviving the tender feelings he thought they shared.

He ran his hand over his hair. "Guess that's a little hard when you're paid to judge me." He stepped back from the door, giving her plenty of space to leave. "I'm taking Logan to the Poconos with some friends next weekend so we won't be here. Rest assured, he'll be fed and cared for in a manner the state would find acceptable."

"Shane..." Her head lowered, her voice shaking, but he wasn't sure if it shook with anger, regret, or pity.

He didn't want her fucking pity. "Goodbye, Ms. McAlister."

She hesitated and then quietly left. Whatever he thought they shared no longer existed in his mind. All possibilities of getting to know her better vanished the moment she pulled away.

CHAPTER 13

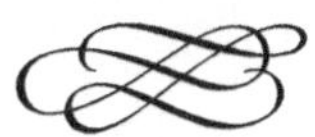

Over the next two weeks Shane threw himself into work. They'd gone to the Poconos where Lisa's family had a house and it was a nice break. Lisa had four girlfriends there and they all doted over Logan. He was a lady-killer.

Her one friend, Tammy, had really taken a liking to Logan. After he put him to bed the first night, she sat by the fire out back with Shane and asked a whole bunch of questions about babies. The second night they drank around the fire as he played guitar. Tammy stayed up later than everyone else and they talked. He even talked about Noel, which he didn't usually do.

She was a nice girl. It became clear she was interested in him on the second night.

Logan woke up and Shane had gone to get

him back to sleep. When he came out of the bedroom, shutting the door quietly, she was waiting for him. They'd hung in the dim hallway for a few minutes and the next thing he knew they were kissing. Her kisses tasted like sweet tea and vodka.

After that initial kiss she'd invited herself to sit by him and touch his leg the rest of the night. She was throwing out clear invitations for more, but Shane wasn't feeling it. Using Logan as an excuse, he'd snuck back into his room and had gone to sleep alone.

Sue was also there, but Sims had moved in on that territory. He was actually glad. Turned out Sue had an annoying habit of hitting people when she laughed. And her laugh, after a few drinks, resembled a cat's cries when in heat. He'd dodged a serious bullet there.

As the weekend dwindled to an end, Shane found himself anxious to return home. While everyone else made a sport out of getting wasted, he'd remained surprisingly sober.

On Sunday he left early and forced Duce to drive with him so there wouldn't be room for anyone else. The following week he was transferred to a new job site and looking at another few weeks of steady work.

Logan was growing like a weed. His first tooth broke through and he was picking up new tricks left and right. His most recent thing was his awesome belly flop dance. The public wasn't ready for it yet, but he was a trendsetter. Shane had no doubt they'd be doing it in all the cool clubs soon.

It was mid-July and Shane's birthday was coming up so he decided to do something special for himself. He'd arranged for Lisa to babysit so he and his boys could go out and blow off some steam. It was the first time he really allowed himself to drink in months, but he didn't go crazy.

It was difficult to let go like he used to. What if there was an emergency and he needed to be sober? Rather than throw away money on booze, their plans took a detour and he and the guys went to an establishment they'd frequented many times in the past.

"How's this look?" Chris, an old friend with a bright blue Mohawk and several lip piercings, asked as he held up a sheet of paper.

Shane smiled. "Awesome. What do you guys think?"

The guys looked at the drawing and all agreed it was perfect.

"Where?" Chris asked.

Shane removed his shirt and pointed to his chest. "Right over my heart."

"Nice," Chris commented as he pulled his stool closer to the table.

He pressed the drawing onto Shane's chest and applied water, setting the ink to the skin.

When he handed Shane a mirror he checked out the placement. It was awesome.

The letters *LOGAN* ran beneath the wings of three abstract angels, two smaller ones set back, and one with long flowing hair resembling the virgin mother. The center angel held a harp with the word *NOEL* scrolled over the bar.

When the needle drove into his skin he welcomed the familiar ache. He would forever be a part of him now. His Logan.

When Chris finished he held up a mirror to show Shane the final product. "What do you think?" Shane asked the guys.

They all smiled and nodded. "Beautiful," Sims said.

Duce nodded his head tightly in agreement.

"Come on," Tucker said, interrupting the moment. "Let's go before Duce starts to cry."

"Shut up, man," Duce said, his voice slightly hoarse.

The days following, Shane forced himself to stop obsessing about what Kate had said. She didn't know him. She had no right to judge him. He could waste his time trying to prove her wrong, but the only person he had to prove anything to was himself, himself and Logan. His only concern was that she knew he was a good guardian and gave the courts a good report.

But like an annoying echo, her words kept

rattling around in his head. Some of what she'd said was true. He wasn't offended that she'd insulted him as much as he was concerned that she saw him that way. The curious thing was that his apprehension had nothing to do with her being his caseworker, which it should have had *everything* to do with. He didn't like the idea of Kate holding such a low opinion of him. The fact that her opinion could influence his life only complicated matters more.

He filled out the survey she'd asked him to complete and stuck it with his other papers for the court. When she came to visit the following Thursday she was, again, all business. She asked questions and made a shit load of notes, but never looked him in the eye.

The longer she sat, buttoned up in her little cardigan, the more he grew uncomfortable with the distance between them. She shouldn't have to think of him as anything more than a case, but he wanted her to. He wanted her to like him as a person and not see him as some loser. Maybe he wasn't setting the world on fire, but he wasn't a bad person either. He worked hard and did his best. Well, maybe not his best, but he worked damn hard.

As he watched her write down something about Logan's daycare teacher he frowned. Why did this bother him so much? Growing annoyed with himself, he pushed all thoughts away and tried to focus of the real reason Kate was there—Logan.

This was good, concise, to the point, no bullshit or mixed signals getting in the way. She was here to see how he was doing as a parent and he was there to prove he was a capable adult. Convincing his conscience that this was the best solution—mainly because it was his only choice—was difficult, so he lied to himself.

He decided—telling himself adamantly, but not at all convincingly—that he preferred their meetings this way, so he was surprised when she asked, "Are you still playing at the Grill?"

He looked at her, considering if he should answer. He really couldn't lie if it was about work. "Three nights a week."

"My friends were there about a week ago. They said the singer was great. I wondered if it was you."

He tipped his head to acknowledge the compliment, but said nothing.

"How did Logan like the Poconos?"

She wasn't writing any of this down, so he assumed it wasn't for her report. Working so hard to convince himself their relationship was strictly professional, it wasn't fair for her to blur the lines again. Studying her for a moment, he finally asked, "What are you doing, Kate?"

"What—what do you mean?" Her cheeks flushed. She knew exactly what he meant.

"Is the judge going to ask how our trip to the mountains went?"

She swallowed and looked down. "I was just trying to make small talk."

"Why?" He honestly didn't know. And it wasn't cool to throw him off when he'd finally started to accept that she didn't want him as a friend or anything more than a case.

She shrugged. "I just thought maybe we should talk."

He frowned. About them? She said there wasn't a "them". He was trying to give her what she supposedly wanted. Was the distance getting to her?

He wanted to believe she missed him, but she'd given no sign of such emotions. Her sudden interest in his personal affairs threw him. He didn't want to get too excited. If this was just about Logan, she should be writing it down. Maybe she made notes after she left. And if this were all about the courts, she'd shoot him down the moment he trespassed on *her* personal territory.

It seemed there was only one way to test his theory. She was allowed to ask him personal questions, but her personal business was off limits, unless something had changed. "Have you been back on any dates?"

She met his gaze. Was she going to chastise

him for crossing a line again? They stared at each other silently for a long moment until she finally answered. "No."

His heart raced. She didn't shut him down. Maybe she was finally admitting to herself he was more than just a case. Almost afraid to ask, he rasped, "Why not?"

They stared at each other for another long while. Her mouth tightened as if she were holding a pretty serious mental debate. "You can trust me, Kate. I'd never do anything to deliberately hurt you or jeopardize your job. I'm a fairly decent friend."

Her eyes shut briefly and he wanted to know what she was thinking. "I shouldn't be talking to you like this. It's unethical. My personal life stays out of it."

"But you don't want that?"

She sighed. It wasn't an agreement of any sort, but he took it as such. Slowly sliding his palm across the table, he let his fingertips graze her. It was a barely existent caress, but her gaze latched on to his the moment his fingers brushed hers. "Tell me why you haven't gone on anymore dates," he whispered.

Her finger grazed his. Her nails were trimmed in a neat little row. She pulled her palm back and he assumed the moment was over. Then she surprised the shit out of him by admitting, "Because the idea of socks and missionary only on Tuesdays terrifies me."

His jaw nearly hit the floor. God damn she was a cool chick. Trying to play it cool himself, he teased, "Yeah, that should definitely only happen on Fridays and sometimes Mondays."

She laughed then looked regretful. Her brow pinched as her gaze shifted to his. "I'm sorry about what I said."

Perhaps he was so drawn to her, because she continuously surprised him. He hadn't expected her to revisit the topic of them. Nor had he expected her to toss sex into the combo. But most unexpected was her apology.

He didn't want to care that she was sorry. He wanted to be over it and be able to say her words didn't affect him, but they did. She'd cut him down by pointing out exactly who he was, making him feel less than good enough. At first he was angry, but then he'd slowly admitted she hadn't really said anything that wasn't true. This was who he was.

"What happened to Blake?"

She grimaced and he held his breath. That prick better not have crossed a line with her or Shane didn't know what he'd do. Her eyes closed as if recalling something painful or embarrassing. He braced himself, hoping he didn't have to track the pink panther down and make a rug out of him.

Quietly, she mumbled, "He asked what a Goonie was."

His head fell back as he barked out a laugh. "Are you kidding? Was he raised under a rock?"

She laughed. "At one point I felt like I was out with Emilio Estevez's character in *The Breakfast Club*, right before he cries."

"Oh no," he laughed again, totally understanding the comparison.

Her giggles faded and her face lowered. There was something real in that moment, something intangible, but impossible to ignore. Kate wasn't meant to be as cold as she led the world to believe. He wasn't even sure why she'd want to hide the sweet girl he sometimes glimpsed behind the façade.

His laughter died. He nudged her knee with his. "Are you Claire?"

She drew in a deep breath and sat back in her seat. "I don't know." What she did next was probably one of the all-time highest ranking cool chick moves he'd ever been witness to in his life.

Her fingers swept her hair over her shoulder and undid her earring. It was a perfect diamond stud. She attached the clasp, reached for his hand, uncurled his fingers, and closed them over it.

He was totally the John Bender to her Claire.

His fingers bent over the stud and he smiled. "Did you just Ringwald me?"

She smirked, her eyes a little sad. "I believe I did."

He fisted her earring and dropped his hand to his lap. There was no way he was giving it back. His heart raced as he brain tried to figure out what this meant. "What now?" Was this a green light? Was she throwing caution to the wind? God, he hoped so.

She shrugged, a bashful tilt to her eyes. Letting out a jagged breath, she admitted, "There are a hundred reasons not to go back to where we were, but I can't seem to get past that night."

Me neither. "What about your job?"

She swallowed, as her gaze turned pleading. "No one can know." His head shook, assuring her he wouldn't say a word. "And you can't be upset when I have to do my job. I can't let my personal feelings cloud my judgment. No matter which way you look at it, it's completely unethical for us to have anything more than a professional relationship."

"But?"

Her hands fidgeted in her lap as she bit her lip. "But… the feelings are there. I can't make them go away. I should have your case reassigned—"

"No."

"—but I don't want to delay your life any more than necessary. You're a good guardian and it isn't fair to Logan to start the process all over with a new caseworker. My asking for a reassignment could also give the wrong impression about the job you're doing, which I don't want to do."

That was all true. He didn't want anyone thinking there was something so wrong with him that Kate couldn't work with him. That would be bad. He also didn't want to lose the time he'd invested. It weighed on him, knowing his custody could still be revoked. The sooner his court date came the better.

"I don't want another caseworker. I want you. You know me and you know Logan."

"Exactly. So…I don't really know how to proceed."

Shane really had to concentrate on playing it cool. "Why don't we just hang out and keep it honest. You know I like you. I'd like to know you better, but there's no rush." He just couldn't deal with her shutting him out again.

"I've never *hung* out with anyone like you."

"Meaning?"

"You're…"

"Rough?" he supplied.

She shook her head. "That's not the right word. I'm not sure what to call you."

"Why don't you try not to put a label on me and I'll offer the same courtesy to you?"

Her head shook and he secretly smirked at how nervous she appeared. He liked that he could set her a little off balance. She'd knocked him clean on his ass plenty of times, so off balance seemed a fair trade.

"Okay," she agreed on a soft exhalation.

He wasn't sure what to do. Did he kiss her? Ask her out on a date? Just then Logan announced he was awake. Shane stood then turned back to her. "Don't leave."

Her smile was shy. "Okay."

He went in the bedroom and found Logan rocking his moves in his crib. He quickly changed his diaper and snapped up his shorts. "We have company, little man," he said as he carried him into the living room. Logan squawked his approval when he saw Kate. Shane put him in the highchair and fastened him in.

"He's getting so big," she commented, leaning over and whispering sweet words to him. Logan shamelessly flirted. Shane totally understood. He was a sucker for her too.

"I know. He's such a cool kid. Watch this." Shane squatted in front of the highchair so he was eye level with him. He pulled his lips over his teeth and pretended to eat Logan's hand. Logan squealed and let out a deep belly laugh.

When Kate laughed in concert he turned and smiled at her. She was so pretty. He wanted to kiss her. But not in front of the children.

He stood and mixed together some cereal,

coming back to nibble Logan here and there. As he passed Kate he took a nibble of her neck. She squealed too. He loved her laugh, loved breaking her little by little out of her shell.

She watched as he fed Logan. "Aw, he's showing off, eating all good in front of his lady caller." Logan yodeled and stretched. Such a flirt. Shane leaned in and whispered, "Laying it on a little thick, don't ya think, buddy?"

Logan spit a mouth full of goopy cereal out, which dribbled down his chin. "Now you're just being a show-off," Shane admonished.

Kate giggled and went to get a napkin. She blotted up Logan's face and he batted his long lashes at her. Shane swore he saw something in her melt. If only Shane had moves like that.

Once he finished feeding him, he rested Logan on the floor with some toys. Kate slipped off her shoes and joined him. Her toe-nails were painted green today.

Shane pinched her big toe, which really wasn't big at all. "You're a surprise, Ms. Mc-Alister."

She stilled, a touch of self-consciousness showing in her eyes. "What do you mean?"

Shane stretched out beside Logan. "I mean, I can't figure you out and I like that."

She shook her head, modestly disagreeing. "I'm boring." Her hand scooted a rattle Logan had been eyeing within his reach.

"You're far from boring," he informed her, his mind going over some of the many fascinating parts of Katherine McAlister. He hid a smile, mentally picturing her sweet, little, heart shaped ass, her dainty, bold colored toenails. Not every woman could pull off preppy *and* vintage punk.

She was classy and sophisticated, yet fun and silly. Originally, he found her unapproachable, but the more he got to know her, the more he realized she was had a story of her own. His goal was to make her an open book. Katherine was Kate and he wanted to learn the multifaceted woman hiding behind the simple name.

She met his gaze and energy pulled between them. Shane shifted, his body growing inappropriately hard. "You shouldn't look at me like that in front of the child."

Her lashes lowered, as her face tipped away hiding a kissable smirk. "Sorry."

He wanted to groan when her cheeks flushed. She was killing him. "Don't be. If we were alone right now…"

Her lips parted as curiosity stole over her eyes. "You'd what?"

He laughed, enjoying how familiar her expressions were becoming and knowing which ones hinted of hidden desires. He longed to know all of her desires. "Oh, the socks would be off."

Her lip twitched and a delicate dimple formed in her cheek.

"Will you come over this Saturday night? I mean, not for work."

She stilled, her eyes studying him. "What time?"

"I put Logan to bed around seven-thirty. Say, eight o'clock? We can order dinner and maybe watch a movie."

Her smile was slow perfection. "All right."

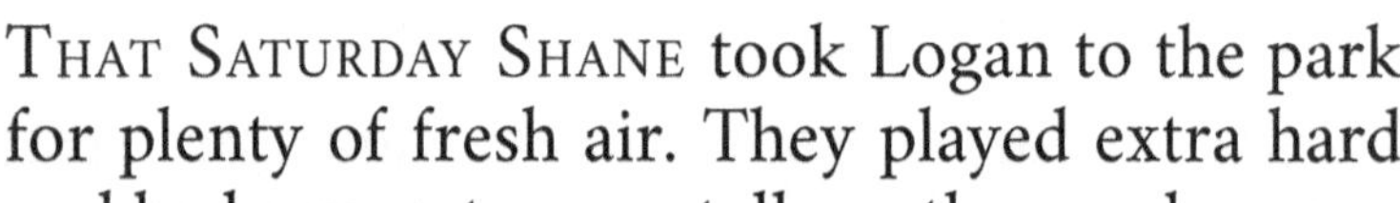

THAT SATURDAY SHANE took Logan to the park for plenty of fresh air. They played extra hard and had a man-to-man talk on the way home.

"Now, I promise to be cool when you start dating if you play it cool tonight. Let's go over some ground rules. No massive diaper explosions in front of the lady friend. I'm sorry, but you've been known to clear out a room. Also, let's try to keep the crankiness to a minimum. I'll let you stay up an extra ten minutes, but you have to agree to not start any trouble once the lights are out."

Logan let out a high-pitched babble.

"I know you like to nap on her boobies, but so do I. And you're too young for that anyway. I'm onto your games."

The baby prattled something that sounded like "Ladle, ladle, ladle…"

"You can be mad all you want. I've given up a lot since you came along. I'm not negotiating this one. Especially if she shows up in the Madonna shirt again."

When they got home Shane cleaned the trailer, paying special attention to the space around the toilet seat and the couch. There wasn't much he could do about his furniture, so he pulled off his bedspread and draped it over the couch, tucking it in like a slipcover so he didn't look too optimistic.

He found a half empty bottle of wine in the fridge and dumped it. Outside, along the perimeter between his property and his neighbor's, tiger lilies grew. He plucked three of the long stemmed orange flowers and carried them inside. Filling the bottle with water, he arranged the flowers and put it on the coffee table as a centerpiece.

He fed Logan an extra heavy dinner that night, making his cereal thicker and leaving him all carbed up and tired. Around seven he did some bicycles on the carpet with him, which led to an impressive poop—Logan's, not his. That would also help him sleep better.

By seven-thirty his little man could barely keep his eyes open—so much for his extended curfew. Shane gave him a bottle and put him to bed.

He grabbed a quick shower, shaved, and pulled his hair into a ponytail. He decided on wearing his favorite Zeppelin shirt and a dark pair of jeans. He left his socks off, opting to go barefoot.

She pulled up at eight on the dot. He cued up his stereo with an unarguably perfect album for seduction. U2's *All I Want is You* opened the evening.

She came to the front door wearing a faded *Back to the Future* t-shirt. Holy shit, if Sims was there he'd be all over that. He held the door for her and tried to hide his nerves. "Hey."

"Hey."

Her shoulders pulled tight as he brushed a kiss over her lips and slowly she relaxed into him. She tasted like cherries. As he pulled away her lashes hung low and her cheeks were flushed.

"I brought this." She held up a bottle of red wine, her hand slightly trembling. "I didn't know if you only drank beer and Wild Turkey, but I figured…"

"Thanks." He took the bottle and placed it in the kitchen, desperately trying to quell the surge of anxiety suddenly assaulting his senses.

"You cleaned." Her face split with a full on smile as she admired the tidy space.

"A little. Do I need to let this breathe or anything?" That's what fancy folk did with wine, right?

She shrugged. "I usually just give my wine mouth to mouth."

Her humor was so unexpected, he laughed. "Sounds good to me." He cracked it open and poured her a glass. "Sorry I don't have any fancy cups."

"That's okay." She took the glass and sipped, turning and looking around the trailer as if it were her first visit. "I like U2."

He smiled. "I like you too. Sorry. That was corny. Did you want to order dinner?"

"Sure. What did you have in mind?"

"There's a Chinese place that delivers or we could do pizza."

"Chinese sounds good."

He went to get the menu off the fridge. Fuck, he was nervous.

"Is Logan asleep?" He peeked back and caught her admiring the new slipcover he finagled.

"Yeah. He was an animal today. We went to the park and he had all the other girls rubber necking from their strollers."

"I bet their mommies were getting an eyeful too." She sat on the couch.

He stilled midstride. "Are you suggesting it wasn't Logan drawing all the attention?"

"Women are suckers for cute dads."

I'm not his dad. He laughed nervously and handed her the menu. She had jeans on and gray plaid slipper shoes. He squeezed her foot. "I like your shoes. You never wear the same ones."

"I'm sort of weird like that. I don't like to repeat outfits."

"So what? Do you follow some sort of wear and toss standard?"

"No, I just remember what I wore and try to not repeat it for a while."

"Did you last wear this in eighty-seven?" he asked, his finger pulling at the sleeve of her t-shirt.

"Are you making fun of me?"

"God, no. If it was in my size I'd totally steal it from you."

She appeared relieved. "I collect retro shirts. It's really from the eighties, you know? Not one of those reproductions they sell at Wal-Mart."

"It's awesome. I love how you can rock your little cardigans and then pull off a vintage classic."

Her smile twitched as she passed him back the menu. "I'll take the chicken lo mein." When he didn't immediately take it, she asked, "What?"

He realized she was nervous too. It was perhaps the most adorable thing ever. "I want to kiss you."

Her lips parted and she seemed to hold her breath. "Okay," she whispered.

He leaned in and gently traced his lips over hers. Cherries. She trembled slightly as he brushed his hand over her shoulder and slipped his palm under her hair and around the back of her neck. As soon as he pressed his lips more firmly to hers she opened.

He breathed deep, wanting to swallow her whole. Her hand came to the side of his face and slid over his ear. Jesus, everywhere she touched him his flesh seemed to purr for more.

Her fingers tugged on his earlobe where he'd stuck her diamond stud and he groaned. He wanted her to touch him everywhere.

Fingers gently trailed over his jaw and to the back of his neck. She played with the damp strands of hair in his ponytail. Shane leaned into her and she eased back. Had he ever wanted anyone like he wanted her?

He needed to slow down. He was already hard and he didn't want to scare her. After a few minutes he pulled back. She stared up at him, her lips a bit swollen and her cheeks flushed.

"Should we order?" he asked.

She nodded, but her eyes said she didn't give a shit about food at the moment. He turned and took in a deep breath. Attempting to walk it off, he stood and went to the kitchen. His dick was so hard he could barely get his phone out of his pocket. Turning, he shifted, attempting to make room in his pants without drawing too much attention to his pre-*dick*-ament.

Jesus, grow up, Shane!

He called and placed the order, not even

sure what he got for himself. When he returned to the couch she was hiding a smirk.

"What?"

"These are nice," she said, motioning to the tiger lilies. "Did you do that for me?"

"Well, you know… you or one of the other women who visit often."

Her smile fell.

"Fuck, Kate, I was kidding!"

"Oh." Her grin was shaky when it returned.

He sat next to her again. She wouldn't meet his gaze so he pinched her chin and turned her face. "Hey, let me make one thing clear. You're it. As long as we're doing this, I don't have any interest in anyone else."

She blinked, relief transparent in her eyes. "Okay."

"I mean it. I'm not a complicated guy. When I say something I mean it. I don't want anyone else."

Her smile grew confident. "Me neither."

Her words shouldn't have hit him so hard, but they did. She wanted him. He drew in a deep breath and released it slowly. This was going to be a long night.

When the food arrived they moved to the kitchen table to eat. They were on their second glass of wine and discussing various things like where Kate went to school, where she grew up.

"I have an older sister who lives in Tennessee."

"What's in Tennessee?" he asked as he worked through his shrimp and rice.

"Her husband. He's in the Army Reserves. They moved there after he finished his time in Italy. They made friends there so they sort of stuck around."

"What about your sister with the two kids?"

"That's Melissa. She lives just outside of Tobin County."

It occurred to him he had no idea where she lived. "Not to sound stupid, but where do you live?"

"In Columbus. I have a small ranch house. Nothing special. It's just me so…"

His brows lifted. "You own your own home? That sounds pretty special to me. Don't discredit it. Some people spend their entire lives trying to own a home."

"Well, I mean, I have a mortgage. It won't technically be mine until I'm in my fifties."

"Still an accomplishment. I told you how we used to have a nice house, but after my parents died and the money ran out, we couldn't make the payments and the bank foreclosed. I know how hard it is to own a home."

"What did you do when you lost the house?"

That had been such a scary time. Noel was only fifteen, three more years until she was an adult. If he couldn't put a roof over her head, the state would have taken her. "That's when we moved to Lakota."

"When did you get the trailer?" she asked.

"When Noel turned eighteen and could be on her own."

Her expression tightened at the mention of his sister. "Were you close?"

"Yes and no. Noel was different. She was smart, but acted entitled in a lot of ways. She definitely had her little sister moments. But when I think back, think about all the times I thought she was just being annoying…now I see it differently."

"Differently how?"

"Like she was trying to get closer to me." His fork pushed around the peas in his rice, sorting them away from the edible parts. "I wasn't always a good brother."

"You were young."

"That's no excuse. The last night I saw her she came looking for help. We had a fight and she left mad. I tried to find her afterward. I looked for months. You'd think in this day and age it would be impossible to lose someone, with all the technology out there. But once her phone got shut off and none of her friends knew where she went, I didn't know where to turn. Then out of the blue there was an officer at my door."

Her eyes softened with empathy. He didn't usually discuss his regrets with others. Vocalizing his mistakes made the shame inexcusable and real. Her head tilted as her fingers fiddled with a fortune cookie wrapper. "How much time passed?"

"Eight months. I didn't even know about Logan."

Her eyes expanded. "What?"

He shook his head. "Last time I saw her she dropped the bomb that she was pregnant. She wanted money for an abortion. I guess she changed her mind." His stomach tightened painfully. "I think of Logan and I can't even believe that was once an acceptable solution to me or her. I can't imagine him not being here. I'm glad she changed her mind."

"So you didn't know you had a nephew?"

"Not until after her funeral." He laughed, imagining how dumb he must have seemed. "I thought I was in trouble when Tabitha found me, like I had to pay off some debt Noel owed or something. I never in my life expected to get a baby out of all this."

A sound of shock escaped her throat as she slowly shook her head. "You've handled it really well."

He smiled and the back of his neck heated. "Thanks. Half the time I don't have a fucking clue what I'm doing, but…"

"But what?" she asked when his words faded.

He shrugged. "I just realized I probably shouldn't be telling you that."

Glancing down, she shook her head and

tsked. "Stop. You should see some of the other parents I'm dealing with. You're doing an amazing job." She hesitated. "To be honest… when I first came here…I thought you were going to fail in a week. I'll be the first to admit I was wrong. You're doing an incredible job, Shane. And Logan loves you."

His head jerked up. "You think he loves me?"

She laughed. "Are you kidding? The kid lights up when he sees you. Of course he loves you. You're all he's got in this world and he knows he can count on you—as much as a four month old can grasp that sort of concept."

Warmth spread through his chest. In a hoarse voice he admitted, "I love him too."

"I know you do."

When they finished eating Kate helped him clear the table. They returned to the couch and Shane changed the CD to Van Morrison. *Tupelo Honey* filled the living room, softening the mood.

When he sat down, she scooted close to his side. He glanced at her and she turned away. They each sort of stared at the television even though nothing was on. Cool fingers slid into his hand and laced through his fingers. They sat, holding hands, listening to the song. It was probably one of the coolest moments of his life, but he didn't know why.

Everything seemed right in that moment.

Kate was there, holding his hand. Logan loved him. He felt…good, balanced. It was as though the planets were suddenly aligned. He didn't want to do anything to mess up this feeling.

Luckily he didn't have to. Kate turned suddenly and climbed onto his lap. He sucked in a breath, not sure what was happening or where such boldness came from. Her arms wrapped around his neck and her lips found his.

He held her hips, sliding his hands over her curves to cup her butt. Her supple body leaned into him, her figure all soft and yielding over his harder parts. He was rock solid in a second. As Van Morrison crooned, he kissed her with everything he had.

He didn't know what the rules were with a girl like Kate, so he fisted his hands behind her to keep himself from going too far. Her sweet mouth pulled at his lips as she ground her body over his. Dear God, she was killing him. He actually feared he'd embarrass himself if she kept moving like that.

Her mouth worked over his jaw as her fingers pulled at the tie holding back his hair. Once she got it undone, she sat back and pulled his hair over his shoulders. "You have such pretty hair," she whispered. "It's so dark and thick."

"Thanks." It wasn't every day a girl said a part of him was pretty, but he took the compliment for what it was.

Her hands moved over his chest and stilled. Her brow puckered and she tilted her head. "Is this the shirt Logan was wearing the first day I visited?"

"Uh, yeah, but it's been washed several times since then."

She smiled. Her touch moved over his arm. She mapped out each tattoo there with her fingertips. It was erotic, the way she explored him.

"Do you have tattoos in other places?"

The side of his mouth kicked up. "Yeah." What would she say if he showed her his newest tat?

Her pupils dilated "I want to see."

"Are you asking me to take off my clothes, Ms. McAlister?"

"You don't have to if you don't want to."

"How about I take off my shirt if you remove the DeLorean?"

She gazed down at her *Back to the Future* shirt. Maybe that was too big of a request—or maybe not. Her hands went the hem of the shirt and it was suddenly on the floor.

Jesus. Her breasts were round and beautiful and encased in a purple lace bra that looked fancier than any shit he'd ever seen before. Even her underwear was out of his league.

"Your turn." Her breath came fast as she waited.

He swallowed. "I think you got ripped off. I can't compete with that."

She leaned in and nipped his earlobe with her teeth. "Drop it like a lead balloon, Zeppelin."

His cock was going to explode. Her mouth seemed to have a straight connection to his body. His heart pounded, pulsing all the way down to his balls. He grabbed the hem of his shirt and lifted. Darkness loomed as he drew the shirt over his head and then he was staring at her once more.

She sobered her smile falling into an unreadable expression. Her hand went to his heart where she traced the still raised edges of his new ink. "This is new?"

"I got it last week."

Her eyes blinked softly as her thumb gently traveled over his heart. "Shane, it's beautiful."

Her finger trailed to his ribs where he had some scrollwork done.

"What does this say?"

"'*Can you help me remember how to smile?*' It's a line from the song *Runaway Train* by—"

"Soul Asylum."

"Yeah," he said quietly, surprised she knew it.

"What does it mean?"

"I got it after I lost my parents."

"How did they die?"

"A train derailed. They were two of the four that didn't survive."

Her brow creased with what he took as

sympathy. Her mouth tightened as she ran her fingers over the verse. "Have you remembered? How to smile?"

"I think so. Logan helps. So do you."

Her eyes met his and there was so much emotion behind her gaze. The blue irises seemed to blaze with hidden secrets. Softly, she whispered, "You scare me, Shane."

He tensed. "Why?"

Her head gently shook. "Because you're nothing like I thought you would be. You have more depth than any guy I've ever known."

He didn't want her to overcomplicate things and take off again. "I'm just a simple man."

"No, you're anything but simple."

His fingers traced the swell of her breast, tripping slowly along the lace-scalloped edge of her bra. "Take this off," he whispered. She hesitated and his voice shook. "Please."

Her arms stretched behind her and she undid the clasp. Purple lace slid down her arms. Her nipples drew tight, like two perfect blushing points. A flush worked its way down her neck, darkening the tips of her breasts to a deep shade of mauve.

Shane leaned forward and closed his mouth over one turgid point. Glancing up at her through his lashes, he watched as her eyes glazed with lust. He sucked and she sifted her fingers through his hair, holding him to her.

He pulled the tip between his teeth and she

moaned. Kissing his way to the other nipple he licked over her curves. Her body moved over his, riding him. His fingers traced up and down her spine. She was so small in his arms, perfect.

Her head lowered and her mouth kissed and licked over his shoulder. Her moans became breathy and pitched a little higher. He wanted to touch more of her.

As if reading his mind, she scooted off his lap and stood between his knees. She gazed down at the bulge in his pants and smirked. Her fingers went to the snap of her jeans and she hesitated, looking to him for some sort of signal.

He was incapable of speech so he nodded tightly. Her fingers undid the button and slowly lowered the zipper. The peek of purple lace had him groaning. Fuck, matching panties. She was a classy lady.

"Don't laugh."

Was she nuts? "Why would I laugh?"

She lowered her jeans, doing a sexy shimmy as they passed the flare of her hips. He couldn't help it. He laughed.

Her mouth tightened, but she was trying not to laugh as well.

He wiped his palm over his lips and stared. "Is that Gizmo?" Right beneath the string of her panties, just at the small of her hip, a gremlin stared back at him. It was only the size of a silver dollar, but there it was.

"They really shouldn't let you get tattoos when you're drunk," she admitted bashfully.

He cracked up. "Do you have any more?"

"No. I learned my lesson."

His mouth pulled to the left. "What happens if you get him wet?"

She pushed his shoulder. "Jerk."

Leaning forward, he placed a kiss right between his fuzzy ears. His hands held her butt, massaging affectionately and her knees softened. She had great curves. "That is, hands down, the hottest mogwai I've ever seen."

She giggled, but sobered as he slowly dragged the thin straps of her panties down her thighs, revealing a soft, golden thatch of hair. The sweet scent of her arousal tickled his nose and he wanted to get closer.

As the panties reached her knees he let go and they dropped to the floor. He placed his fingers over Gizmo. "Look away, mogwai, things are about to get crazy."

He gripped her hips and picked her up. She squeaked as he tossed her on the couch. He came down on top of her, his mouth finding the sensitive part of her neck. Her hands ran through his hair and over his shoulders as he kissed his way down her body.

He cupped her breasts, taking time to lick and suck them both until she was writhing beneath him. His hand roamed over her flat belly and tickled the damp patch of soft curls between her legs.

She parted her thighs and his knuckle grazed the little nub of her clit. She moaned. Her cream coated his fingers as he explored lower. Smooth folds parted and he slid a finger slowly inside of her. Her body was burning hot.

She arched, pressing into his palm. She was tight. Real tight. His finger pressed deep and slowly withdrew, gathering her cream and spreading it over her clit. His thumb teased her nub and she moaned and arched.

Her arms stretched over her head. She was likely the most beautiful vision he'd ever seen, spread out beneath him, naked and twisting with desire and need. Scooting lower, he trailed his tongue around the slight indent of her belly button.

His hands cupped her thighs and pulled them apart. She was glossy and pink, everywhere. Lowering to his knees, he spread her folds with his thumbs and tasted her. Sweet tang met his tongue. "God, you taste amazing."

She pulled her legs wide and he pressed his tongue deep, sipping from her, unable to get his fill. As his fingers found her clit again she gripped his hair, pulling tight against his scalp. She seemed insatiable and he loved it. It became his life's ambition to make her come.

He licked and sucked and rubbed. Twisting his wrist, he slid his middle finger deep inside of her channel. His lips curled around her clit. She cried out as he nibbled and sucked.

The first flutters tightened, deep within her sex. Her knees drew up, soft skin tickling his shoulders. He inserted another finger and she squeezed around him.

"Shane…"

His cock pulsed at the sound of his name passing her lips in a breathy sigh. He sucked, and fucked her with his fingers. Her body bowed, fingers tightening in his hair to a point of delicious pain, as she cried out.

She was loud, but he liked it. Heat coated his knuckles. Her body expanded and contracted. Her little toes dragged up his sides and her one heel dug into his back.

His mouth kissed at her thighs. He bowed his head, resting his face on her lower belly. Hands combed over his hair as they both breathed.

"You're really good at that," she rasped.

He smiled against her leg and kissed the cute gremlin there. Eyes shut, he rested. Van Morrison played on—*Into the Mystic*.

She turned and cuddled into him, twisting and scooting until they were both crammed chest to chest on the couch. He opened his eyes and the prettiest brown irises blinked back at him.

"Hi," she whispered.

"Hi."

She smiled and pressed her lips to his. He wondered if she could taste herself. Those shy moments would be forever cataloged in his mind as one of the most intimate times of his life.

"You're still wearing pants," she said, causing his brow to arch. Tentatively her fingers pulled at the button of his jeans. "I want you."

Had there ever been more beautiful words? He eased onto his back and she filled the space between his thighs. "I'm yours."

Sitting up, her hair was a wild halo of gold and wheat. Her breasts hung heavy as she leaned over and undid his pants. Lifting his hips, he gave her room to ease them down. She pulled them off and he lay before her clad in only his boxers.

Her fingers teased along the elastic band of his shorts. Looking at him with drowsy eyes, she asked, "Do you have a condom?"

"In my wallet."

She looked around and lifted his jeans off the floor, handing them to him. He withdrew his wallet from the back pocket and fished out a foil packet. He'd been carrying it for months. He held it up and she smiled.

Her fingers wrapped around the packet and he heard the tear of foil. She lowered his shorts and seared kisses along the head of his cock.

His eyes closed as he drew in a long breath through his nose.

Warm lips closed over him, sucking gently. His spine extended and his butt clenched. She wasn't necessarily blowing him. She was seducing him.

He lifted as his shorts came down, drawing out one leg then the other. She sat up, her mouth glossy. Her teeth nibbled on her lower lip and her dimple appeared. Latex slid over his flesh and she met his gaze. She was so fucking hot. He hoped he lasted long. It had been a while.

"No socks. Does that mean I'm on top?" she whispered.

Where did this woman come from? Trying to play it cool, he whispered, "However you want it."

Her hair fanned over her face as she climbed over his hips. He stretched and flattened out on his back, holding her hips as she found a comfortable position. She held him in her grip, lining his erection up with her sex, and slowly seated her body over his.

Heat engulfed him. She made a slight sound of duress as she lowered herself, but continued to take him slowly inside of her. Head tipping back, he sighed. Heaven.

Once she was completely seated, she was breathing fast. A starburst of color expanded behind his eyes. She was so tight and warm. His fingers dug into the soft flesh of her hips.

Her hands opened wide, like little five point stars, as her weight balanced on his chest. "You're big," she said as she adjusted to him.

He laughed silently. That was always nice to hear.

Slowly, she lifted. His body pulled from hers in a gradual glide. He stared as her cream coating the latex. He wished he wasn't wearing a condom, but he knew better. She lowered herself and his grip tightened, fingers flexing over her hips as they both moaned. He couldn't recall ever fitting so perfectly with another human being.

Again she lifted and fell into a controlled slide. She was taking him with measured patience. It was glorious. He guided her and soon her rhythm increased.

His cock stroked along her tight channel. Her breasts swayed slightly with each thrust. The temptation was too much. Sliding his hands up her back, he curled forward and sucked a nipple into his mouth.

She arched in his hold and rode him faster. Needing more, he sat up and turned, taking her with him. The cushions of the sofa supported his back and his feet pressed into the floor. This position allowed them a bit more support. As he guided her hips, she rode him hard.

His hands and mouth were everywhere.

Their flesh became dewy with perspiration. He ran his hands through her hair, gripping a handful of the spun silk at the nape of her neck, forcing her to angle back.

His lips opened on her throat as he sucked. He nibbled to her shoulder. Nails dug into his back.

Suddenly he turned, flipping her so she was beneath him. His hands gripped the soft underside of her knee and lifted it to the back of the couch as he pounded into her heat. She cried out with each hard thrust. He filled her, forcing himself as deep as he could go.

Her cries echoed off the walls, words of begging, pleas for him to never stop. His hair hung over his face. He thrust into her. When the tingle started at the base of his spine and he knew he was close, he reached between their bodies and found her clit, rubbing in tight little circles and she came apart.

She was a wild wind he couldn't capture, arching and scratching and bucking into him. Her hands gripped the back of his neck and pulled him low. Her mouth fused with his.

"Yes!" she whispered against his lips.

His cock pulsed and his balls drew up tight. He thrust hard as his seed pumped out of him, filling the tip of the condom. Bolts of electricity zipped up his spine and locked him in a moment in time, so potently saturated in all things human. He stiffened, reveling at the peak of his release and collapsed onto her soft, welcoming body, careful not to crush her.

His mind came back to him slowly, sensing her lips kissing his shoulder. He pulled himself off of her, giving her room to breathe and wanting to check if she was okay. She smiled up at him.

"You're amazing," he said.

"So are you."

CHAPTER 14

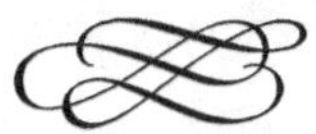

Shane awoke to the sound of the television playing softly and quiet chatter.

"And then maybe we can take a walk later. Do you have a stroller? It's a nice day out, yes it is, little man."

He opened his eyes and found Kate sitting in his kitchen wearing his Led Zeppelin shirt, creamy, bare thighs crossed delicately beneath the worn surface of the table. You'd think she was wearing a suit, considering how properly she carried herself.

Logan sat in his pink highchair and babbled back at her as she spooned something into his mouth, scraping the spoon slowly along his chin. He was handling the solid food a lot better for her than he did for him.

She continued to talk to Logan as she fed

him, unaware she was being watched. Seeing her feeding him, chatting with him, did things to Shane.

He sat up and she turned. "Hey, sleepyhead."

"Hey." He smiled and stretched. Sliding off the blanket, he found his jeans and pulled them on. Strolling into the kitchen, he bent and kissed her head. She smelled like a mix between him and her. It was the best perfume in the world.

"Hey, big man," he said, running a hand affectionately over Logan's head. He smiled and cooed at him. Turning back to Kate, he said, "Thanks for getting him up."

He went to the bathroom and cleaned himself up. When he returned Kate was sitting on the couch with Logan watching Sesame Street. Logan had a fistful of her hair and was happily tugging it. It was a nice picture.

He grabbed a Gatorade and joined them. "What are your plans for the day?"

She shrugged, her fingers being used as a teething toy, which she didn't seem to mind. "I'm free. How about you?"

"I have a gig tonight, but that's not until later."

They spent the morning watching television and playing with Logan. Around lunchtime, Shane put him in his swing where he quickly fell asleep. He turned and stared at Kate.

"He's a really good baby," she said as she picked up rattles and placed them in a basket.

"Yeah. He is."

She stood and a moment passed where they simply waited for the other to speak. He knew what he wanted to do.

"Come here," he said as he locked the front door.

She smiled and followed him. He took her hand and pulled her into his bedroom. The covers were still on the couch. Shutting the door, they stood in the small, dim room. He faced her and knew she understood his intentions.

Tucking a strand of hair behind her ear, he ducked down and kissed her slowly. She kissed him back and soon they were all over each other. "I love you in my shirt."

"I can't believe I'm wearing what was once a diaper."

"Not for long." He toppled her to the bed and her laughter filled the room as he removed her shirt.

She reached for him and undid his pants. Shane kicked them off and pulled away her panties. There was something so sexy about rolling around on his bare bed with Kate completely naked.

Their legs twined and the brush of her sex against his bare cock made them both groan. Reaching in the drawer in the bedside table, he found a condom and slipped it on. She lay beneath him, anxious and waiting. He filled her on one quick motion.

Her legs curled around him, heels digging into his ass as he slowly fucked her. She gripped him and met each thrust. Her head tipped back as she came and once her pleasure was handled he began fucking her in earnest.

He liked that she didn't need it to always be gentle. His hands cupped her breasts and he sucked at the tips, pinching the other nipple with his fingers. When he came he felt as though he gave her part of his soul.

They panted and held each other. Slipping off the condom, he dropped it in the wastepaper basket on the floor. They each lay on their backs, hands entwined, thumbs slowly gliding over the other's fingers.

Shane never had a girlfriend like Kate. She was a grown-up. She had a job and a house. Having her in his life made him want to be more of a man.

He contemplated how tight his budget had become, trying to figure out ways to save some money. His mind always seemed to return to finances, even in post-fuck languor. It was hard, having a kid and being lower class. Kate was middle class.

"Will you put this in your report?" he asked, joking.

She laughed. "Perhaps."

They hung out all day, not getting fully dressed until he needed to shower and prepare for his show. Kate seemed nervous when he came out of the shower. She was back in her jeans and had pulled her hair into a clip. Logan bounced happily on her knee.

"Does the same girl always watch Logan?" she asked.

"Yeah. Her name's Lisa."

"Lisa's Tucker's girlfriend, right?"

Was she nervous because he saw another woman regularly? It was nothing like that, nothing remotely close to what he and Kate had. Lisa was his babysitter. That was it. "Yeah. She's good with Logan. He likes her."

She nodded quietly and her expression seemed tense, despite her effort to appear calm.

"Hey, you okay?"

"What? Yeah."

He pulled on his shirt and frowned. Something seemed to be bothering her. As he laced up his boots he watched her. She put Logan on the floor and situated him with some toys as she tidied up, straightening pillows on the couch and tucking in the kitchen chairs.

"You don't have to do that."

Pausing, she wrung her hands. He walked to her, not stopping until his front was pressed to hers, and pinched her chin between his fingers, tilting up her face. Her lashes fluttered and their eyes met.

"What's the matter?"

"N—nothing. I just…I'm not sure what happens now."

Confusion tightened his brow. "What do you mean?"

"I mean…with us."

"Well, I'm going to work and I won't get home until late, so you probably won't hear from me until tomorrow morning." Relief showed in her eyes. "Hey, what did you think this was?"

"I didn't know."

"I'm not like that, Kate, certainly not with you. I like you. I like you a lot. This wasn't a one time thing, okay?"

She smiled at him and nodded.

It seemed her nerves were contagious, as he was suddenly worried everything might slip through his fingers. "Can I call you tomorrow?"

"I'd be mad if you didn't," she told him. He kissed her and when he pulled away she said, "I should probably go before your friends get here."

"Why?"

She shrugged. "I don't want them to think anything."

"Kate, do you think they aren't going to find out?"

"Well…it's just…maybe we should try to keep this to ourselves for a while, because of the situation with Logan."

Disappointment had his brows lowering. He understood not broadcasting it to her supervisor or the judge, but not telling his friends…that seemed a bit much. "Is that what you want?"

"No, but I think it's what's best."

Maybe she was right—for now. "Okay."

They kissed goodbye and she said good night to Logan. After Shane watched her leave he got his guitars together and waited for Lisa. His face was sore from smiling so much, something he didn't think he'd every experienced before.

Tucker arrived with Lisa. As they came in, Logan gave a gummy grin. Lisa scooped him up and Tucker scanned the trailer and frowned.

"Dude, flowers? You okay?"

Shane's face burned. "Shut up. I'm trying to make it nice around here."

"Nice or gay? Why don't you throw down some doilies while you're at it?"

Shane ignored him and went to say goodbye to Logan.

The night was uneventful. He played, got paid, and thought of Kate the entire time. He wanted to do something for her. Take her somewhere nice, maybe. His budget was tight and he'd have to consider Logan, but he'd figure something out.

∾

THE FOLLOWING MORNING, after Shane dropped Logan off at daycare, he called Kate.

"Hey," he said when she answered.

"Hey."

A thrill raced through him at the sound of her voice. It so was surreal that he could now call her whenever he liked. "How was your night?"

"Good. How was your gig?"

"Okay. What are you doing today?"

"I have a few home visits then I have to go to Lakota and swing by the office. I'm getting a new case today. I'll have lots of paperwork to do tonight."

"Oh." So she wouldn't be able to come over. "I was thinking…we should do something."

"Like what?"

"I don't know, but don't make plans for next Saturday."

"My weekend's all yours."

He smiled, liking the way that sounded.

As he pulled up to the job site he said good-bye, wishing he had more time to talk to her. The sun beat through his t-shirt and the air tasted wet, but he didn't mind. He whistled as he clocked in and his lips twitched as he tried to hide the grin that kept trying to show.

Work was more tolerable than any other day. The warm and happy sensation he had that morning remained. As he worked he didn't let mild dilemmas upset him. He was patient and even went the extra mile when a buddy of his needed a hand, not worrying about how it would affect his own objectives.

On the drive home, he hit all green lights and the radio played only good songs. It was a perfect day, a day in which Kate kept his mind company through it all.

~

TUESDAY, he spoke to Kate briefly in the morning and she said she'd call him when she finished work. His day went fast and on the way home he continuously checked his phone. At seven o'clock, when she still hadn't called, he tried her cell.

"Hello, you have reached Katherine McAlister. I'm unable to take your call at the moment, but if you need immediate assistance you can contact the Children and Youth department at…"

He hung up.

After he put Logan to bed he called her again, but got her voicemail. It wasn't until eight-thirty when his phone finally rang.

"Hello?" he answered anxiously.

"Hey."

He breathed a sigh of relief. "Hey. Where have you been?"

She sounded irritable. "Working."

"Oh. How was your day?"

She sighed. "All right. Long. How was yours?"

"Mine was good. Why was your day long?"

"This new case I have is a tough one."

"Can you tell me about it?"

She hesitated. "It's confidential. Sorry."

He didn't expect that, but supposed he had to respect it. "Oh, okay. I didn't know you'd be working this late. I thought I might have been able to see you tonight."

"Sorry. My weeknights are sort of busy."

"Oh." He was getting an odd vibe. "Is everything okay?"

"Yeah, I'm just…tired."

"Do you want me to let you go?"

"Yeah, I have some paperwork I need to fill out and I have to iron my clothes for tomorrow."

"Ironing, what's that?" he joked. She laughed, but it wasn't her genuine one. The smile he'd been wearing all week faded. "Okay, well, I'll talk to you tomorrow?"

"Sure."

They hung up and he couldn't shake the uncomfortable feeling he had. Was she pulling away from him again? Maybe she was just having a shitty day. He tried not to dwell on it, but his mind kept replaying their conversation.

The next day he called her on his way to work and she sounded better. That night he had a gig at the Grill so he could only send her a text telling her he missed her and was thinking of her.

By the time he got home the week must have caught up to him. He crashed as soon as he walked through the door.

Thursday morning he was excited. Kate usually stopped by on Thursdays. Her visit was part of her job, of course, but it still meant he got to see her.

When he got home he tidied up and gave Logan a bath. Trying his best not to make a mess, he stirred the boiling spaghetti and simmered a jar of sauce as Logan banged his spatula on the tray of his highchair. He was straining the pasta and pouring the sauce over it when he heard her pull up. Carrying the bowl to the table he went to the door.

She was professional Kate, wearing white slacks and a black cardigan. Her shoes were black as well. She grinned when she saw him waiting at the door.

Reaching for her bag, she shut the car door and walked up the steps. "Hi," she whispered.

"Hi." He kissed her, backing her into the trailer and taking his time giving her a greeting that made the waiting worthwhile. When he released her she was slightly flushed. "I missed you."

"I missed you too." She turned. "You cooked?"

"It's just spaghetti and Ragu. I'm not real gifted in the kitchen."

She smiled. "That's okay. You have other talents."

They sat and ate, talking about their workweek. Kate looked tired. It bothered him when he asked about her other clients and she hedged, giving vague answers. He knew she had to keep things confidential, but it wasn't like he knew the other people. She could still talk to him about general things without giving away too much. However, when he thought about her telling strangers about his personal shit he didn't like it, so he respected her privacy.

She stayed until Logan went to bed, but sadly, left shortly after. Something was off. He sensed space between them that wasn't there the other day and he didn't like it.

Friday morning he called her on the way to work and she sounded like a totally different person. She sounded normal again.

"Sorry about yesterday. I, uh, wasn't feeling real good."

"Is everything okay?" he asked. God, he hoped she wasn't sick. What if she was? She'd played with Logan a lot. He didn't want either of them to be sick.

"Oh, everything's fine. Just...women problems. I'm good now."

Women problems? *Ohhh...*

"So, all back to normal?" He wanted to see her Saturday. He had big plans. And not to be a pig, but a lot of those plans involved a naked Kate.

"Yup."

That night he played at the Grill. He couldn't wait for the weekend to officially start, wondering how early Kate would come over on Saturday. He had what he thought was a pretty decent plan for the day.

That night he couldn't sleep. It was after midnight when he got home, but she didn't have work the next day so he called her. "Hey, were you sleeping?"

"No. I was reading."

He asked about her day and they talked for a few minutes. Her voice was soft and he loved listening to it. As he lounged on the couch holding the phone against his shoulder, he stretched. *Crocodile Hunter* was on mute on the television. His hand slipped past the band of his pants as he sprawled out. Just her voice made him hard.

"I wish you were here."

She was quiet for a second. "I could come over."

He stilled. "Really?"

"Yeah."

"Oh, please do…"

She laughed. "Okay, give me a few minutes."

"Can't wait. Drive safe."

He hung up the phone and grinned. She was coming over. He anxiously waited for her, trying to pass the time by watching TV. When she pulled up excitement exploded low in his gut.

He went to the door and watched her climb out of her bug. She wore soft pants and a t-shirt. What would it be this time? His grin widened when he made out the silkscreen. Vintage Rainbow Bright—totally awesome.

She came through the door and stared up at him. "Hi. I'm here."

He traced a finger over her brow. "What do you want to do now?"

Her eyes searched his and she gave him a pointed look. Yup, him too.

Their bodies crashed together in a fury of need. He stripped off her shirt and groaned when he saw her pale pink, lace bra. Her petite fingers undid his pants and he removed his shirt. Her mouth went to his chest and bit his nipple.

He hissed and moaned. She was a frisky little thing. He scooped her up and her legs wrapped around him. Turning, he sat her on the kitchen counter.

"God, I fucking missed you," he said as he yanked down the straps of her bra and pulled a tight nipple into his mouth.

Fisting her hands in his hair, she arched into him. "Me too."

His fingers slid into the waistband of her pants, grabbing a handful of her plush ass. She lifted as he tugged off her pants and panties. Holy fuck, Kate was completely naked on his kitchen counter.

Something inside of him told him to stop and take in the moment. He eased back and stared at her. She was balancing her weight on her palms braced behind her. Her breasts bore the wet marks from his mouth and her eyes were heavy with lust. As he looked at her she smiled and slowly parted her legs.

Glistening pink folds flashed at him and he practically came in his pants. He growled and dove for her, lifting her legs over his shoulders and fastening his mouth to her clit. Her voice cried out as he stabbed his tongue into her slit. She tasted fucking magnificent.

Her fingers tightened in his hair as he feasted on her. When she came, it was loud and hard. Moving up to her breasts, he dragged his lips over her silky flesh then found her mouth. "Taste yourself," he whispered as he sealed his lips to hers, pressing his tongue deep.

She moaned and gripped his jaw as if she couldn't get enough. Suddenly, she broke the kiss and disappeared. He blinked and looked down as her body slid off the counter and she was on her knees, quickly unfastening his pants.

She pulled him free and gripped his flesh,

tugging long, sure strokes. He thrust his hips forward. "Put your mouth on me," he practically begged. Never in his life had he experienced this sort of fury to be with a woman. Every encounter was urgent and erupting with shared lust.

Leaning up off her heels, she opened wide and took him deep. Holy fuck! Her mouth was a tight, wet suction of heat. As she looked up at him with big brown eyes, her cheeks drawn tight over his flesh, her lips sealing him in, he nearly exploded. She was so fucking sexy.

Her hand cupped his balls while the other gripped the base of his cock, stroking as she bobbed up and down over him. His hands went to her hair. He didn't want to hurt her, but the moment he tightened his grip, she moaned and sucked harder. She liked it a little rough.

He twitched and jerked as she gave him the best blowjob of his life. When he got close, he tightened his fist in her hair and began to fuck her mouth. She took all of him, her mouth open wide, hands squeezing his hips.

"I'm gonna come," he warned.

She slanted her mouth over him and grabbed the base of his cock again, not letting him pull away. Holy shit, she was porn hot. He'd never seen a girl do it like that in real life.

She pulled at the end of his dick then opened her mouth and jerked him fast. Her little pink tongue caught the first jets of come as they shot into her mouth. Another ribbon of white pulsed over her tongue and she swallowed. Leaning forward, she took him deep, milking every last drop of his release.

His knees shook. He couldn't take anymore. Dropping to the ground, he toppled her to her back and kissed her with everything he had. Her tongue was salty with his taste.

He cupped her head and drew her body over his. She laid her cheek on his shoulder and played with his nipple. His head was spinning. "That was the best blowjob I've ever had in my life."

She laughed—a soft genuine show of amusement. "Glad to be of service."

He kissed the top of her head. "You're amazing."

She sighed. They lay on the floor for some time and then they quietly shut out the living room lights and went to bed. The three of them slept in the bedroom, he and Kate in the bed, Logan safely beside them in the crib.

CHAPTER 15

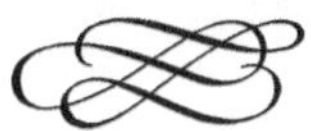

Saturday they woke up, had breakfast, and Shane left Logan with Kate so he could run to the store. She offered to go with him, but he didn't want her to see him paying with his food stamps card. It was stupid. She was aware he was getting assistance, but his pride took a hit every time his situation was brought into the light. Once he had everything he needed he returned home.

Logan was sleeping in the swing and Kate was just coming out of the bathroom. Her hair was wet and she wore only a towel. He dropped the grocery bags on the counter and cornered her in the bedroom.

"You're naked under there," he said, shutting the door.

She pushed past him and he snagged the corner of her towel. She squealed as he picked her up and tossed her on the bed. He pinned her down and kissed her.

Moaning, she bit at his lip and smiled. "What are you going to do to me?" she asked, her tone playful and dramatic. Very damsel in distress and he dug it.

He toyed with her wet hair. Oh, the things he could do with Kate. He breathed in her scent. She smelled like his soap. "I want your pussy."

Her eyes went wide. "You have a very dirty mouth."

"You love it."

"I do," she admitted, her eyes dark with lust and her cheeks flushed.

He rolled to his back and pulled her over him. She rose above him, straddling his hips. Their fingers laced. "Come here," he said as he tugged her.

"Where?" Her head tilted in confusion, trying to make sense of what he was asking.

"Put your hands on the headboard and scoot up."

She lifted and leaned forward. Her breasts hung over his face so he stretched and suckled them. She moaned. His hands glided over the smooth globes of her ass. His palm pressed her forward. "I want to taste you. Scoot up."

"Like this?" she asked as she leaned forward, rising above him.

"More." He adjusted her legs so her knees

rested on the side of his head. "Mmm, yes." Leaning up, he licked at her slit.

Her spine straightened and she tried to lift, but he gripped her hips and held her to his face, slowly fucking her with his tongue. It took her a few minutes to relax in that position, but eventually sensation took over and she rode his mouth.

He could eat her pussy for days. Her scent was so strong there. He loved it. Loved the way he could still taste her on his lips for hours afterward.

His hands squeezed her ass. Throwing her head back, she cried out his name as she came on his tongue.

Not giving her a chance to come down, he tossed her to the bed and quickly stripped off his clothes. Grabbing a condom, he sheathed himself and hoisted up her hips as her face rested on her arms.

Her supple ass rose before him as her spine stretched. Climbing between her knees, he parted her thighs and teased the mouth of her sex with the tip of his cock. Her voice purred and her body pushed back into him, seeking his touch like a cat.

Running a hand from the nape of her neck, down her spine, he gripped her hips, thrusting into her to the hilt. She lunged forward and moaned with each thrust. He wanted her hard and fast and she seemed to want the same.

Their bodies smacked together, his balls tapping against her clit. Her tight pussy gripped him as he fed her his cock. She was the best sex he'd ever had, hands down. Something about her was so confident and at ease with her desires. It was incredibly freeing.

Wanting to see her face, he gathered her damp hair in his fist and pulled, turning her head to the side. He leaned down, blanketing her with his body and kissed her shoulder. When he found her mouth she was ravenous.

He drilled into her as their tongues dueled. His other hand slid over her shoulder and grabbed her tit, hard. He squeezed and she moaned into his mouth.

"Oh God," she cried and her sex tightened around him.

He ripped his mouth from hers and sucked on her shoulder, pulling her back as he sat up. Her body came with his. Her back pressed into his damp chest. He cupped her breasts. "Wrap your arms around my neck."

She did as he instructed and he pinched her nipples hard. "Oh, God, Shane…"

He ground his cock into her, his one hand sliding over her belly to where their bodies met. He found her clit and pressed his fingers over it, rubbing up and down.

She jerked and tightened her arms around his neck. "I want you to come with me," he whispered into the curve of her neck.

He thrust deep and bit at her shoulder. Her body writhed. Sliding his arm around her ribs, he held her to him as he fucked her, sensing his release climbing. Pinching down on her clit, he pressed into her, seeking the soft curve of her G-spot.

"Ohmygod, ohmygod!" she cried.

His cock twitched as her sex clamped down him. His muscles locked and he twitched as his release ripped through him. They both shouted as they came.

They fell onto their sides and panted, still stuck together. He was too sensitive to withdraw. He squeezed her tight, just wanting to hold and hug her for a while. She tightened her arms over his and sighed.

"I need another shower now."

"*Shh*, let's just lay here for a while."

WHEN LOGAN WOKE up Shane fed him and dressed him in a pair of swim trunks and a badass muscle shirt.

"Are we going swimming?" Kate asked, admiring Logan's little suit.

"Yup."

"I don't have a suit."

"We can swing by your place on our way," he said, applying a hearty amount of sunscreen to Logan's arms and shoulders.

"Were are we going?"

"You'll see. Hand me the purse."

She frowned. "Purse?"

"Yeah, the baby purse. Right there."

She giggled.

He self-consciously faced her. "What's so funny?"

"Shane, it's called a diaper bag."

He flushed. "Oh, well…that's a little more manly. Wish I would have known that. Hand me the *diaper bag*, please."

She passed it to him and pressed a kiss to his cheek. "You're adorable. Here's your purse."

Kate gave him directions to her place. She lived in a really nice neighborhood. Everyone had clean yards and nice cars. Growing uncomfortable the closer they drove to her place, he slowly navigated the way.

He tugged at the collar of his shirt. When he glanced at her she looked serene and comfortable.

"Turn left here."

He turned onto a small suburban road with neat curbs and sidewalks and mailboxes at the edge of each drive. He grew up in a neighborhood like this, but no longer felt like he belonged.

"That white house over there is mine."

He pulled up at the curb. It was nice. *Really* nice. The siding was new and white and although it was small, it was pretty. Red shutters butted up against the two front windows and the door had a shiny brass knocker.

"Do you want to come in?"

He was curious, but feared seeing how well she lived would only embarrass him and make him more self-conscious. God, she probably thought he was a total dirt ball. He glanced back at Logan. "I better stay here with Logan."

"Okay. I'll only be a few minutes."

He watched as she unlocked the door and disappeared inside. Even her hedges were perfect. He sat, waiting, his cynical thoughts taunting him, reminding him he'd never measure up. When she reappeared she had a bright yellow polka dotted bag slung over her shoulder.

She wore short white shorts and a blue tank top. He could see the strings of her bathing suit tied at her neck. Big black sunglasses perched over her head like a headband and her hair was pulled up in a bun. She should have been on television she was so cute. The sight cheered him and pulled him from his pity fest.

She opened the door and dropped her bag behind the seat. "Ready?" she asked as she buckled her seatbelt.

He nodded and pulled away.

He was taking them to a state park about an hour away. It had a free, man made beach and a calm lake. He couldn't wait to see how Logan liked the water.

They drove in silence, only the radio filling the quiet. He fiddled with the dial, looking for something decent.

"Are you okay?"

Distracted, he quickly glanced away from the road and toward her. She was frowning. "What? Yeah. Why?"

"You're being really quiet."

He was nervous. Since seeing where she lived his goal to impress her seemed ten times more daunting. "Just driving."

She turned and looked in the back. "Logan looks like he's going to fall asleep."

Logan didn't usually nap at this time. That would probably mess with his schedule. Maybe the water would tire him out and it would all even out in the end.

Kate played with the radio and settled on a Doors song. They drove in silence. He hoped she wasn't disappointed with the day. He spent a lot of time thinking of something fun for them to do that didn't cost a lot of money. He filled his tank that morning and pretty much cleared out his spending money.

They pulled into the parking lot and Kate glanced around. "A park?" She smiled and he hoped she was pleased.

"Yup." He parked the car and shut off the engine. When he glanced at her, she was staring out the window and he worried he hadn't done enough.

"Is there a beach here?"

"A lake, yeah. It's a little different than the beaches on the coast. Come on."

He climbed out and unloaded the car seat. Logan was sleeping. He grabbed the *diaper bag* and popped the trunk. He brought a blanket, a cooler, and towels, but wished he had the forty bucks to buy the beach chairs he saw that morning.

Kate took the blanket and towels and he lifted out the cooler. The beach was only semi-crowded. The sand was coarse and warm. They found a spot a few feet from the water and he put Logan's carrier down, facing him away from the sun.

The sun baked sand was warm under his bare feet. Kate unfolded the blanket on the sand and removed her tank top. A tangerine string bikini with little pink ruffles at the trim clung to her curves. It was fucking sexy.

She kept her shorts on, but kicked off her flip-flops. He watched as she dug in her bag and pulled out a tube of sunscreen.

Shane took off his shirt and shoes and sat on the blanket. "Want some help?" He needed to touch her.

"Sure," she handed him the tube.

"Eighty, huh?"

"I'm Irish. The sun is not my friend."

She smiled, but her glasses hid her eyes. Was she mad they came there? He should have brought an umbrella for her, but he didn't own one. He was German so his skin sort of stayed tan year round.

He squeezed some of the white cream on his palm and dabbed it on her shoulders. Small wisps of blonde hair slipped from her bun and got caught in the lotion. His sticky fingers brushed them off her neck and placed a kiss on her shoulder when he was finished. This was her smell. She must wear sunblock often, because she always carried a sweet, beach like fragrance.

"Thanks," she said, taking the sunscreen back. He rolled a towel behind his neck and lounged, making no secret of watching her as she applied lotion to the rest of her body.

She rubbed sunblock over her belly and the swells of her breasts. "I could have done that for you," he teased.

Her lips pursed in a smirk, her delicate dimple winking at him. "This is a family place."

"I can behave," he pouted, poking her knee with his toe.

She looked at him. "Who says I was talking about you?"

His brow lifted. "Kate, you're a naughty minded girl."

"You have no idea," she warned and lowered herself beside him on the blanket.

His finger ran over her hip, tugging lightly

at the waistband of her shorts. "You keeping these on?"

"Yeah. I don't like my butt."

He turned his head, giving her a leveled look. "Excuse me? I happen to have it on good authority that you have a fine ass. As a matter of fact, I could spend days exploring it, maybe sing to it a little, kiss it, whisper sweet nothings to it."

"You're going to sing to my butt?" She giggled.

"Sure."

"What would you sing?"

"*Brown Eyed Girl.*"

She shoved him and blushed. "You're disgusting."

He laughed and pulled her so she was half lying over his chest. She stared down at him and he could see himself smiling in the reflection of her glasses. "I'm just kidding, but I would sing to you. All of you."

Her lips remained curved in a pleasant expression. "Sing to me now," she whispered.

He sang the first thing that came to his mind. Her face lit up as he whispered the words of *If I Fell* by the Beatles. It was probably too soon to be using those words, but for some reason it felt right to sing songs of love to her.

When he reached the last line she lowered her head and gently kissed him. People were probably staring, but he didn't care. His fingers traced over her shoulders.

Logan made a sound and they parted. "Somebody's awake," she whispered.

The moment was quiet and magical. His eyes squinted against the sun. All he could see was Kate, a white halo forming behind her. "I better get him."

They ate the sandwiches he'd packed and took Logan to the water. The little guy didn't know what to make of it. He seemed to like it, but the cooler than bath water temperature startled him every time.

They stayed at the park later than the rest of the beach goers. All in all it was a spectacular day. Better than any day he'd had in a long time. When they arrived back at the trailer it was dark.

Shane unloaded the car and filled the kitchen sink with warm soapy water. "I remember when my mother used to bathe me in the sink," she said as she watched him wash the sand off of Logan. He splashed and laughed, then made a comical expression of shock when water landed on his face.

Shane couldn't remember his mom ever bathing him, but he did have a memory of Noel sitting in the sink playing. "Yeah," he said, chest tightening with bittersweet nostalgia.

He dried him off and changed him into his PJs. Kate followed, seeming to take it all in. "Do you think you'll ever have more kids?" she asked as he gave Logan his bedtime bottle.

Shane stared at her, visions he'd never entertained dancing in his mind. "With the right woman? Definitely." She'd be a good mom, but it was way too soon to suggest anything of the sort. "Babies are awesome."

"How many kids would you want?"

The answer came with little thought, carrying logic as if he'd already decided such things, but he couldn't recall doing so. "At least two, in case anything ever happened to me. That way they'd always have each other. I'd hate for Logan to be lonely."

Her eyes studied him and he couldn't tell what she was thinking. He hand pressed to his arm. "You're a good dad, Shane," she said softly.

His instinct was to say he wasn't Logan's father, but as he looked down at his sleeping face and took in all his belongings scattered around their home he realized he *was* a father. It was the first time he had the courage to acknowledge such an assessment. "Thank you."

Her opinion should've mattered because she was his caseworker and as his caseworker it was *her* opinion the judge was interested in. But his case had nothing to do with the warm, satisfying pride blooming inside of him. Her opinion mattered, because he cared what she thought as a person. He didn't want Kate to look at him and see a disappointment. He needed her to look at him and see a dependable man, a man capable of taking care of others. Her praise meant something personal to him.

She spent the night and hung around until late Sunday, just before Lisa showed up to babysit. He wanted her to meet Lisa. Maybe they could become friends, but again, Kate said, until the custody hearing was over, they should probably keep their relationship to themselves. He didn't necessarily see the harm in letting his friends know about Kate, but he didn't argue.

There were only three weeks until his court date and then all of this would be over. No more caseworker reports. No more judges. No more being under the microscope. It would just be him, Logan, and Kate.

He'd have Logan forever and Kate, well… she'd be there too.

CHAPTER 16

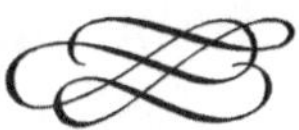

The next week went by incredibly fast. Lisa had gotten her class roster and managed to work around his schedule. She said the extra hundred bucks a week helped and she wanted to keep babysitting. That was the good news of his week.

There were other times he'd rather forget. Sims had swung by one afternoon. Shane was vacuuming and trying out his new baby back-pack kangaroo pouch thing a guy from work had given him. It was the same guy who gave him the pink highchair. Unfortunately, said pouch was also pink...with ruffles...and little hearts.

He'd debated using it, but Logan was being a little fuss monkey that day and Shane was trying to get things done around the trailer. So on went the emasculator—that's what he decided to name it—and in went the kid.

Once again, Logan didn't seem fazed by the feminine salmon bisque color. He happily hung from him like a munchkin in a harness and Shane was able to run the vacuum.

Classic rock played on the stereo. Unfortunately, *Dream Weaver* by Gary Wright was playing when Sims pulled up in the DeLorean. Shane didn't hear the car, or the door open.

Shane was pushing the sweeper over his dated carpet and bellowing out the slow lyrics as Logan swung from his chest, happily babbling along. He'd turned and stilled when he saw Sims standing between the stereo and the door, pie-eyed and looking a bit uncomfortable.

Not moving his feet, Sims reached over and switched off the music at the same time Shane shut down the vacuum. *Awkward...*

Sims deliberately cleared his throat. "Uh, what's up, Hazel?"

Shane glanced down at the pink kangaroo pouch and mentally cataloged what his friend was seeing. Damn it, even his hair was tied up in a bun. It had been getting in his way and making him hot.

Shane rubbed the back of his neck, cleared his throat, and used his manliest voice. "Hey, man, what's up? I'm just getting some of this shit cleaned up before I crack open a beer." Yeah, beer was manly. *You don't even have beer.*

Sims stared at him over the rim of his Clark Kent framed glasses. "Oh, okay. I just came by to see if you wanted to take a ride to the mall, maybe pick up some tampons or get your nails done."

His eyes closed as he surrendered to the ribbing. Trying to draw his testicles back out, he said, "Ha, ha. Seriously though, this thing is pretty cool. I can do all sorts of stuff now, without having to give up one hand to hold Logan."

Sims had shaken his head. "Dude, that thing on your chest is a lot of things. Cool is definitely not one of them."

Shane took abuse for that afternoon ever since. He couldn't get the damn pink pouch off fast enough and Sims had snapped several pictures of him with his phone, sending the pic out in a mass text to all their friends. *Fucker.*

There was no denying Shane's life had definitely changed. As much as getting his balls broken sucked, he couldn't say he had any regrets. Logan made his days fuller and he really liked the direction he was headed. Parenthood, oddly enough, suited him. He hoped Logan liked having him around, because he loved the little bugger.

❧

LATE AUGUST, Shane was finishing up a job and was told to swing by the general foreman's office on his way home. He left a few minutes early so he wouldn't be late picking up Logan.

The company office was in Lakota, not too far from the daycare. It was where they went every Friday to get their checks. He knocked on his boss's door and entered.

"Hey, Shane."

"Hey, Bruce."

Bruce was a good guy. Shane worked for him a few times before. Shane sat down in the chair across from his desk and stretched. It was exhausting doing concrete in the summer sun. "What's up?"

"Well, they're cutting back the job now that we're closing in on it. You've been here past your thirty days, so you're up on my list."

His pleasant mood toppled. "But there's still plenty to be done."

"I know, but they only contracted for so many hours and we've exceeded our time. I gotta cut back on men."

"You're laying me off? But I have a kid to take care of."

"I'm sorry, man. Everyone has responsibilities. More work will be here in the fall, I'm sure. We got that big contract coming up for the civic center."

Fuck! This sucked. It beyond sucked. He

couldn't afford to be laid off right now. "Can I at least finish out the week?"

"Tomorrow's Friday, but sure. I'll give you your check now to save you a trip tomorrow."

Shane took the check and went to get Logan. How appropriate that his tuition was due. He basically handed over a check only a few bucks shorter than the one in his pocket. At least he still had the Grill. That was under the table and he'd need every penny of it over the next few weeks.

When he got home he couldn't form the slightest smile. His back was tense and everything agitated him. Logan was cranky too, likely picking up on Shane's grouchy state. He called Duce.

"Yo," his friend answered.

"Hey, what are you doing?"

"Nothing. Haven't heard from you in a while. How's parenthood?"

Shane bounced Logan on his knee. "Good. What are you doing tonight?"

"Nada."

"Wanna come over and have a beer?"

"Sure," Duce said, his tone a bit surprised.

"Cool. Could you grab some on your way?"

Duce laughed. Shane had bought enough beer in his lifetime that he was owed plenty. "Sure."

About twenty minutes later Duce was there with a case. They sat on the couch watching television and drinking. After such a hot day a cold beer tasted spectacular.

The sound of gravel crunching had him turning. "Fuck."

"What?" Duce asked.

"It's Thursday."

"So, what's that mean?"

"That's Kate." He hadn't even thought about dinner, not having much of an appetite.

"Do I need to leave?"

"No, you brought the beer. Stay. Just be polite."

"When am I not?" Duce asked.

Shane stood and went to the door with Logan balanced on his hip. "You know what I mean."

Kate stepped in, smiled, and stilled as she was about to kiss him, noticing Duce sitting on the couch.

"What's up?" Duce greeted.

"Hello," Kate said, clearly taken off-guard.

"How was your day?" Shane asked.

"Good." Her gaze went to Duce who was now engrossed in something on the television. She looked at Shane, her eyes wide and pointing out the fact that they weren't alone as she'd likely expected.

"Kate, this is Duce. Duce, this is Kate."

They each nodded at the other. Kate went into the kitchen and sat down. She didn't have her bag. She obviously wasn't comfortable with their company. Her expression was tight and observant. When she spoke her voice remained low.

"How's everything going?"

He shrugged. "I got laid off today." Why hide it? She'd find out eventually.

"Oh, no. Will there be another job soon?"

He plopped into the chair next to hers and took a swig of his beer. "There should be something in a month or so."

Her mouth opened. "That long? Will you need to go on unemployment?"

Goddamn it. "Yeah. I don't have any other option. I'm just a regular government statistic, aren't I?"

"Shane," she whispered. "Stop. It happens. You'll go back to work and everything will pan out."

Yeah, that was what he usually told himself, but that was before he had another human being depending on him. After a layoff he was always in a bit of a hole. He'd live off Cup-of-Soup for a month and do what he had to do, but now he had Logan to consider. At least he'd be able to spend more time with the little guy.

"Did you have dinner?" she asked.

"Not hungry." He should offer her something, but he really didn't feel like playing the host. She probably had a whole pantry full of gourmet food at home.

After a few minutes of silence, she turned to

glance at Duce then said, "I guess I should go. The hearing's in twelve days. I need to work on my report for the judge."

"I'm sure my new job status is gonna look great to the court," he said sarcastically.

She frowned at him. "The economy's a mess right now, Shane. You aren't the only parent out of work."

He stood and grabbed another beer. She slowly walked to the door and waited awkwardly. He couldn't kiss her in front of Duce. Her rules, not his.

"Well, I guess I'll see you soon."

"Yeah. See ya." He saw the confusion in her gaze, perhaps even hurt, but chose to ignore it. Logan started to fuss so he turned away from the door to make him something to eat.

~

THAT FRIDAY SHE CALLED, but he was in the shower. He meant to call her on his way to the Grill, but didn't. He was embarrassed and avoiding her in an attempt to avoid talking about his pathetic situation. Maybe it was for the best. What was she going to do with a loser like him?

He played through his set on autopilot. When he got home he crashed. His phone woke him up the following morning, but he silenced it. Logan played in his crib while Shane sat in bed thinking about how the fuck he was going to make ends meet.

He was in the kitchen feeding Logan when there was a knock at the door. Kate was there and she didn't look happy.

"Hey," he said, holding the door for her.

"Hi." She looked around to make sure they were alone. "I've been trying to call you."

"Yeah, sorry. I've been busy."

She blinked at him. When he turned away she grabbed his arm. "Shane, what's going on?"

He shrugged. "Nothing."

"You aren't talking to me. Did I do something wrong?"

God, he was a total ass. He didn't want her to take it personally. His mood had been in the shitter for days and he didn't want to dump his problems on her or draw more attention to all the ways he was coming up short. But he also didn't want her to think *she* did anything wrong.

Pulling her into his arms, he kissed her head. "No. I'm sorry. I've just been in a bad mood since Thursday."

She wrapped her arms around his waist. "Because of your job?"

He stiffened. He was willing to apologize, but still didn't want to open up a discussion about shit he hadn't figured out how to solve yet. "Yeah, that's one reason." He pulled away and went back to feeding Logan.

"You know, you can talk to me."

No, he couldn't. Not about this. Eventually someone would point out all the ways he wasn't good enough for her. It didn't need to be him. The minute she realized what a loser he was, she'd likely bail—and he couldn't lose her too.

She sat down beside him and smiled at Logan. "Do you want to do something today? We could go to my place."

"What's wrong with my place?"

She drew back at his accusing tone. "Nothing. I just figured it would be a change of scenery."

Yeah, nice *scenery for a change... No thanks.* He didn't need more reminders of how much better than him she was. He stood and dropped the bowl of baby food in the sink. "This scenery's just fine by me."

She looked down and chipped away the corner of nail polish on her thumb. "Do you want me to go?"

No. He wanted to lose himself in her. He wanted her to hold him and kiss him and make him forget about all his stress. Why he couldn't just say that, he had no idea. He didn't talk about his emotions and had no idea how to explain to her how broken he felt at the moment. "You can do whatever you want."

He was totally uncomfortable with the feelings pummeling him. He felt smothered and wanted them to go away. Somehow, that came out sounding like she was smothering him, which only added to his fucking stress, because he didn't want her to leave at all. When she blinked at him her eyes looked glassy. Fuck.

There seemed to be some crossed lines between his brain and mouth. Everything he said came out wrong and he was fucking everything up. "Look, Kate, I'm not good company right now."

"We don't have to do anything, I just wanted to spend time with you. It's Saturday."

Saturday was their day. They also got part of Sunday, but the rest of the week was eaten up by work and other obligations. Well, he wouldn't have that problem anymore. His schedule was wide open. "Sorry." It was all he could say.

She sat for a few minutes as if considering her options. When she stood, she kissed Logan on the head, went to the door, and left. She didn't even say goodbye.

He brooded from his chair as he waited for the sound of her car taking off. *Go get her. Say sorry, you dick! She's trying to be nice and you're fucking shutting her out.*

His gaze bore into his shitty screen door as his conscious berated him sand insisted he call her back and explain that he was lashing out because he was scared, but his pride refused to let him move.

When the engine of the VW hummed to life and the press of gravel under its wheels crunched, he knew it was too late. He lost his family, his job, why not move the inevitable along and lose her?

~

Shane and Logan had a lazy weekend. He went to play at the Grill on Sunday night and really wasn't feeling it. Kate never called and before he knew it Monday arrived. Problem was, Monday felt like Sunday, and Tuesday felt the same. On Wednesday he waited until the very last minute to shower and get ready to go to the Grill.

On Thursday she didn't come by. He was starting to really miss her. He should call her, but every time he considered picking up the phone, Logan needed something.

There was one week until court. If he didn't get things back to normal with Kate, would he ever see her again? If she wasn't his caseworker she really had no reason to talk to him.

He needed to fix this, but couldn't. Giving her space was perhaps the most honorable thing he could offer at the moment.

He was an unemployed, broke musician, on food stamps with bad credit, a child he could barely afford, and living in a trailer park. She'd seen the real him and fought their attraction, because she knew then he was no good. Things had only gotten worse. Kate was too observant not to put it all together. And he liked her too much to put her through a life made up of de-hydrated soup, overdue bills, and no money for propane when it suddenly ran out the second winter hit.

Fuck. It was bad enough he'd face times like that with Logan. It pissed him off he was the kids best option in life when all he wanted was to provide a good life for his little man. When would he catch a break? Logan didn't have a choice, but Kate did. And eventually, she'd choose someone more successful like she deserved.

Cutting her off hurt like a fucking bitch, but it had to be easier than watching her walk away in utter disappointment. Knowing all this and accepting that he might've pushed her away before he was ready to let her go, only made him panic. He *should* let her go. It was the right thing to do, but he selfishly wanted her to stay. Someone had to love him.

He was fucking pathetic and his thoughts were giving him emotional whiplash. Even he was sick of himself. He was being a pussy, but he didn't know how to get out of the pity fest going on in his head.

The weekend passed and she never called. At that point he didn't know if she'd answer even if he contacted her again. He had nothing to offer her and maybe she was finally getting that.

On Tuesday night Tucker, Sims, Duce, and Lisa all stopped by unannounced. Logan was in bed. Shane opened the door and immediately picked up on some bad mojo.

"What's up?" he asked, not liking a single one of the expressions staring back at him.

Duce looked concerned. Sims wouldn't look at him at all. And Tucker was fidgeting. "Tell him, Lisa," Tucker said.

"Tell me what?"

Lisa went to the couch and sat down. "I was at a party this weekend with my friend Liz. I don't know if you know her, Liz Erickson?"

He shrugged. He'd never heard of her.

Lisa wrung her hands and went on. "Well, Liz's brother has been in jail for the last eleven months. He was busted for possession and intent to sell. He worked out a deal and he's getting out tomorrow."

"Okay...and this matters to me why?"

She swallowed. "I didn't realize there was any connection—I never really met her brother —but Liz and I were talking and she mentioned him having a girlfriend when he got arrested. Liz of course wasn't really a fan of the girl, because as soon as her brother got busted she disappeared, never once coming to visit him in prison."

"So?"

"Shane, his girlfriend was Noel."

He stilled, shards of ice forming in his veins. "What?"

"I think Will's Logan's father. I saw a picture of him and he has dark hair and sort of looks like Logan."

His blood turned brittle in his veins. "But Logan doesn't have a father..." he said. There was no way Logan's real dad was some criminal.

Lisa looked like she might get sick. "There's more."

"Go on." He might as well hear all of it.

"Well, when she mentioned the name Noel I immediately started asking questions. I was so taken off-guard by all this that I told Liz Noel died a few months ago. She was shocked. I told her how I knew you and before I realized what I said, she was staring at me. It occurred to me that their family didn't have a clue about Logan."

"*You fucking told them?*" Fear and rage exploded inside of him, forcing him to his feet. He instinctively wanted to go to Logan and hold him close where no one else could reach him.

"Hey! It's not her fault," Tucker said defensively.

"I'm so sorry," Lisa cried. "I never would have said anything, but I swear, everything happened so quick. I'm not used to thinking we have to keep Logan a secret. I love that little boy. I'd never do anything to purposefully hurt him."

She was really upset, but he was too overwhelmed by all of this to even process her emotions. "Well, what did she say? What happens now?"

Lisa frowned. "I talked to her today and… she told her brother. He was really upset when he found out about Noel. I don't know what'll happen now. All I know is that he's supposed to be released tomorrow."

They all sat silently for a few minutes. Sims finally said, "Maybe you could go somewhere and hide for a few days, until your court date. If he can't contest the guardianship then you'll be awarded custody and he'll be too late. That's if he's going to try to take Logan."

A queasy, sick sensation churned in Shane's stomach. No one was taking Logan from him. No one! "It isn't that easy. First, I can't run. That would look terrible on my part. Second, it isn't like I go into court next week and sign a paper saying Logan's finally mine. It's a process." He ran his hands over his head. "Fuck. I don't know what to do."

"Maybe this guy won't care. Not everyone wants kids," Tucker said.

"Maybe you should call your caseworker," Duce suggested.

Yeah, Kate would probably know what to do. "We aren't really speaking right now."

The four of them frowned. "What do you mean? She's gotta talk to you. She's your advocate," Lisa said.

"Holy shit," Sims said and they all turned to look at him.

"What?" Duce asked, a confused twist curving his brow.

Sims eyes were wide. "You banged the social worker!"

Four sets of eyes turned on him. "Dude, seriously?" Tucker barked.

Shane looked away, his face burning under their scrutiny.

"Holy fucking shit," Tucker said. "I can't believe you diddled the caseworker."

"It isn't like that," Shane snapped. "I...like her."

"Well, I would hope so! Isn't that completely unethical? What if her job finds out?" Duce asked.

"That's why we didn't tell anyone."

"Well, she's definitely gonna help you if she has feelings for you. I think you should call her," Sims said.

Shane considered it. It wasn't like he had a lot of time. He looked at the clock. It was after eight. "Fine. Give me some privacy."

They all nodded and shuffled outside. He smelled cigarette smoke and knew Sims was still smoking. He dialed and hoped she answered.

"Hello?"

"Hey."

"Hi, Shane." She didn't sound happy.

"I'm sorry I haven't called." She said nothing so he went on. "I, um, sort of have a situation. Could you come over?"

"Is everything okay with Logan?"

"Yeah, Logan's fine. It's something else."

She hesitated. "Shane…you haven't called me in days. I don't understand what's going on, but if you're calling so I come over there and fuck you—"

"Fuck. No, Kate, it's nothing like that." Jesus, he'd never heard her curse. "I just…I have a problem. Could you please come here?"

A beat passed and she sighed. "Fine. But I'm still mad at you."

"I understand."

"I'll see you in a few minutes."

He hung up the phone and invited the others back in. They waited on the couch as Shane paced by the door.

His mind was going a hundred miles a minute. What if this guy wanted Logan? He couldn't give him back. There was no way. The courts had to give him some credit. He'd done everything he could to make Logan's life easy and happy. It was wrong to separate them from each other.

All this time he'd thought the biggest threat to losing Logan was himself. He'd never expected a biological father to turn up out of the blue and take his boy. *Fuck!*

Kate's green bug pulled up and she climbed out. She was wearing a Thundercats T-shirt and gray stretch pants. Her head turned, noting the various cars outside and her steps became sluggish. He held the door for her and she stepped in and stilled the moment she saw everyone.

Tucker, Lisa, Sims, and Duce all waved and said, "Hi," all at once. They sounded like an AA meeting.

She looked at Shane. "What's going on?"

He took her hand and pulled her to the table. "Here, sit down."

She hesitated, giving him an unsure look. "Shane," she whispered. "What's wrong? Where's Logan?"

"Logan's sleeping. He's perfectly fine."

"Then why am I here?"

He stepped close and she tensed, glancing quickly back at their audience. The four couch sitters all turned away and pretended great interest in the carpet.

Shane cupped her face. "They know. Please don't be mad."

Her lips pressed tight. She was mad.

"They just guessed," he whispered.

Her eyes closed, her mouth tight with regret. "And you told them."

"They're my friends, Kate. They love me. They aren't going to expose me or risk my situation with Logan in any way. Trust me."

She pursed her lips, scowled, but nodded. Once she finally sat, Shane introduced her to everyone again and turned her attention to Lisa. Lisa retold the story he'd heard only a half hour before and his nausea grew. He watched as Kate's face paled.

"But no one knows for certain if he's the father?"

Lisa shook her head. "No."

Kate pressed her face in her hands and groaned. She looked apologetically at Shane. "I have to report this. If there's any reason that I see why you couldn't rightly be granted full guardianship of Logan, I'm obligated to let the court know immediately."

"But what if he's not the father?" Shane asked, instinctively expecting her to put his best interest first.

"But what if he is? Shane, he could contest your guardianship. That would be a nightmare for everyone involved. I think I need to talk to my supervisor and see what she says."

"Tabitha?"

"Yes. She likes you. I've talked to her about what a great job you've been doing. She wants what's best for Logan. I think she'll know what's best."

He got quiet. They all did. He voiced his greatest fear. "But what if that's not me?"

She placed her hand on his. "I think it is. Logan sees you as his father. You need to have faith in yourself."

Easier said than done. Blood was blood and if this guy was Logan's biological father, there wasn't a court in the world that would choose Shane over him.

When everyone left Kate stood. "Are you leaving?" he asked nervously.

She looked at the floor. "Shane, everything just got ten times more complicated. I don't know what's happened over the past few days with us, but…you hurt my feelings."

"I'm sorry. I'm an asshole. Please stay."

"I think, in light of everything, I should go. I need to think. It's late and I have work tomorrow. I need to figure out how to handle this."

His chest tightened, making it hard to breathe. "Do you think I'm going to lose him?" The words hurt to say.

Her expression was pained, but he knew she wouldn't lie to him. Quietly, she admitted, "I don't know. He may not even be related to Logan. Try not to worry about it until we have more information."

He nodded, knowing that was an impossible

request. When she left he gave her a brief kiss, but she turned away. He'd hurt her and for that he was sorry. Once again, he'd only been trying to do the right thing and somehow fucked it all up.

~

THE FOLLOWING day he waited for his phone to ring. When it didn't, he called Kate. He couldn't just sit around doing nothing. He held Logan more than usual, needing to feel his weight safely in his arms.

The call went to voicemail, but he left a message. "Kate, it's me. Please call and let me know what's going on. This is killing me. I can't lose him. I just...can't. He's...he's all I've got."

He went to the Grill and checked his phone between every set, but she never called. When he got home a frantic panic struck him, nearly knocking him to his knees. Lisa's car was gone and in its place sat Kate's little green bug.

He walked in and she was sitting on the couch. He was disoriented and scared. "Where's Logan?"

"Asleep. Hi."

He put his keys on the table, his entire body trembling on the inside. "Hi."

She took a steadying breath. Shit. This wasn't going to be good. She was still in her work clothes.

He didn't move, only waited for her to say something.

"I met William Erickson today."

"And?"

"And he's pretty sure Logan's his son."

"Fuck." He rubbed his eyes. "Is he going to try for custody?"

Her expression was an image of professionalism, totally unreadable. "If the paternity test comes back positive, yes. I'm so sorry, Shane."

His jaw locked. He swore even his organs were shaking. Logan was his boy! "What can I do?" His voice sounded strained.

"You can appeal. You know I'll speak on your behalf."

He stood, shoving the chair into the table and she flinched. "Doesn't anyone care that this guy just got out of *prison*?"

She was quiet. "Our job is to advocate for the child in question. If we can prove that this is where Logan would be better off then you could win."

"You and I both know the chances of them removing a child from his biological parent is something that hardly ever happens."

"Will's on probation. We don't know where his head is. He could mess up—"

"And risk Logan's safety? No way. I can't hope for that."

She folded her hands on her lap. "I'm sorry."

"What happens now?" he asked.

"Tomorrow he'll have the test. You'll need to make an appointment with Logan's pediatrician to have a swab done—"

"I'm not sitting in a doctor's office with this guy!"

"No, you wouldn't have to see him. The doctor will send the results to a lab. You don't need to see him."

His mind clouded with fears he couldn't name. His opponent was faceless, but threatened everything he loved in this world. "What was he like?" he whispered.

She gazed up at him from the couch. "He resembles Logan. He's tall. He asked about your sister, about the hit and run. I think he cared for her."

"Didn't care enough to be there for her," Shane mumbled snidely. "If he wasn't off doing drugs he wouldn't have been arrested. Noel wouldn't have had to come to me for help and then she might not have run off to Jersey and been killed."

His heart was racing and he didn't know how to let out the nervous energy pumping through him. He was terrified. The helpless position he was suddenly in was intolerable. This fucking criminal was going to take his baby. No!

His hand swept across the table. Papers went flying through the air. "*God damn it!* This is so fucking unfair!"

Kate jumped. "Shane—"

He turned on her. "Don't sit there and act like everything's gonna be all right! You know it isn't!"

"I don't know anything! I'm not the judge. Custody hearings happen every day. There's no set answer. Every case is different."

She silently moved to the couch and eventually lowered herself. Pacing, he stifled the urge to hit something. Falling into the couch, he palmed his face and growled, tugging his hair in his fists. There was no outlet for the rage inside of him.

Growling in frustration, he got in her face, his arms on either side of her, boxing her in. "What am I going to do if they take him from me? I've changed my entire life for him. I don't remember what I used to do, who I used to be, before I had him." He was frantic.

"Shane, you're scaring me. You need to calm down. You aren't helping anyone like this. You need to keep your head."

He searched her eyes and shook his head. "You don't get it." He grabbed her hand and held it to his chest. "Here, this is where he is. Taking him from me would be like ripping out my heart."

With her other hand she cupped his jaw. Tears shimmered in her eyes. "I'm going to do everything I can to not let that happen. I promise."

He was breathing heavily. Her hand filled his as he continued to press it to his chest. He shut his eyes and breathed in her smell, drawing comfort from her presence. Why did he lose everyone he loved?

He was losing everything, his parents, Noel, his job, Logan, Kate. His world was crumbling and every time he tried to grab onto a wall it turned to dust in his fingers. He needed to be a man and keep it together, but he had no one but himself to lean on.

When he opened his eyes Kate was watching him, a crease marring her brow. "Stay with me tonight. Please. Please, don't go."

She looked ready to turn him down, but she hesitated. He knew he'd made a mess of their relationship and the recent turn of events only complicated everything more, but he needed her, needed someone to be by his side for once.

Her lashes slowly lowered. "Okay."

Relief and gratitude tunneled through him as he kissed her. Their mouths sealed and he pulled her to into his arms, needing someone to hold him. His mind couldn't cope with all of this. He was terrified, unable to imagine a world without Logan.

"Stay with me, Kate," he whispered as he pushed her to her back.

"I'll stay," she assured him, kissing him in response.

He could tell she thought he was only

asking for tonight, but he wanted so much more. Just once he wanted to know someone would be there forever, through all the bullshit, all the ups and downs. He needed to know there was at least one person who saw him as enough.

He unbuttoned her cardigan and slid it off her shoulders. His fingers shook as he unsnapped her pants. He should have been gentle, but he was too high strung. The most he could do was force himself to go slow.

When he filled her, he thrust hard. He moved as though he meant to punish her, his intensity borne of fear, because he knew, just like everyone else he loved, she'd eventually leave too.

His head pressed into her shoulder. His hips snapped forward with hard, measured thrusts. She held him and he wanted to weep with how good her touch felt. No one touched him anymore.

He missed his mother's hugs, his father's guidance, and his sister's biased admiration. All he knew was that moment—Kate. Her touch was warm like sunshine. It heated him from the inside out, made him feel safe.

He was so scared.

He came without taking care of her pleasure. He was a selfish prick. Everything was wrong. Nothing made sense. He was losing ground in every aspect of his life and his fear made his common sense lock up. There were things he could have done to come off as less of a prick, but when the opportunities presented themselves, he lost his grip with reality and simply reacted, leaving him with more hollow regret in the end.

He felt like a scared little boy pretending to be a man. He wasn't complicated, but life was and it was swallowing him whole.

Kate breathed beneath him. Her breasts bore the mark of his touch. He brushed a finger over her tender flesh and she winced. "Are you okay?" he asked, apologetically.

"Can I have some water?"

"Sure." He eased out of her and cursed. "Fuck."

"What?"

It was the first commandment, but in the back of his head, that quick, he saw a silver lining. Maybe this would seal her to him. "I forgot a condom."

She swallowed. Her expression didn't betray her concern. Maybe she didn't think it was such a bad thing either. Having a child with Kate would be amazing. Logan could possibly have a little brother or sister—

"I started the pill. We should be safe."

His hope died. He got up and went to the kitchen, turning his back on her so she didn't see his disappointment. She was on the fucking pill? Wasn't that something couples usually discussed? Was the idea of having his child so abhorrent to her that she had to take such measures?

He was being ridiculous. He could barely afford Logan. Now was not the time for a baby and he and Kate were so far from that stage his thoughts were laughable.

He filled a glass with water and returned to the couch. She'd pulled the blanket over herself and sat up. He touched her knee. "I'm sorry I was rough."

She sipped, her motions a bit jagged, and nodded. "It's okay."

"No, it's not. Did I hurt you?"

She put the glass on the table. "I'm not going to break, Shane. When will you learn that I'm here and you can lean on me?"

"I'm afraid to push too hard. One day you might not come back."

"So long as you're honest with me and let me in, I promise to come back. It's only when you shut me out that those walls separate us. Don't shut me out."

He nodded, wishing he didn't have that habit, but life's experiences had shown him that sometimes it was easier to be solitary. "I'll try."

They moved to the bedroom. He lifted the covers and she curled into his side. He needed to get his life together or he would lose her too. No matter how much he thought letting her go was right, he no longer possessed such selflessness. She would only put up with so much before someone pointed out that she was too good for him.

He kissed her ear, wanting nothing more than to whisper words of love to her. That was one thing he could offer. He wasn't complicated. His world consisted of simple things. He hadn't lied when he told her he was a simple man. He didn't need wealth or fancy things. All he wanted was a family to love. With that, his life would be square.

CHAPTER 17

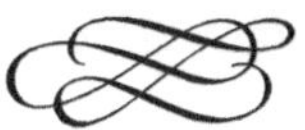

On Friday, he got the news. Will Erickson was Logan's paternal father. Court was on Tuesday and his situation didn't show any signs of improving. He was going in, asking for full custody, and doing so without a job and nothing but sixty-seven dollars in the bank account.

The weekend passed way too fast. He took Logan to the park and played with him non-stop. Kate came by on Saturday and had lunch with them. She had a family thing she couldn't miss so she didn't stay.

Shane worked at the Grill Sunday night as usual. When he came home he took Logan from his crib and brought him to his bed. He pressed kisses into his cherub cheeks and nuzzled him with his nose, a thousand wishes rushing from his heart to any angles listening above.

On Monday, Shane actually considered running. Where could he go? The only thing that stopped him was the constant realization that, no matter how entitled he felt, it would be kidnapping.

Tuesday morning he packed up Logan's diaper bag and loaded him in the Kia, a nauseated dread tightening his stomach enough to bring him to his knees. He moved on autopilot and numb terror. Their appointment was at ten. He entered the courthouse like a ghost. He felt himself fading away, and nothing he did could put him back on solid ground. He stared at each person waiting, wondering if they could see him, see his agony and smell his fear.

A tall guy with dark hair was eyeing Logan's car seat like it was a naked woman. The sense of being violated cut through him and Shane knew in that instant the man was Logan's father.

He took the farthest seat from Will Erickson as possible. He didn't even want to share the air with the man, let alone Logan. Tabitha appeared and smiled at him. Where was Kate?

He was told to enter the court and sit at the table on the left. Every breath seemed rationed to his lungs, a painful proof that he was still living and life fucking sucked. Kate waited for him at the table and he knew there would be no hiding his anxiety from her.

"Hi," he whispered, placing the carrier on the table, unable to say more. He wanted to hug her, but that was inappropriate.

"How are you?"

His insides shook and he fought back the urge to vomit. "Terrible. Scared. Nauseated."

She subtly brushed her hand over his. "Me too."

The judge appeared and took his seat. Everyone stood and, again, he was made to swear on the Bible to tell the whole truth. Kate swore too.

"There have been some developments since we last met, I see," the judge announced, all too detached from the emotional turmoil strangling his heart.

Tabitha walked the results of the DNA test to the judge. He asked Will a few questions. The sound of the other man's voice made his molars lock and he had to shut his eyes to steady his breath. Shane wanted to point out that Will had just finished being incarcerated, but no one seemed interested in that tidbit.

Everything seemed a bit too impersonal for Shane's taste. What was the point of all the visits and personal questions if no one wanted to hear about how far he'd come as a caregiver?

"Ms. McAlister, you have a statement?"

"Yes, your honor."

"When you're ready." The judge nodded.

Kate stood. She opened a folder and withdrew a typed letter, her hands slightly trembling. Aside from that, she carried herself beautifully, as though she didn't have a worry in the world, her pressed suit only making her appear more capable.

She cleared her throat. "When I first took on this case I saw a young man who knew nothing about babies or parenting, for that matter. In my experience, in cases such as these, I see a lot of shortcomings in our nation's system to provide the best service to children in need of care. Even when those charged with the care of a child are in fact the child's biological parents, sometimes they fail. I feared, when I met Shane Martin, I would see another struggling guardian fail a child, but I could not have been more wrong.

"Mr. Martin took his responsibilities as guardian beyond the outlined requirements. He took baby Shane into his life and made him a home. Being a parent, for Mr. Martin, was more than simply attending appointments or meeting a standard. He made it his priority to give baby Shane a father. He gave him back the family they had both lost.

"During my many visits to Mr. Martin's residence, I witnessed the wholesome love of a father and son that I don't see very often in my profession. It is the love that's supposed to exist between a child and their guardian, the love we hope to advocate when we place children in the care of another.

"Mr. Martin provided something for baby Shane that, I believe, has helped him flourish and develop beyond any measuring stick we use to weigh the system's failures and successes. He's given him the only kind of security a child of baby Shane's age can understand. He's met his every need in a way that equates to love in an infants mind.

"When I observe Mr. Martin and baby Shane, I see a son looking to his father. Baby Shane knows that if he needs something Mr. Martin will be there, no matter what. Mr. Martin has reorganized his life in order to make baby Shane his number one priority. His affection for his nephew is evident in the way he plays with him, the way he cares for him, and the way he always, without question, puts him first.

"I understand that there's a decision to be made today and paternity will play a strong role in deciding who is the right guardian for baby Shane. I don't know Mr. Erickson. Neither does his son. What baby Shane does know is that the man who brought him here today is his father in every sense of the word. Genetics mean nothing to a five month old. Their minds can only comprehend things in the simplest form, but I do believe, even as infants, they can understand one of the most complicated concepts of life. That's love, Your Honor. And I have no doubt in my mind, Mr. Martin loves this child with all of his being. And it is with complete certainty, that I believe Baby Shane loves Mr. Martin.

"I ask that the court consider what's best for the emotional wellbeing of baby Shane and not those of us here who are able to rationalize the unfair moments of life. Baby Shane lost his mother with no explanation. He will never fully understand why she was there one day and suddenly gone the next. Don't take the only father he's known away from him as well."

She sat down and he stared at her. She wouldn't meet his gaze. Her eyes remained fused to her paper and he watched, speechless, as a single tear rolled past her lashes.

Knowing he may be jeopardizing his case, he struggled not to take her in his arms and hug her, thank her for speaking such beautiful words on his behalf. He did the only thing he could. Reaching under the table, he put his hand over hers and squeezed. She turned her palm up and clasped his hand tightly.

The judge finished making notes and turned to Will. "Mr. Erickson, do you have a statement?"

"Yes, sir."

"Go ahead."

Will stood. His clothes were wrinkled and

his hands shook. "I just found out that I had a son. I appreciate that Noel's brother cared for him while I was unable to do so. However, I feel it only right that I have the opportunity to be a father for my child. No matter what, Shane Martin will always be Shane's uncle. On that same note, nothing will ever change the fact that I am his father."

He sat down. Short, nothing poetic, but enough to destroy Shane's world all the same.

"Do you have anything to add, Ms. McAlister? Mr. Martin?"

"No, Your Honor."

Shane stood and Kate looked startled.

"Your Honor." He hadn't prepared anything, but he couldn't leave without saying his peace. His heart pounded as he heard his own voice stumble over words, trying to express everything he was struggling to keep inside. "I love my nephew as though he were my own. He's a part of me. All I can say is that taking him away would be like taking away my heart or a chunk of my soul. I don't know how to live without those parts…I take good care of him. Before my sister died, she told her caseworker that if anything should happen to her, that it be me who raise her son. In the few short months I've had him, he's somehow become my greatest accomplishment. He's my pride and joy…Please don't take that away from me."

He remained standing, reading sympathy in

the judge's eyes, but not conviction. Shane swallowed. "Your Honor, the convoluted truth is…" Nerves choked him. He cleared his throat. "The truth is, Your Honor, Logan has a home. It isn't much, but I like to think he's happy there. He has everything he needs, food, shelter, love. I just don't think this should be a question of genetics. It should be a question of what's ethically right for Logan. He may not have been born my son, but I know," his voice broke and he swallowed. "I know…without a doubt, I was born to be his father."

He stared at the table, for the first time facing the inescapable possibility that he was losing his boy and no matter what he said it might not be enough. "That's all." He sat.

"We will take a recess and I'll return shortly with a verdict." Everyone stood and Logan stirred.

"Are you okay?" Kate asked, her eyes glazed and her brow tight with concern.

He couldn't lean on her, not with everyone watching. "Yeah. I need to change Logan. I'm going to take him outside for a minute. Will you come get me if anything happens?"

She nodded and he took the diaper bag and lifted Logan out of his chair. He found a bench and quickly changed him. Shane was giving him a bottle when Will came out of the courtroom.

Shane softly hummed the beat of Jack Johnson's *Better Together*, breathing in Logan's soft hair, never taking his eyes off the serpent that threatened their happiness. As Will approached, Shane's courage shook. No man should have this much power over another.

He unassumingly walked toward them, stealing some of the air from Shane's lungs. *Go away.*

On a shaky breath, Shane braced himself and faced the other man. He slowed a few feet away from their bench.

"Can I see him?" the other man asked.

There was no way Shane was letting him hold Logan. He knew this guy never did anything wrong to him personally, but he hated him. Hated him more than he ever hated anyone, but he had to be nice. God forbid—if Will got custody—and cut off his ties with his nephew completely, Shane would die.

He tilted Logan so the other man could better see his face—it was the most he could offer. Logan gripped his bottle and eyed the other man indifferently.

"He looks like your sister."

"Yes," Shane managed.

Will shifted his posture. "No matter what, I would hope you would still stay close with Shane."

"His name is Logan."

Will blinked at him and the door opened. Kate stepped out. "Shane," she paused when she saw Will standing there. "The judge is about to come back in."

Shane stood and gathered the diaper bag. He left Will to find his own way back, unable to tolerate his presence a second longer. When he sat down beside Kate she whispered, "What was that about?"

"Nothing. I'll tell you later." He shifted Logan on his lap and helped him get comfortable with his bottle again.

The judge entered and took a few minutes to get situated. Shane swallowed. This was it.

"There's a lot of emotion in the courtroom today. I must say, it's nice to see adults vying to prove their love for a child rather than serve some ulterior motive. However, knowing that two people want this child does not make my decision any easier. What matters is what's best for the child.

"Mr. Martin, I have reviewed your case thoroughly. Ms. McAlister has made it abundantly clear that, in her professional opinion, you're a caring and capable guardian. However, your love for your nephew is not enough to negate the fact that, while one parent is deceased, another is still very much alive and willing to take responsibility for his son."

Shane's grip tightened on Logan. His heart pounded and he thought he might puke all over the stuffy little courtroom.

The judge turned to Will. "Mr. Erickson,

your situation is what it is. I'm not going to pretend there was no reason you only just found out you are a father. For reasons none of us will ever know, Noel Martin asked that her brother look after her child in the event that she was unable to do so, rather than yourself."

He looked at Logan who unknowingly smiled and babbled in Shane's lap. "This is not a decision that should be made lightly and therefore I've decided to order a trial period of one month in which Shane Logan Martin will be put in the custody of his paternal father. After that trial period, in which you will adhere to the same requirements as Mr. Martin, under the supervision of another caseworker, we will reconvene here and decide what's best for the baby. This judgment will go into effect today and we'll meet here in one month."

The gavel came down and Shane's breath shook out of him. No... *No!*

People stood and began moving out of the courtroom. An officer approached. He couldn't breathe.

"...Shane? Shane?" Kate's voice barely registered, but he heard her concern.

People began to crowd him. She snapped, "Just give him some room, will you!"

Everyone backed up and she filled his line of vision, her expression pained. "Shane, listen to me. We'll appeal. We'll do everything we can."

"We lost," he breathed.

"Nothing's final yet."

A woman came to stand next to Will who waited to their right. She looked like she might be his mother. She held a knitted baby blanket in her arms. Shane couldn't move.

Kate whispered in his ear. "I'm so sorry."

He held Logan, who knew nothing about what was happening. Shane's stomach felt like it was flayed wide, his guts on the floor. He drew Logan to his shoulder and hugged him as tightly as possible without hurting him. His little arms squeezed him back and he cooed.

A cold, dead settled over Shane. He had flashes of things that made absolutely no sense running through his mind. Noel. Trains. Speeding cars. Hollowed graves. Bottles of drain cleaner. His friends dressed and waiting for him the day of the funeral outside of his trailer. Tabitha handing him a card. Joanne explaining his sister had a son. Duce gagging over the smell of a dirty diaper.

Kate—the first time he saw her, all prim and proper in her buttoned up cardigan. The first time he saw Logan smile. The first time he saw him roll over. The first time he got sick. The many nights he held him, simply staring at his angelic face in awe. Making love to Kate. Playing with Logan in the lake. Giving him a bath. Doing the Bill Cosby.

It all flashed through his mind in the blink

of an eye and when he looked forward he realized he was here and there was no escaping the horrible moment. He pressed his face into Logan's pudgy cheek and breathed in his smell. There was nothing better than that smell.

He looked into his curious eyes, which had faded from baby blue to brown, just like his own. "I love you, little man." He kissed his nose, a pained sound slipping from his throat as he tried to hold it together and failed.

Somehow the weight of Logan disappeared from his arms, a heavy, hollow ache in its place. He watched as the woman with the blanket cradled him to her chest. Logan looked at him, wonder in his little brown eyes.

Will leaned over and said something to Logan. They turned and began to walk away.

That's my son! Shane stepped forward, going after them, when something pulled at his sleeve.

"Shane, no."

He turned and saw Kate. Tears shimmered in her eyes.

"They're taking him," he said, dumbly.

"Only for a little while," she whispered.

He looked back and they were gone. He began to hyperventilate. Nothing had ever hurt like this—not his parents' deaths, not losing his sister. Nothing. He bent, holding his knees, and dry heaved. The ground wobbled as his vision blurred. He wiped at his eyes and stood, angrily, storming out of the courthouse.

Kate somehow managed to get him into her car and drove him home. He walked into his trailer and the first thing he saw was Logan's swing. He turned around and stormed out.

Kate watched him as he kicked the gravel. He walked to the trashcan at the edge of his property and booted it, stomping in the side as it toppled over, all the garbage spilling onto the sandy ground.

"Fuck!" he screamed. Birds scattered from a tree up above.

"Do you want me to call someone?" she asked.

"Who? Who the fuck are you going to call, Kate? *They took him!"*

She burst into tears. "I know. I'm sorry. I don't know how to make this easier for you. It's killing me, seeing you like this. Please don't yell at me."

He should apologize, but he couldn't even think. He looked at her, crying by his shitty front door, and turned. He needed to get out of there.

Shane walked without paying attention to where he was going. He didn't care. He walked to the very end of Sunny Acres and then walked some more. His feet hurt and he was sweating and parched, but he continued.

His phone rang a few times, but he shut it off. When he finally returned to his trailer, staggering and exhausted, it was dark. Kate was gone and he was alone.

He hesitated at the door, knowing the moment he stepped inside signs of Logan would be everywhere. Taking a deep breath, he crossed the threshold.

He marched straight to the cabinet and pulled down the bottle of Wild Turkey that had been collecting dust over the past few months. He brought it to his lips and took a long swig. The alcohol burned a trail to his belly and he drank some more. When that bottle was empty he grabbed another.

Once he drank enough that his thoughts no longer made sense, he grabbed a trash bag and filled it with rattles, toys, books, and baby clothes. He filled two tall bags and shoved them in his closet.

When he went into his room he saw the crib with its *ROCK STAR* bedding. He pulled the sheet off his bed and draped it over the crib then went to find another bottle.

He had no idea what he was drinking or what time it was. At some point he woke up to puke, barely making it to the bathroom. When he finished vomiting, he crawled back to the kitchen and chugged a beer, wishing it were drain cleaner.

He sat on his kitchen floor, his back against the cabinets, and stared at the ground until he finally passed out. Utterly alone.

CHAPTER 18

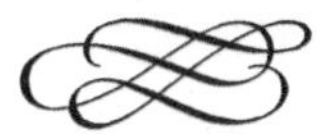

When Shane woke up he was disoriented. His head felt like someone parked a Mac Truck between his eyes. He slithered to the shower and stood, as best he could, under the water.

When he came out, he barely dried off before collapsing into bed and falling back to sleep. The next time he opened his eyes it was after five. He dialed Duce and told him to come over and bring something to drink.

Duce showed up with the guys and they began doing shots of Jack the moment they arrived. It wasn't long before the room was spinning like a Tilt-a-Whirl and Shane came to terms with not driving his car full speed into a tree.

Music blared and voices shouted throughout his trailer. At some point Lisa showed up with some friends, including Sue and Tammy. Sims stuck with Sue like a rash, but even wasted, Shane could see she was no longer interested in the guy. Tammy tried to talk to Shane, but he didn't feel much like talking.

He wanted to drink himself into oblivion. His friends were merely a precautionary measure so he didn't do anything overly stupid. At some point Tucker pulled out a bag of weed and a bunch of them sat at his kitchen table passing a joint. Shane sat that one out. Pretty sure with all the alcohol filling his system smoking would only give him a coronary.

The trailer existed under a thick smog of dirty air. Everyone was laughing. He tried to smile at all the appropriate times, but felt nothing inside. The music, which was blaring suddenly cut off and everyone got quiet.

Shane opened his eyes and saw why. Kate stood at the stereo, scowling. Oh, pretty Kate. She was so good.

"Shane, what the hell's going on?" she hissed.

She wore a shirt that said *Save Ferris.* "I like your shirt," he slurred.

She shook her head. She wasn't amused.

"Hey," he yelled, trying to hoist himself off his couch. "Do you guys know that Kate has a tattoo of a gremlin?" The others acted interested, but Kate eyes widened with fury.

"Can I talk to you? Outside?"

God. Déjà vu. Noel, standing in that very spot, saying those very words, shimmered in his memory. He laughed, even though it wasn't funny. "What's up?"

"Outside. Now."

She turned and marched through the door, which slammed behind her. She had a great ass. "Hate to see you go, but I love to watch you leave," he grumbled as he stumbled to his feet.

He tripped out the front door and saw her standing by his car. Kate did nice things, like bring his car back when he left it places. He clumsily walked up to her and hugged her.

She stiffened and pushed him away. He pulled her back and kissed her, jamming his tongue in her mouth until she shoved his face hard.

"What is wrong with you?"

He glowered at her, disliking the sharp sting of her open rejection. "Nothing. What's wrong with you?"

"You stink."

"Gee, thanks."

"Shane, what are you doing? Do you think acting like this is solving anything?"

Anger made him turn away. What could he say? His head wasn't thinking clearly. She was smarter than him and he had nothing intelligent to bring to the table. He walked to the trailer and pushed against the siding. "Why are you here?"

"Because I'm worried about you?"

"Why?"

"Because I care about you?"

He laughed and spit in the sand. "You're supposed to be smart, Kate. When are you going to get it? I. Am. A. *Loser.*"

"You're sure acting like one now."

He pivoted and nearly fell. Catching his balance, he scowled at her. "Don't be like that. You're not a bitch."

"And you're not a loser so stop acting like you are."

"Really? I don't have a job. I live in a trailer. I'm on fucking food stamps. And I just lost the only person, aside from you, that I care about in the whole world. It won't be long before you wise up and leave me too. Yeah, I sure sound like a winner."

She marched up to him and jerked a fistful of his shirt. He looked down at her. It was like being attacked by an elf, which was kind of funny.

"You listen to me, Shane Martin, the only way I'm leaving you is if you push me away. Now stop acting like an idiot and grow up!"

"I am grown up!" He'd been a grown up since he was seventeen fucking years old!

"No, you're being a child right now! If you're unhappy with your life, do something about it. Don't sit here and drink your liver away, waiting for situations to fix themselves, because it's not going to happen."

"What do you know? You have *everything*!"

She got in his face. "Do you think those things were just given to me? I worked my ass off for everything I have—"

"And I didn't? I sweat my ass off pouring concrete in a hundred degree weather. I bust my balls trying to make extra money playing guitar when I can. I've been struggling to make ends meet since I was seventeen fucking years old and God decided to pull the rug out from under me! I follow the rules. I play the game, but no matter what I end up getting fucked! I didn't have the opportunities in front of me that you did, so excuse me if I don't see us as equals."

She shook her head. "You may not have had the same opportunities as me, but don't act like this is your only option. You have yourself so pegged as this lower class bum, because you're afraid if you try to be anything more, you'll fail. It's a shitty self-fulfilling prophecy and if you think that way, you've already lost."

His jaw locked as he breathed rapidly through his nose. "You don't know what it feels like to be me."

"You're right. I don't. But I could say the same thing about you." She put her hands on her hips and looked down, taking a deep breath, as if collecting her thoughts.

"I've watched you, for months, go against all odds and do something most men could never do. You sit here and claim to be this simple man. Well, I don't see a simple thing about you. As a matter of fact, you're so complicated, I was afraid of getting too close to you. I knew, the minute I let you in, I'd fall for you. Shane, I love you, but this," she waved her hand in front of him. "This is not the man I love."

He looked down. Everything he loved, everyone that ever loved him was always taken away. "Don't love me, Kate."

Her hands cupped his jaw. He fought her hold, too ashamed to meet her gaze. She turned his face until he finally looked at her. "Too late."

It was too much. Everything finally collapsed inside of him and he broke. Shutting his eyes tight, he fought the tears, but it was a losing battle. His face twisted as a sob broke painfully from his chest. "I'm dying inside."

She wrapped her arms around him. "I know."

He hugged her tight, probably tighter than she could take, but she let him. He wept into her shoulder. He hadn't cried actual tears since he was a child. Not when Noel died. Not when his parents died. But he cried now.

"I miss him so much." Her hands ran over his hair. He fell to his knees and she fell with him, never letting him go. "I'm so scared that now that he's gone I'll lose you too and have no one."

"I'm right here."

"Please don't leave me. I need you. You and Logan, you're everything."

Her lips pressed into his temple. "I'm not going anywhere. But Shane, you can't do this. You're better than this."

He wiped his eyes, digging the heel of his palm into his socket, mortified to be crying. "You're the only one who believes in me."

She pulled back and gripped the sides of his face, forcing him to meet her gaze. "Everyone in there believes in you, Shane. You are *not* a loser. The only person who doesn't believe in you is *you*. When are you going to see yourself the way everyone else does?"

"I let everyone down. I let Logan down. I let Noel down. There will be plenty of times I'll let you down. You'll see."

"And there'll be times I'll let you down. Nobody's perfect. That's why we need others to help us through."

"I'm sorry."

"I know you are."

His body shook with every escaped sob he failed to contain, each one slipping past his lips in a horrible moan. "Nothing's ever been this hard."

"No one said it would be easy." Her forehead pressed to his, her fingers combing through his tangled hair.

He sat on the sandy ground and she knelt across from him. "I can't even bring myself to look at his stuff. I had to bag it all up and put a sheet over his crib."

"You know you could go visit him. I could petition the court for visitation."

"I'm afraid. Leaving him is hell. I don't think I can—"

"I know, but don't you think Logan misses you too?"

He started to cry again and she hugged him. When he finally calmed down she said, "I want you to go inside—"

"I don't want to see them."

"Just go in and walk right into your room and shut the door. I'll take care of them. I'll meet you in there."

He stood and spent a few minutes searching for the thinnest veneer of composure. Once he found it, he walked inside and crept quietly past the others who barely noticed him. He shut the door, stifling the music and laughter.

The stereo cut off. He heard Kate, but couldn't make out what she was saying. A few minutes later he heard everyone leaving and soon his bedroom door opened and she stepped in.

She quietly slipped out of her pants and

climbed into bed beside him. He pulled her close. He just needed to hold her.

She rested her arms over his as they spooned.

She was here. At least she was here. He kissed her ear, no longer willing to let another opportunity slip away. "I love you, Kate."

Her fingers tightened around his. "I love you too, Shane."

They lay in silence, neither one of them ready to sleep, but too emotionally exhausted for anything else. She began to hum as he stroked his arm.

Quietly, he sang the words to *If I Fell*, the same song he sang to her on the beach that day, praying she could help him understand, just as the song said.

CHAPTER 19

Shane stood in the unemployment office and waited for the woman with the bottled red hair to look up from where she clicked at her computer. Her fingers tapped over the keyboard. She hummed and pursed her lips, a frown working its way between her penciled eyebrows.

"And you've checked with your union hall for work?"

"Yes, ma'am."

"I see. But you aren't interested in extending your claim?"

"No, ma'am. I want to work."

She sighed and folded her hands. Addressing him as if he were a child, she said, "Mr. Martin, according to our last contact, your claim doesn't run out for another six weeks. Your local business rep has you on the call list and says that you'll be up for the next job, should you prove willing and able to work."

"I'm willing and able to work *now*," he told her.

"But you'll lose your benefits with the union if you seek work elsewhere. You'll also be taken off the list. Young man, I can put you in our job placement program, but the chances of you making as much as you do for the union are slim to none."

"Look, I need to work. Whether that's schlepping burgers or concrete, I don't care." No wonder so many people milked the system. Once you were in it, they made it almost impossible to get out.

She frowned and turned back to her computer, typing in a few more things as a printer next to her desk spewed out paper. "Here, fill this out."

He went down the list of skills and checked off what he thought to be honest attributes of himself. When he finished he slid the paper back to her. She read over it and again turned to her computer. She input some more information and said, "We'll be in contact with you."

He left the unemployment office and went home to clean the pigsty that awaited him.

～

His phone rang at four o'clock. He sighed when he saw it was Kate. "Hey, beautiful."

"Guess what!"

Her excitement jarred his senses, stabbing through the gloom. "What?"

"If you're up for it, you can see Logan tomorrow."

He drew in a breath, his heart stuttering hard in his chest. "Really?"

"Yup! And again on Saturday and every Tuesday until the appeal."

His face split with a wide grin. "Why aren't you here so I can kiss you?"

"Why don't you meet me at my place and kiss me when you get there? I'm heading home now."

Kate's place. "Okay."

"Great. I'll see you in a few."

Shane locked up and drove to Kate's. When he got there, her car was in the driveway. He walked to the door and knocked as he stepped in.

The first thing he saw was a blue sectional with bright, sunny pillows set in the corners. "Kate?"

"In the kitchen."

He walked through the unfamiliar house. *Lucky Star* by Madonna was playing from somewhere. Something smelled delicious. When he found her, she was still in her work clothes, but her shoes were off.

He came up behind her at the counter and wrapped his arms around her. "Hi."

She leaned into him and hummed pleasantly. "Hi."

"What are you making?" He kissed her ear.

"I'm making a rotisserie chicken. And by making it, I mean I'm removing it from its package and putting it on a plate so that you're impressed and think I've been slaving over a hot stove all day."

He smiled. "I'm quite impressed, Ms. McAlister."

"And so you should be. I have sides too. Shut your eyes as I remove them from the deli containers and put them in my own dishes."

He did as she asked, but didn't let go of her. His arms clung to her hips as she quickly worked around his hold.

"There. You can open." She carried the dishes to the table, which was set for two.

"This looks amazing," he said as he took a seat. The table was a chunky white country looking thing.

"Thank you. As you know, I've worked very hard."

"Very," he agreed. Truth was, this was the best meal he'd sat down to in years.

She filled their plates with chicken, green beans, roasted potatoes, and salad. It was incredible.

"So tell me about today," he invited.

She shrugged. "I talked to Tabitha and she got back to me with an answer right before the end of the day."

She was amazing. "Thank you," he said sincerely.

She smiled, her gaze shyly meeting his. "You're welcome. How was your day?"

"I put myself on a job placement list."

"For the union?"

"No."

She stilled, her fork halfway to her lips. "But, if you work somewhere else the union will take you off the call list."

"I know. I need to work, Kate. A man needs to work. I don't care if I'm paid to dig holes and fill them. I just need to know I'm doing something."

"But you've been with the union for years. You make good money there."

"When there's work. Winters coming and that means I may be out of work for months, depending on how the weather holds out."

She looked unsure.

"Look," he said. "Pouring concrete used to be enough. When I was a kid, it was great. I lived like a king compared to my friends, but after the past few months I realized I'm never going to make enough to do the things I want to do."

"Like?"

"Like get a real home, have a family. I want… more." *I want you.*

She looked at him and smiled. "Then I think you're doing the right thing."

They finished dinner and Shane helped her load her dishwasher. After dinner they settled onto the couch and watched television.

"Have you heard anything else on Logan?" he asked.

"No." She looked disappointed. "I do know who Will's caseworker is. Her name's Stephanie."

He didn't know what he was trying to find out. No matter what news he got regarding Logan it made him feel sick. Kate seemed to notice the dip in his mood.

"Hey," she whispered. "We'll get through this."

"I know. Sometimes it just seems like a month is going to take a lifetime. And I'm sitting here telling myself a month, a month, a month, when in reality a month may not make a bit of difference, because it could end up permanent."

"Just think about getting through tomorrow. One day at a time."

He nodded.

They watched some TV and he must have dozed off. Kate woke him and as she shut off television, she asked, "Do you want to stay?"

He looked at her through drowsy eyes. She was so pretty. "I don't want to go."

"Come on." She took his hand and he followed her through the house as she locked up and shut off the lights, leading him to the back room.

She flipped on the light. The furniture was black and the accents were all white or pink. There wasn't a speck of dust anywhere and her bed was made as on display at Macy's. Yeah, this was Kate.

She went to the closet and hung up her cardigan. He observed as she removed her watch and earrings. He still had his John Bender earring in his ear that she gave him.

Stepping out of her pants, she draped them over a white chair against the wall. Her blouse followed. She stood before him in white lace bra and panties. She was exquisite.

"You're staring."

"You're beautiful."

She blushed.

"Come here," he said in a hoarse voice.

She slowly walked to him. Reaching behind her back, he unclasped her bra, pulling it away from her arms and tossing it to the chair against the wall.

Dropping to his knees, he slowly drew down her panties, pressing a kiss to Gizmo. "Step." She stepped out of the puddle of lace at her feet. He pitched them aside and stood, dragging his fingertips up her calf, over her thigh and around her hip.

She stood perfectly naked, quivering as he stared at her. His fingers gently dragged over the swell of her breast, around her nipples, and across her shoulder.

Unclasping her hair, he arranged it over her shoulders. She looked up at him, her face relaxed and serene. "I'm so glad I have you," he whispered, never meaning anything more.

She smiled and tugged on his shirt. "Take this off."

He lifted his shirt and placed it over the footboard of the bed.

She leaned forward and kissed the Logan tattoo over his heart. She untied his hair and also arranged it over his shoulders. "You're too pretty for a man."

He laughed. "You say that too much. I'm gonna get a complex."

"Don't. I see women looking at you. You've got that manly thing working for you. Musician, tattoos, tall, dark, and handsome…you can handle pretty."

"*You're* pretty," he said, stepping close and nuzzling her neck. She turned into him and wrapped her arms around his neck.

"Make love to me, Shane."

He found her mouth and kissed her, long and slow. As they kissed, he nudged her toward the bed. "Lie down."

She sat on the bed and scooted back, tossing the pillows out of the way. He removed his pants and boxers, knowing she watched him. In the dim light she sprawled out, stretching her arms above her head. Shane shook his head, still finding it hard to believe she wanted him.

He climbed onto the bed, making space between her thighs. His hand slowly cupped her breast, his thumb teasing over her tight nipple. Leaning in slow, he kissed her.

Her body came to life beneath him, slowly writhing. Her tiny hands gripped his shoulders as her knees cupped his hips, holding him close. Shane was breathing heavily. His palm caressed her sex, finding her warm and wet.

He fingered her gently, plucking and probing.

"Shane, I want you."

He kissed her throat. "Condom…" His teeth caught at her ear.

"We're good."

Right, she was on the pill. His lungs filled with breath as he found her channel. Nudging her folds, she spread wider for him. With excruciating slowness, he entered her.

Kate watched him from beneath her lashes, her hands resting on his shoulders. As he filled her, sharp little nails pressing into his muscled back. Heat engulfed him. Her body wrapped tightly around him. His cock stroked in and out, their breathing a lyrical backdrop to the rhythm of their bodies.

His chest pressed to hers as he glided over her. Sex was amazing with nothing between them. This was how it should always be, just the two of them, no walls between them. It was beautiful.

She came in quiet sighs, gripping him tightly, holding him firmly. Her body pulsed, triggering his release. Sighing, as he filled her, pressing his head to her shoulder. "I love you, Kate."

"I love you too."

CHAPTER 20

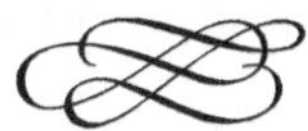

They met at the park. Logan arrived with Will's mother, in a very expensive looking carriage that Shane didn't think was Logan's style at all. When he saw them approaching, he stood.

The tightness in his chest eased as if his lungs were filled with helium. He was more excited to see his little man than he thought possible. Will's mom strolled over to him and smiled uneasily. "Hello."

He barely acknowledged her. Leaning in, he greeted Logan. "Hey, big guy!"

Logan's face lit up like a firecracker. He held out his arms to Shane and squealed. Shane looked back at the woman. "May I?"

She gave a shaky nod. He undid the buckle and scooped Logan into his arms, a thousand racing sensations tickling his stomach as his slight weight filled Shane's arms. "My man!" He hugged him and there were no words to describe the feeling of Logan's little arms wrapping around him.

Spinning, he returned to the bench he'd been waiting on and sat. "How are you, buddy? I've missed you so much." He kissed his head. He was wearing clothing Shane didn't recognize. His shirt had a bear on it. It was probably killing Logan's little ego to rock something so lame.

He chatted with Logan as he climbed up his chest. Shane supported his weight then helped Logan grip his thumbs. With his feet on Shane's knees, he pulled himself up to a standing position and did a wobbly hip and butt thrust as he tried to find his balance. "Look how strong you're getting!"

"Ba, ba, ba, ba, *baaah*," Logan said back.

Shane supported his torso and his little hands grabbed his lips. Shane nibbled and blew raspberries in his palm and he laughed.

He looked back at Will's mom. That was Logan's grandmother, his only one. A pang of sadness burned through him that his mother wasn't there to be a grandmother. She would have been an awesome grandmother.

He played with Logan and watched Will's mom out of the corner of his eye. She seemed transfixed on the baby, but something about her expression appeared sad. He decided to breach the awkwardness and be polite.

Logan tugged on Shane's hair and he turned him to sit on his lap. "Has he been sleeping through the nights?"

She seemed startled that he was talking to her. "Well, not the first two nights, but he's adjusting."

"I wonder if he misses his crib," he said to himself. The woman pressed her lips together in a sad smile. "How's Will with him?"

She opened her mouth and looked nervous. "Will's learning to be a father." She stepped closer. "May I sit down?"

Shane nodded and scooted over.

"Thank you. I'm so tired. It's been a while since I've had to take care of a little one."

He frowned. "Do you watch him when Will's...at work?" Was Will back to work already? It had only been a few days since he got out. What kind of job did he have?

"Well, he's looking for work, but we're all in one house together. Will lost his apartment when he went away."

She said it like her son had been studying abroad. "Does Logan have his own room?"

She frowned. "You call him Logan?"

"Yeah. It was confusing having two Shane's so we started using his middle name."

She nodded. Her finger brushed over the collar of Logan's lame bear shirt. "Logan," she said, testing the name. Logan turned at the sound of his name and babbled.

Where was Will? Maybe he didn't want to see Shane.

"He really is good for you," she said.

Shane grinned. The compliment registered as genuine praise, which he believed it was. He nibbled Logan's cheek and made him laugh. Logan grabbed his nose, digging his fingers into Shane's nostrils—secret handshake.

They sat talking and watching Logan for the next hour. When he fussed Shane gave him the bottle Will's mother had brought. Logan was getting really good at holding the bottle himself. Soon he'd be moving onto solids like Cheerios and biscuits. He was sad that he wouldn't be there for those firsts. He'd looked forward to them.

When their time was up Will's mother stood. He reluctantly stood as well. Pain slowly eased into his chest, tightening and forming a knot there. It was time to say goodbye again.

"Would you like to see him tomorrow?"

"I thought…" That wasn't what the court had ordered.

She shrugged. "Logan's happy when he sees you. I see no reason for you not to see him."

"Sure. I'd love to."

She smiled. "Same time then?"

"That works." Shane suddenly felt lighter "Um, what's your name?"

"Nadine."

"Thank you, Nadine."

"Thank *you*, Shane, and you're welcome."

He helped her load Logan back in the stroller and watched as they walked away. Logan's cries tore at his heart something fierce. Shane only survived the difficult moment because he knew he'd be seeing him again in less than twenty-four hours. One day at a time, that's what Kate had said, one day at a time.

SHANE MET Nadine at the park every day that week. On Saturday she actually dropped him off at the trailer for the day. She was an older woman, in her late fifties and seemed tired, but Shane didn't know if that was just how she always looked.

That Saturday, Kate came over and they played on the floor with Logan like old times. Nadine came to pick him up just before his bedtime. It was hard to say goodbye, as always, but knowing he'd be seeing him again soon helped.

Shane never saw Will, which started to annoy him. "But where the hell is he?" he asked Kate one night in bed. "I feel like Nadine's acting like his mother more than he's acting like a father."

"I don't know," she answered honestly. "I'll

see Stephanie tomorrow and I can ask her, but you know I can't break confidentiality."

He rolled over so he was leaning slightly on her chest. "You would tell me though, if something was wrong, I mean."

She kissed him. "Shane, I was Logan's advocate for three months. You know I would step in if I saw something that wasn't right."

He turned and rested on his back. He was beginning to like Nadine. She was good to Logan, doted over him the way a grandmother should. Shane was grateful Logan had someone in his life like that.

On Monday he got a call from the woman at the unemployment office. "Mr. Martin?"

"Yes?"

"This is Merriam Costel from the Labor and Industry bureau. We have an opening for a labor position in Tobin County you might be interested in."

He muted the TV and grabbed a piece of paper. "I'm listening."

"It's a maintenance position working for Lakota Township. The job's going out to ten candidates who meet the requirements. The final selection will be made through a raffle. If you're interested you'll have to be at the township building Thursday morning for an interview."

"Okay." He got the address from her and jotted it down.

"Mr. Martin, this is a very rare opening. The pay's substantially more than what you were making for the union, because it's salary. You may want to collect some letters of recommendation to bring with you for the interview."

He wrote down letters of recommendation and put five exclamation points after it. "What's the starting salary?"

"The position starts at sixty-five thousand a year and tops out around eighty."

He stilled. *Sixty-five thousand?* His brain went blank. That was like a thirty grand pay increase. His hand trembled and he swallowed nervously. "Is there anything else I should bring?"

"Just yourself. Good luck."

He thanked her profusely and called Kate to tell her the news.

"That's fantastic!" she said over the phone.

"It's not a sure thing. I need to interview and then make it to the final list. From there it's a raffle. Do you…do you think you could write me a recommendation?"

"Of course. Whatever you need."

When he got off the phone with Kate he called Bruce, his last general foreman. It was difficult explaining that he might be leaving the union. That was frowned upon in a big way, but Bruce had a family and he was aware of Shane's situation over the last few months. He agreed to write him a letter, but asked Shane to keep that between him and the people conducting the interview.

After he visited with Logan that afternoon he went to the bank. He had eighty-four dollars to his name, but his bills were paid. He withdrew forty and went to the Salvation Army store. There he found a nice white polo shirt and a decent pair of dress jeans for under twenty bucks.

He gassed up the Kia and drove to the strip mall outside of Sunny Acres. As he waited in his car he took a deep breath. This was it. He gripped the steering wheel and decided this opportunity totally justified his decision.

He pulled his keys from the ignition and locked the car. When he entered the establishment, a woman in a black apron greeted him. She walked him back to a chair and he sat down nervously. They went over what he wanted.

"Ready?" she asked.

He met her gaze in the mirror and took a deep breath. "Ready."

The sheers sliced through his ponytail and he shook his head, hair tumbling around his ears. No going back now.

She proceeded to snip away at his hair until he barely recognized himself. The length of his ponytail was being donated to Locks of Love to make wigs for children undergoing chemo.

When he left he had four dollars in his

pocket. His ears were cold and he felt like a different person. He stopped by a convenience store on his way to Kate's and spent his last four dollars on a red rose.

Rather than simply walking in when he arrived at Kate's, he knocked. She opened the door and was wearing a dusty sage cardigan and brown dress pants. She looked like a centerfold for fall.

He held out the rose and her eyes bulged. "Oh my God, your hair!"

"Do you like it?" he asked nervously.

She jerked him through the door and yanked his head down so she could run her fingers through it. "It looks amazing. I can't believe you cut it all off."

"But you like it?"

She met his gaze, her soft brown eyes burning as they stared into his. "It's incredibly sexy."

He held out the rose. "I got this for you."

She blushed a delicate shade of pink and took the rose. Then she kissed him.

His arms wrapped around her and he pulled her close. She must have really liked his haircut, because she started taking off his clothes right there in the doorway.

Shane peeled off her cardigan and tossed it on the floor as she shucked her pants. He scooped her up and her legs went around him. Leaning her against the door, he ravished her mouth. Her fingers burrowed in his short hair as she ground her body against his.

Her fingers made quick work of undoing his zipper. She gripped him and he slid her panties aside.

"Put me inside of you," he growled against her mouth.

She lined their bodies up and Shane drew back, snapping his hips forward and filling her to the hilt. Kate's head tipped against the door as he withdrew and thrust into her, hard.

Muscles burned as breath and blood and lust pumped through him. His body pounded into hers so hard the small brass knocker on the other side of the door rattled with each cock of his hips. Kate was a maniac. She scraped her nails over his shoulders. If he hadn't been wearing a shirt she'd probably have drawn blood.

He loved her. God, he loved her.

They came together and he remained inside of her as he carried her to the couch. Collapsing, he held her to him. When he caught his breath, he laughed and said, "I should bring you flowers more often."

She giggled. "I decided on doing that to you before you even got here, but yes, flowers are nice."

After dinner she handed him three envelopes. "What's this?" he asked.

"Open them."

He opened the first envelope and withdrew a slip of paper.

To Whom It May Concern,

I became acquainted with Shane Martin when I was assigned by the court to be his caseworker after he volunteered to act as guardian to his nephew after the death of his sister. I have never witnessed Shane on a job, but I did get a chance to witness him in his day-to-day life.

Shane is a man who takes responsibility very seriously. If he is expected to do something, it becomes a top priority. He is honest in all things. He is prompt, dependable, and possesses great people skills.

While I cannot vouch for his abilities as a township laborer, I can assure you that he is a person I hold in high regard and believe capable of many things. According to Shane, he's a simple man, but in the short time I've known him I've come to the decision that extraordinary is a better word for the type of man he is.

Please accept this letter of recommendation on his behalf. While Shane would benefit greatly from this opportunity, I also believe the township would be acquiring an employee who would prove to be a great asset.

Sincerely,
Ms. Katherine McAlister
Licensed Social Worker

Children and Youth
Advocate and Liaison for the Department of
Welfare

HE LOOKED at her as she waited anxiously for his reaction. "Wow, Kate." He shook the letter. "That's twice you've gone to bat for me on paper. Thank you. This is incredible."

"I hope it helps."

"Even if it's never read by anyone but me, it helps. Thank you." He kissed her. He held up the other two letters. "What are these?"

"Their from Joanne and Tabitha."

"More recommendations?"

She nodded. "I told them what you were doing and they insisted on writing up something."

"I didn't know you talked to Joanne," he said.

"We keep in touch. Tabitha called her and she faxed the letter right over."

He shook his head, speechless. The other two letters were equally as praising but nothing meant as much as reading Kate's commendation.

~

THURSDAY MORNING HE SHOWERED, shaved and changed into his new clothes. He cleaned up his work boots and stuck his recommendation letters in his pocket, including the one from his old foreman that arrived the day before. He was at the township building before it was even opened.

He interviewed with a man named Russ Myers. There were about forty guys there for the job, which was intimidating. Because there were so many applicants, the interviews were short and sweet.

Russ was a nice guy in his mid-forties. The applicants ranged from their early twenties to their late fifties. The job would be labor intensive and Shane was glad to see that he ranked among about ten percent of the guys applying when it came to a healthy physique.

He left feeling unsure. It was a crapshoot.

That afternoon when he visited with Logan he went to the Erickson house. Nadine invited him in, saying that now that the weather was getting cooler there was no reason to keep meeting at the park.

Logan lifted his arms to be held the moment he saw him. He recognized Shane's voice, but curiously looked at his head as if trying to place what was different.

"You look nice today, Shane," Nadine said as she placed a glass of iced tea on the table for him. "Got your hair cut."

"Yeah. Thanks. I had an interview."

"Oh, that's wonderful. When will you know if you got the job?"

"Not for a while."

Their house was nice. Simple. The furniture was clean, but dated. Old pictures hung along the wall behind the staircase leading to the second floor. Baby toys dotted the living room and dishes waited in a drying rack to be put away.

There were a lot of prescription bottles on the counter. He didn't want to be nosy, but he noticed they all said Nadine. Will wasn't home.

"Would you like to see Logan's room?" she asked when Logan pooped and needed a change.

"Sure."

He followed her down the hall. Their carpet was royal blue and didn't really match the rest of the decor. But again, it was clean. The Erickson's appeared to be normal people. As they passed more pictures sitting on a hutch in the hall, Nadine said, "This is Frank, my husband." She ran an affectionate hand over the frame. "He passed away six years ago."

Shane didn't know what to say to that so he nodded and looked down.

Logan's room was done in bears. He hid a smile. After being a *ROCK STAR* at his place, this baby bear motif had to be killing him. It was totally softening the badass image the little guy had been trying to cultivate.

When they walked back to the kitchen Shane noticed a bedroom with sports jerseys hanging on the wall and knew it was Will's.

After sitting and talking for a while Shane stood. "Do you mind if I use the bathroom."

"Go right ahead," Nadine said. "It's down the hall on the left."

Shane headed in that direction, but rather than go to the bathroom he returned to the room that had to be Will's. The room was immaculate. The nightstand only held a lamp. The bed was made and the drawers of the dresser were all closed tightly. He frowned. Did anyone live there?

He pulled the door partially closed and went to the bathroom, flushing the toilet and washing his hands. Something was off. Although he didn't want to see the guy who took Logan away from him, it was weird they never crossed paths.

That night, Shane couldn't sleep. Kate was at her home, because he'd played at the Grill. He lay in his bed worrying. Worrying about his interview, worrying about Logan, worrying about Kate, worrying about what kind of father Will was, and worrying why Nadine had so much medicine on her counter.

She had dark circles under her eyes today. When he'd returned from the bathroom he saw her before she saw him and she looked run down and sad. Nadine did that a lot, frowned when she thought no one was looking.

He liked Logan's grandmother. He wanted to do something nice for her. He didn't know what kind of man Will was other than the absent kind, and being that she was a widow, he'd be willing to bet that the patched up cabinet in the bathroom had been waiting to be fixed for quite some time. He decided he'd fix it for her.

The next day when he knocked at the Erickson's door he had his tools with him.

"What's all that?" Nadine asked, holding Logan on her hip.

Shane was suddenly self-conscious. "I, uh, noticed your vanity in the bathroom was broken. I thought I'd fix it for you."

She blinked at him and he frowned when he thought he saw tears shimmer in her eyes. "Oh, Shane…"

"If you don't want me to—"

"Oh, no," she quickly interrupted. "I'd really appreciate it. How about I set Logan up in his playpen in the hall so he can watch his daddy work and I'll make you something to eat?"

He frowned, but nodded. Did she realize what she'd said? His gut tightened uncomfortably. Was Will there? Was she referring to him? He took Logan as she got out the playpen. Once it was set up he went to work on the bathroom cabinet.

When he realized Will wasn't there, he relaxed. Logan sat up babbling and clapping and drooling all over a teething ring as he worked. He was getting so big. Everyday Shane noted a difference.

The cabinet was a quick fix. When he was finished they ate chicken salad sandwiches. Shane was completely distracted by the fact that Logan was eating Cheerios. Cheerios! He was growing up too fast.

The front door suddenly opened and closed. Nadine noticeably tensed.

"Ma?" Will walked into the kitchen and stilled. "What's he doing here?"

Shane stared at the other man. He had a drawstring bag slung over his shoulder. Nadine cleared her throat and said, "Will, you know Shane."

"I thought visitation was only on Tuesdays and Saturdays?"

Shane noticed that Logan didn't give a flying fuck about the guy's presence. Nor did Will greet Logan. What the hell was going on?

"Shane came by to fix the cabinet in the bathroom."

Will eyed him. Shane was slightly embarrassed, but tried hard not to let it show. As he held Logan on his knee he stared back at the other man. Something wasn't right.

"Oh, yeah, I've been meaning to get around to fixing that."

Nadine stood and carried their dishes to the sink. She remained standing at the counter.

"Well, I'll just put this in the laundry room." Will said and walked away. A door in the hall closed. Was he sticking around?

There was a long, uncomfortable silence. Logan was getting cranky and probably needed to go in for a nap. "I should probably go," Shane said.

Nadine took Logan and smiled. "Thank you for fixing my cabinet, Shane." She squeezed his arm. "Come back any time."

On the drive home Shane tried to make sense of the situation at the Erickson's house. The more he thought about it the more pissed off he got. Will didn't even say hello to Logan.

When Kate called that night, he told her what happened. She was quiet.

"Do you know something?" he asked.

"Shane, you know I can't talk to you about this."

He blew out a frustrated breath. "Can you at least tell me if Logan's in any trouble? I mean, I know Nadine loves him, but Will's never there. It's weird."

"You see him. Logan's fine. Nadine's very good with him, you've said so yourself. You see for yourself that he isn't in any danger."

He finally said what had been bothering him. "But she isn't his mother."

"I know. Listen, I talked to Stephanie today

and I think you may have a really good chance of getting Logan back, not because he's in any danger there, but because you're a good father figure and the circumstances are turning in your favor."

Her words reminded him of what Nadine said that day. "She called me Logan's daddy today."

"Who did, Nadine?"

"Yeah."

She was quiet. "I don't know how things are going to work out, but you're more that child's father than anyone else in this world. No one can ever take away the time you raised him, Shane. It's okay to call yourself his dad."

But he wasn't his dad. "I'm not ready to say that, not when the court doesn't see it that way."

"What about the way Logan sees it?"

Her question jarred him. At one point, Logan had a mom too. Did he miss her? Remember her? Wonder why she wasn't around any more? He didn't want to fall into the same category as his sister.

He thought about her question, as he got ready to go play at the Grill. Did Logan see him as his father? Shane definitely saw him as his son.

CHAPTER 21

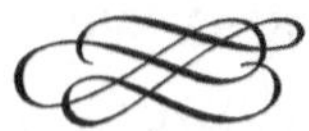

His phone was going crazy. Shane rolled over and reached for his cell. When he found it, he rubbed his eyes and squinted at the screen. He didn't recognize the number.

"Hello?" he answered in a scratchy voice. What time was it?

"Hi, Shane?"

"Speaking."

"This is Russ Myers from the township."

He sat up. "Oh, hi."

"Is this a good time?"

"This is a great time." Shane looked at his clock. It was eight-thirty, but raining out, so his room seemed darker than usual.

"Good. I was calling to let you know that we really liked meeting with you and have decided to push you forward. If you're still interested, we'd like to submit your name for the job."

He was smiling so wide it was difficult to form words. "That's fantastic! Thank you."

"You're very welcome. The raffle will be drawn this Friday and we should have a final answer for you by Monday. Best of luck."

"Thank you. Thank you very much."

He ended the call and dialed Kate. She'd already be at work.

"Hello?"

"Guess who made it to the top ten…"

"Really? That's great!" she shouted then lowered her voice. "I have news too, but I can't talk to you about it now."

"Is everything okay?" he asked.

"Everything's great. I'll call you tonight when I leave here."

"Okay. I love you."

"Love you too. Bye."

∼

SHANE WAS TUNING his guitar when Kate called.

"Hello?"

"I'm coming over," she said by way of greeting.

"Okay. Everything all right?"

"Everything is perfect!"

"Good day?"

"Great day! I just need to know if I should pick up pizza or Chinese on the way."

"Whatever you want." Shane didn't have the pockets to be picky. A little of his manhood withered each time she bought him dinner, but he loved her all the more for never making an issue of it.

"Pizza. Can you call ahead and order?"

"That I can do."

A few minutes later the green bug pulled up and Kate climbed out holding a steaming box of pizza. She bounced up the step of the trailer and gave him a smacking kiss. Her happiness, whatever it was about, was contagious.

"I have a bottle of wine in my trunk. Will you grab it?"

Shane went to get the wine and when he returned Kate was carrying two plates of pizza from the counter.

"What's going on?"

"Wine first," she said, digging in the drawer for the bottle opener.

He pulled down glasses and she uncorked the bottle.

He poured them each some wine and waited.

"Sit," she said, cheerily.

He sat.

"Okay." She took a deep breath. "I talked to Stephanie today."

His stomach flipped at the mention of Logan's new caseworker. "And?"

"And you know I'm not allowed to talk to you about that."

He frowned. "Then why are you bringing it up?"

"Did you ever play Hot and Cold when you were a kid?"

"Yes."

"Let's play that game. The warmer you get me the more naked I'll get."

"*Um*, okay."

"Guess how my day was," she said.

"You're day was good." They'd already established that.

She removed the thin purple scarf around her neck and dropped it to the floor. "Try to guess what else happened."

"You talked to Stephanie about Logan and Will."

She unbuttoned her cardigan and put it on the back of her chair. She wore a purple slinky tank top underneath. "What else?"

"They said I could have Logan back," he hoped.

She pressed her lips together and picked up her scarf, wrapping it back around her neck.

"Will didn't get a good report," he said, more realistically.

She smiled and removed the scarf again. "And why do you think that is?"

"Come on, Kate. Is Logan okay?"

She tsked at him. "You know I can't tell you the details of his case. Logan's fine." She took a bite of pizza. Cheese strung from her lips and she wiped her mouth with a napkin.

He sighed and thought for a minute. His mind rolled over the facts, Nadine and the house and Will suddenly showing up the other day. He was never there. "Will missed an appointment."

She kicked off her shoes, stood and undid her pants, sliding them down and folding them neatly on the chair to her left. She sat in just her panties and a little tank top. "Keep going."

"It's hard to think with you sitting there half-naked."

"And holding pizza. Give me a fresh beer and I'm a man's wet dream. Keep going, you're almost there."

He rolled his eyes. He couldn't care less about the fucking pizza. He had an appetite for something totally different.

He groaned. "Um, Nadine said something in my favor to the social worker?"

She grinned, reached inside her tank top, undid the clasp of her bra and slid it through the sleeve. It was fucking hot.

He knew this was a long shot, but he hoped. "Nadine thinks I should have Logan."

The tank top came off. His skin tingled as possibilities shot through his mind.

"Are you serious? What did she say?"

She shook her head. "*Ah, ah, ah...* I can't share that information."

She sat at his table eating pizza, her bare breasts tipped with rosy tight nipples and an expression on her face that would give the impression she was dressed in a power suit. How did she do that, come off so confident no matter what?

"Is it because she likes me or something Will did?" She shook her head. He needed to phrase the question as a statement to play the game. "Will did something that broke the court order."

She stood, placed her crust on the plate, and dropped her panties to the ground. She was standing in his kitchen buck-naked.

"Holy fuck, what did he do? This is huge, Kate. You have to tell me!"

"I can't, but you're really good at this. I'm really hot."

He groaned. "You have no idea."

"Think, Shane. What did you tell me the other day? What was Will holding when he came in."

"I don't know. A bag. It looked like laundry."

She gave him a pointed look.

"Oh, my God. He's not even living there!"

She threw herself at him and kissed him. He kissed her hard then pulled back. "What does this mean?" he asked, wanting to truly understand what was happening.

"It means that you'll likely be getting a notice in the mail that your appeal's been moved up. I, of course, can't tell you why or share anything I may have been told in confidence, but I will of course be there when you go to get *your* son back."

My son.

He kissed her again and she began to ride him through his jeans. "You have too many clothes on, Mr. Martin."

"I think I can fix that. I've been told that I possess great resolution skills."

Her mouth bit at his neck. "Then you better resolve to get naked."

He stood, lifting her with him as he headed to his bedroom. "Will this be going into your report, Ms. McAlister?"

"Yes, so you better please me."

"Oh, I aim to."

~

THREE DAYS later he got a letter from the District Court of Lakota. His appeal date was moved to Wednesday. He brought the letter to Nadine's that afternoon.

His greatest fear was that this was all a misunderstanding, that Kate was wrong and nothing had changed. But if she was right and

Will wouldn't be Logan's primary guardian, where did that leave Nadine?

He liked Nadine. She was a good grandmother. But since the beginning, Shane noticed an inherent gift among women to connect with children. What if Will not being there wasn't enough for him to get Logan back? What if the court picked Nadine over him because she was a woman? Who would be seen as the best choice, a child's uncle or grandmother? They both had a link to Logan and, again, Shane feared he wouldn't be enough.

When they sat at the table he withdrew the letter from his pocket and placed it on the table. "Do you want to tell me what this is about, Nadine?"

She sighed and looked sad, knowing he was watching her. "I'm sick, Shane. I have arthritis and my body isn't what it used to be." She smiled at Logan and slid a toy car closer to him. He grabbed it and put it in his mouth.

"Will you be okay?" He cared about Nadine on some level and didn't want to think of her as unwell.

"I'll be fine. I just have to be realistic about what I'm capable of. I raised two kids with a good husband there through most of it. I know you know what it means to be a parent. You worry about everything. Are you loving them enough? Are you smothering them? Did you tell them no when you should have and yes when it was right?

"Liz was a great daughter. She never got into trouble, always did what she was told. I raised her and Will the exact same way, I believe, but from the time they were babies they had their own likes and dislikes and were each their own person.

"When Will got in trouble I was crushed. I always wondered if Will still had Frank in his life…a boy needs a strong role model, a good father to guide him. When your child does something to shock you, something wrong, your first instinct as a parent is to say, no, not my child. But the truth is, we can teach our children the difference between right and wrong, but that doesn't always mean they'll make the best choices when we aren't there for them."

Her head tilted as she gazed at the table. "I never met your sister. I imagine if she was anything like you, Logan lost out on having a wonderful mother. You're so different from my William. You're responsible, patient, and you want—so very much—to be a father."

She picked up a teething ring, turning it this way and that. "When Will told me about Logan I was confused and then, after it sunk in, I was thrilled—a grandbaby to love and spoil. I don't have many friends since Frank died. I told

William he had to do what was right and be a father to his son.

"I didn't realize the mistake I was making at the time. Logan *had* a father, an amazing one who'd sacrifice anything for him. Being a parent isn't about the bloodline you share. It's about what's in here." She placed her hand over her heart. "It's been three weeks and William barely knows his own son. I love that baby boy, but he's not mine. It isn't right that I keep him when he has a father who'd do anything to be there for him."

He held Logan tight and looked at Nadine. "What happens now?"

"I told the caseworker I think Logan should live with you."

His heart raced so fast he thought Logan might feel it pounding through his chest. "What about Will?"

"William won't contest. I sort of pushed him into this in the first place, thinking I was doing what was right. He's been away for so long, he wants to be out in the world, not home with a baby. He's not as mature as you. He just doesn't get that the simple things in life are what makes it magical."

He looked at her and she sighed. Shane's voice was tight. "I don't know what to say."

"I just hope that you'll let me still be a part of Logan's life. I adore him and think of him as my grandchild."

"You're his grandmother, Nadine. I'd never deprive him of that."

"I hoped you wouldn't." She smiled at him. "You're a good man, Shane. I'm sorry I put you through this."

That afternoon when he drove home, his mind was numb. He was getting Logan back—for good. He'd be Logan's legal guardian and Logan would be his son. *His son.* It was almost too good to believe.

As he stepped into his trailer, he looked around. The laundry was all put away. The sink was empty and the counters were clean. His mother's quilt covered the couch and the pillows sat neatly in each corner. There was only one thing missing.

He went to the closet and pulled out the two trash bags. He turned on his stereo and put in his Skynyrd album. Taking his time, he carefully pulled out each piece of clothing and folded it into a pile. Carrying the clothes to the bedroom, he placed them back in the drawers. He set out all the toys and baby paraphernalia. His son was coming home.

~

THAT WEDNESDAY NADINE and Will showed up in the courtroom with a large suitcase. Logan opened his arms to Shane the moment he saw him.

The judge spoke to Stephanie the caseworker and asked Will questions. Nadine didn't speak.

Everything sounded so cut and dry on the surface. The judge asked if Shane was still interested in custody and he immediately agreed. Kate was there beside him the entire time.

Once Will renounced his sole guardianship the judge dismissed them and Tabitha took them to a private room to go over paperwork. Nadine and Kate sat in the hall with Logan while he and Will signed what needed to be signed.

The other man looked resigned. "I really appreciate this," he said.

Shane simply could not wrap his brain around the other man's decision to give up his child. He nodded, too afraid to say too much and maybe cause Will to change his mind.

He signed on the dotted line and they shook hands. It was surreal. He knew there would be more paperwork to follow, but the basics were done.

Will left the private room and Tabitha handed him his set of copies. "Congratulations, Shane. You deserve this."

He smiled at her. "I'm so glad you found me."

"Me too," she said and shook his hand. After gathering her things, she quietly left.

Shane stood alone in the room for a few minutes, feeling the rest of his life waiting for him on the other side of the door. He folded his papers and shoved them in his back pocket when his phone suddenly vibrated.

"Hello?"

"Shane?"

"Yes?"

"Russ Myers. How are you?"

"I'm great," he said calmly. "How about yourself?"

"I can't complain. Sorry for the delay, but I wanted to be the first to tell you that your name came up first in the lottery. The job's yours if you want it."

Breath settled in his lungs as a thousand worries took flight. Tension he'd been carrying for weeks slowly unraveled inside of him. His shoulders unknotted and, for the first time in months, he felt like he could finally breathe again.

He'd lost everything, yet was the richest man in the world. Not because he'd be making money again soon, but because he'd managed to find security in a tumultuous world that came without promises. Emotion locked down on his vocals as he realized he'd done something good for himself. Not one to pat himself on the back, the due praise felt good. He was proud of himself.

He didn't want his new boss to think he was crying, even if he was. He cleared his throat.

"Thank you, sir. That's great news. I'd love to take the job."

"Good, good. Can you come in on Monday and we'll get you all set up?"

"Monday's perfect."

He hung up the phone and wiped his eyes. As he pushed open the door the first vision he saw was Kate holding a sleeping Logan. She smiled at him. He loved them. They were his everything.

"Congratulations. It's a boy," she whispered as he stepped close and kissed her discretely. His hand tenderly brushed over Logan's head and he smiled. His son.

"Guess what?" he whispered.

She looked up at him, asking with her eyes.

He smiled. "I got the job."

She jumped and Logan stirred. She quickly comforted him back to sleep and pressed her face close to his chest as if it took everything she possessed not to kiss him right in the courthouse. "I'm so proud of you."

"I love you," he said back, needing for her to understand how much she meant to him. He pulled back and looked into her eyes. "I could have never done this without you, Kate. Thank you."

She smiled. "Come on, let's take your son home."

They left the courthouse with Logan's new belongings in tow. Shane put him in his car seat, which he was quickly outgrowing, and he drove them all back to the trailer.

That night at dinner Logan dined on mushed up macaroni and cheese while they dined on the non-mushed variety. Shane had never felt more like a king.

After he put Logan to bed he came to join Kate on the couch. They sat in silence, but continuously met each other's gaze and grinned, as though they were communicating telepathically. Their expressions were twin pictures of serenity and relief. This was it. His life was figured out.

Turning to her, he watched a soft smile curl her lips. It was a day of wins, yet something was missing. He took her in. Her toenails were the color of bubblegum. Her pants were pressed and fitted. She wore a sweet, butter yellow blouse and a delicate string of pearls.

That was his Kate, yet he saw the girl within. She was wild and silly and had a little gremlin tattooed right next to her money spot. He laughed.

"What?" She turned, grinning at him curiously.

His gaze dropped to her hands folded primly on her lap. His fingers plucked the tab off his beer and faced her. She blinked adoringly at him. Taking her hand, he fiddled with her fingers, slipping the beer tab over the tip of her ring finger. She looked at him and giggled.

"Marry me, Kate."

She stilled, her expression sobering.

When she didn't immediately reply, he said, "I know I don't have a whole lot to offer you, but it'll come in time. Right now I have my heart to give and I only want to give it to you and Logan. I want to love the two of you with everything I have."

He hadn't planned this. When she still didn't answer he looked down at her finger with the silver beer tab stuck on the end and frowned. He should've planned this better.

"If you don't want to—"

She grabbed his face and made him look at her. "Shut up," she rasped. "I'll marry you, Shane. I'd love nothing more than to be your wife."

A smile split his face. He kissed her and she kissed him back, their lips curling with happiness. He had an idea and suddenly pulled away.

His fingers went to his ear and he undid the diamond stud there. It was his John Bender diamond and she was his Claire. He pressed the post of the diamond earing through the narrow hole of the tab and attached the back. The diamond winked back at them. He grinned at his handiwork. "There, that's better."

"Did you just Ringwald me?"

"I believe I did."

She kissed him. "I love you, Shane Martin. Thank you. That was probably the most romantic thing anyone's ever done."

He felt himself flush. "Let's go to bed."

"Please," she said, and shut off the television.

EPILOGUE

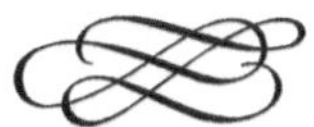

Kate picked up another garbage fry doused in chili and cheese, and God knows what else, and tossed it in her mouth, her wedding ring flashing amber under the dim lights at the Grill. She was getting fat, but she didn't care. These fries were unbelievable.

Shane reappeared and slid into the booth across from her. "Sorry."

"How was he?"

He laughed. "Ridiculous. Nadine said he insisted on saying goodnight before he went to bed."

She laughed. "You really shouldn't indulge his every whim." Her phone rang and she brought it to her ear. Shane gave her a knowing look, his one eyebrow arching high in his beautiful face.

"Hello?" she answered.

"Mommy?"

"Hey, big man. Why aren't you in bed?"

"Mom-mom said I call you."

"I see. And what did you have to call me for?"

"This…" He blew raspberries into the receiver and she laughed. "I sound like Uncle Duce!" he giggled.

She shook her head at Shane. This was his influence. "Yes, you sound like Uncle Duce. Now go to bed."

He laughed. "I love you, Mommy."

"I love you too, Logan." Her heart raced every time he said those words.

"Do it back," he said excitedly.

Kate looked around. Leaning low over her fries, she stuck her tongue between her lips and blew raspberries into the phone.

Logan cracked up. "Mommy farted!"

She laughed. "Goodnight, stinker."

"Goodnight, Mommy."

She ended the call and Shane gave her a dubious look. "You know, you really shouldn't indulge him like that."

"Oh, shut up," Kate smiled, shoving another fry in her mouth.

Shane stood and kissed her. "Do you need anything before I go up?"

"No, I'm good. Break a leg."

"Roger that," he said as he grabbed his guitar case and headed to the stage.

Kate finished her fries and leaned back as the waitress removed the plate. She watched her husband, just like she did every Friday night, as he set up his equipment.

She still had a hard time believing she was married to such an incredible man. She loved him with a fierceness some might call obsessive, but she didn't care. He was hers and she was never giving him back.

Her sisters and her parents had both welcomed Shane into the family with open arms. Having not been around family in such a long time, he was shy with them at first. It didn't take them long to see what Kate saw in him. Everyone saw it. His modest ways seemed to charm everyone that crossed his path. Even her nieces, Keira and Kiley adored him.

The microphone whistled as Shane took his seat. "Good evening, everyone."

She'd never forget the first time she heard him play. She probably fell in love with him in that moment. He was so incredibly talented. His voice was like silk and when he sang, it covered her skin in goose bumps every time.

"This first song's for my beautiful wife. Katie, I love you." His fingers strummed over the guitar as his voice rung out. *Well Momma told me..."*

His hair was getting longer again. She liked it. He *was* the John Bender to her Claire.

When he hit the chorus to Skynyrd's *Simple Man* the crowd applauded. He sounded wonderful. Heat blossomed in her chest. He was her simple man, but she knew deep down he was anything but simple. He was the other half to her soul. He was her world, her heart, her very extraordinary husband.

When they pulled up at the one story home, Nadine's car sat in the driveway. He grabbed his guitar out of the trunk and opened her door. "Come on, sleepyhead."

They walked into the house and Nadine stood from the couch. "How was he?" Kate asked, putting her purse on the table next to a stack of Shel Silverstein books.

"He was wonderful."

She kissed them goodnight and Shane walked her out. Kate tiredly bent to pick up a pile of Transformers scattered all over the floor. Sims convinced Logan they were the coolest toys and he played with them every day.

Shane returned as Nadine's headlights skittered across the back wall as she pulled away. He locked the door and came behind her, hugging her tight.

His hands rested on the swell of her belly, peeking from the opening in her cardigan.

Pressing his lips to the back of her neck he asked, "You tired?"

She sunk into his hold and shut her eyes. "Depends. What did you have in mind?"

He swayed with her and hummed the tune to their wedding song, *Tupelo Honey,* by Van Morrison. "I was thinking about carrying you to bed, stripping you out of these clothes, and making love to you until you passed out."

She sighed. "That sounds wonderful." Her world tilted and she squeaked. "Shane! I'm too big for this."

"Shut up, you are not too big."

"I'm fat," she pouted.

"You're seven months pregnant. You're beautiful."

When he said that, she melted. He truly saw her that way. He didn't see any of her flaws. He never noticed how intimidated she was by others or how much she second-guessed herself. He only saw her best parts. Either that or he saw her worst and still found reasons to love her anyway. She made him a better man and he made her a better woman.

He laid her down on their bed and slowly removed her shoes. His lips kissed her toe and pulled off her maternity pants. She self-consciously covered her belly.

"Stop," he said, drawing her hands to her side and pressing a kiss to her rounded stomach. "You're perfect."

He gently pulled off her shirt and undid her bra, kissing her tenderly. She pulled at his shirt and he crossed his arms at his waist and lifted it over his head.

She could look at him like that for days. His strong arms wore various markings. His left arm was completely covered in a black sleeve of art. She traced her finger over the line at his ribs. She liked to think that she helped him remember how to smile.

Her lips kissed the tattoo covering his heart where their son's name was forever held in a place of honor. And then she moved her lips over to his newest work of art, a tattoo of their daughter, the way they first saw her in the ultrasound.

He slowly kissed her body as if he were worshiping her, anointing every dip, curve, and imperfection with his mouth. Her body arched into his hold and he carefully filled her. When they made love of late, it was always gentle. It was because he was afraid for the baby, but she didn't mind. She'd take him any way she could have him.

Their bodies glided over each other's, becoming one. Like the waves of the ocean, they ebbed and flowed together in a vision of beauty.

Afterward he held her and she reflected on how lucky she was to find such an amazing man. The fact that he wanted her still took her breath away.

He'd come so far from that first day she met him, hair piled up on his head like a run down maid. She smiled and squeezed the arms holding her tight.

He'd gotten the job for the township and that seemed to make him happy. It was never about the money for Shane, it was about feeling like he could provide for those he loved.

It had taken a lot of persuasion to convince him to move into her house. He wanted to live somewhere they'd bought together. She finally agreed the next two years' mortgage payments would come out of his pay and then they'd be even. He was happy with that.

They'd traded in the Kia and purchased a family car. Since he was making better money his self-esteem seemed to take a turn for the better.

Kate knew bad times would come, but she also knew, so long as they had each other, they could overcome anything.

They weren't rich. They lived within their means, but as far as wealth went, they had everything they'd ever need. They had Logan and would soon have their daughter, whom they planned to name Noel Grace, after his sister and mother.

As far as Kate was concerned, they were the

richest people in the world. And she hoped she would always feel that way.

"I love you," she whispered into the dark.

His lips pressed into her ear. "I love you, too."

The End

Want more bestselling romance from Lydia Michaels?
Read *Calamity Rayne Gets a Life* for FREE!

Are you follow Lydia Michaels?
Stalk her on <u>TikTok</u>, <u>Instagram</u>, <u>Facebook</u>,
Goodreads, and BookBub!
<u>TikTok @LydiaMichaels</u>
<u>Instagram @lydia_michaels_books</u>
<u>Facebook @LydiaMichaels</u>
<u>Goodreads</u>
<u>BookBub</u>

. . .

SIMPLE MAN

ALSO BY LYDIA MICHAELS

BOOKS BY SERIES

Many first in series books are FREE

Grab them here!

Free Books Here!

MCCULLOUGH MOUNTAIN

Almost Priest *

Beautiful Distraction

Irish Rogue

British Professor

Broken Man

Controlled Chaos

Hard Fix

Intentional Risk

JASPER FALLS

Wake My Heart *

The Best Man

Love Me Nots

Pining For You

My Funny Valentine

Side Squeeze

CALAMITY RAYNE

Calamity Rayne Gets a Life *

Calamity Rayne Back Again

Calamity Rayne Gets Hitched

BONUS: Calamity Rayne Veiled & Railed

Calamity Rayne Over the Moon

Calamity Rayne Knocked Up

THE SURRENDER TRILOGY

Falling In

BreakingOut

Coming Home

Ruthless Billionaires

One Billion Secrets *

Two Billion Enemies

MASTERMIND

Blind

Untied

NEW CASTLE

First Comes Love *

If I Fall

Shattered Vows

ADDICTED TO YOU

Crush *

Bang

Throb

THE ORDER OF VAMPIRES

Original Sin *

Dark Exodus

Prodigal Son

Immortal Bastard

Primal Kill

Blood Moon

STAND ALONES

ABOUT THE AUTHOR

To receive Lydia's Newsletter and 7 FREE Books, click HERE !

Lydia Michaels is the bestselling and award-winning author of more than forty novels. She writes heart-clenching, unpredictable romance with dark elements and high heat. Her work is character-driven and bursting with broken heroes and badass females. With a sweet spot for overbearing, territorial types, her deeply emotional books are spicy, emotionally satisfying, and guaranteed to leave readers with many book hangovers.

Lydia is the consecutive winner of the *2018 & 2019 Author of the Year Award* from *Happenings Media* and the recipient of the *2014 Best Author Award* from the Courier Times. She has been featured by *USA Today, Romantic Times Magazine,* the *Women in Publishing Summit,* and more.

Michaels started her author career in 2007, becoming a recognized presence and advocate within the publishing industry. She is the CEO of LMC Consulting, a certified author coach specializing in character and plot development, and the founder of the *East Coast Author Convention,* the *Behind the Keys Author Retreat,* and www.LydiaMichaelsBooks.com.

She is happily married to her childhood sweetheart. Her favorite things include cooking Italian cuisine, hosting extravagant dinner parties, sipping espresso martinis, listening to her husband play piano, and escaping to her coastal home on the Jersey Shore. She's an LGBTQ ally, a BLM supporter, a firm believer that the patriarchy must end (women's rights are human rights), and an advocate for pediatric cancer research.

LYDIA

Follow Lydia Michaels on social media!
Facebook | Instagram | TikTok

THANK YOU FOR YOUR REVIEW!

Reviews help authors so much! If you left a review for this book, I greatly appreciate it!
Thank you,
Lydia

Click here to leave your review!

www.ingramcontent.com/pod-product-compliance
Lightning Source LLC
Chambersburg PA
CBHW061546190726
48289CB00004B/1191